THE STAFF AND THE STAKE
Spencer Allen

For Ashley, Eva, and Indiana:
Wherever I go, whatever I do, I'm relieved knowing I do
so with you.

TABLE OF CONTENTS

1

Forgive me, Father

"Forgive me, Father, for I have sinned," the woman said.

The priest's voice traveled through the partition. "It has been how long since your last confession?"

The woman let out a slow exhale. "What's the date?"

"September 15th."

"Thanks, Father. Wait… do I call you 'Father'? 'Miles'? 'Padre'?"

"Father will do."

"Oh right. Thanks, Father." He hadn't confirmed that he was in fact Father Miles Pulaski of Durham's Saint Térèse's Church, so she peered at the hazy outline of the priest to confirm he was the one whom she had researched. He seemed to be: Bald, stocky, middle-aged, mixed-race, thick beard, vaguely monk-ish. She pushed on.

"So it's been 34 years? Or never? Not sure what's the right phrasing. Or why I asked. I'm sorry, I'm just a little nervous. I'm not actually Catholic. I don't think I'm Christian, to be honest." She glanced at the outline in her notebook and affected concern. "I could just use some help."

"That is perfectly fine," Miles said lightly. "You're here now, and that's what matters. What would you like to say?"

The woman took a breath, replayed the plan, cracked her knuckles, then dove in.

"So, Father, I've hurt people. Not directly. And not intentionally. But I was so focused on my work that I didn't consider what might come from it."

"I understand."

"Do you mind calling me Christina?" Since she couldn't rely on eye contact and posture-mirroring to forge a quick connection, she hoped using her name might help. She checked her watch: 10:20. If all went to plan, by 10:30 he would have transitioned to calling her the more informal 'Tina.'

"Of course, Christina. You can tell me more, whenever you're ready."

"So, I guess this started about a year ago. Maybe more. When was the eclipse?"

Miles tried to recall that eery moment when downtown Durham turned dark in the middle of the day. "A year sounds about right."

"A year ago it is, then." She didn't bother to specify that it was a little over 10 months ago. "Well, that would be when I was assigned the case."

"You're a detective?" Miles asked.

"Oh, sorry, no. Clinical trial case. I'm a project manager at Wakestone Trials." She pointed out the door. "A few blocks to the west. Downtown Durham."

"Right," Miles responded. "The big tower."

"Yep, 60 floors. That's where I work. When a pharmaceutical company is developing a medicine, there is a fairly lengthy process to get it approved by the FDA. Less lengthy than it was before the deregulation, but still numerous hoops to jump through. That's what ensures that when a drug is available to the public that it won't have unsuspected side effects. Well, in theory." She paused long enough to let the priest engage.

"I see. Go on…"

Tina noted that this was a request, not a command. His attention piqued, she set aside the back-and-forth and launched into her story.

"So my job is to guide companies through that process. From the monkeys to the masses, we say. We recruit people who would benefit from experimental medicines or procedures, ensure all the appropriate forms and waivers are completed, track the data in our system, and so on and so forth. It's all fairly automated, to tell the truth. Most cases I never even hear the voice of a single doctor or patient involved. Follow the steps, and file the reports, ya know? Wakestone Trials didn't get to be the largest privately run C.R.O. without efficient systems." She paused, caught her breath, then continued. "But this trial was…

different. It didn't seem like it, initially. If it wasn't for one or two things, I probably would've simply rubber-stamped it and never thought of it again… Thank God I didn't."

This last phrase slipped out before Tina could consider how it would be received. When Father Miles didn't interject, she continued.

"In hindsight, the first red flag was how the case was presented to me. Typically they are assigned directly through our internal system and added to our queue with all the relevant details embedded in the notes. This one was added, but instead of being at the bottom of the queue, it was atop the list with a star. Not unprecedented, but not common. And instead of containing the details, it simply featured a note reading 'See me - E.S..' So I did. Tucked my notebook under one arm, laptop under the other, headed out of my cube, and hopped on the elevator.

"Emerson Sinclair's swanky office was on the 50th floor, overlooking Foster Street. What he did to earn that view and that salary was beyond me, considering his only discernable skill was taking credit for others' work. But whatever. I knocked, I entered. And I recall him smiling and saying something along the lines of 'Ah Tina, thanks for your quick response! I knew you were the right person for this job!' This irked me on three levels:

"1) That he was referring to me at all. Almost all of our interactions had been curt demands sent over our intra-office-chat. The few times he did talk to me personally were always just about my brother. Something like 'I'll be spending the weekend at my place in Miami and couldn't help but notice that the Rays will be in town. How about you see if your brother can get me some box seats for the game?' My brother, Robinson, is the right fielder for Tampa Bay, and although he would love it if I were to reach out and ask for tickets, I wasn't about to get them for this sleazeball, so I politely refused every time Emerson asked. Once he realized he wouldn't get tickets out of me, he simply stopped talking to me directly. Which was certainly fine by me.

"2) That he called me 'Tina.' Each message on our chat was always addressed to "Sanders."

"3) That he was smiling. I don't think I had ever seen him smile before, which was ironic considering the unsolicited advice he gave at my annual review: 'You might find more professional and personal success if you smiled more.'

"But a job is a job and money is money, so I set those concerns aside the best I could. He told me that there was an exciting opportunity that the 60th floor thought I would be perfect for. (As if Jacob Wakestone even registered my existence.) He elaborated: 'A time-sensitive trial from a prominent pharmaceutical company. Cutting edge approach to white blood cell regeneration. The type of medical breakthrough that could save countless lives and make countless investors quite comfortable in the process.'

"I recall him pausing and staring at me, expecting... I'm not sure what? Gratitude? Excitement? Whatever he was hoping for, he must not have received, cause he sighed and continued. He explained that this trial would be handled in an 'old fashioned manner.' He used phrases like 'utmost discretion.' After being drowned in corporate cliches, he slid a manilla folder halfway across the table. Not quite close enough for me to reach it while sitting, so I awkwardly stood to retrieve it, catching the title written on the tab: Project Enoch. But as I grabbed it, the folder didn't budge. His hand clamped it to the desk. He locked his eyes on mine. His smile was gone.

"'The utmost discretion,' he repeated, his voice suddenly an octave lower and devoid of emotion. With that, he removed his hand. I took the folder and began to sit, but was cut off when he replied with his previous tone. He told me that I would find a case in the system assigned to me with placeholders recorded for the specifics of the patients. He dismissed me with a head nod toward the door.

"I distinctly remember responding quietly with a 'Yes, sir.' It kills me that I said that. I had never called him 'sir' before and I certainly never will again. It just kind of slipped out. I left his office with a folder in my hand and a lump in my throat."

Tina read this last line verbatim from her notebook and worried she was overselling it. She shrugged and continued.

"So, I got to work. think I knew it was shady. But it's not like I had never worked on a trial for a predatory drug before. Being successful means sometimes you gotta put your head down and do what ya gotta do, right?"

Tina waited to see if Miles would take the bait and share his story from D.C. He did not, so she continued.

"Although it was my only case, it consumed my time in the office (which sadly was most of my waking time). I was in constant communication with Bảo Huynh, the doctor down in Louisiana conducting the trials. Typically we're lucky to scrounge up a handful of volunteers for clinical trials, yet not only was our allotment of 20 patients constantly filled, but those volunteers were also constantly changing, which was quite rare. Each time one of them saw a decrease in their white blood cell count when given a particular enzyme being studied, they were dropped from the case and promptly replaced. It was my job to ensure that each retiring volunteer was wired their funds, and each new volunteer filed their waivers. Not once did a payment get denied and not once did a waiver come back misfilled. I couldn't think of another trial I oversaw where that occurred. I say that now in hindsight. At the time, I was so buried in keeping the system updated with all the forms, reports, and data that I failed to notice it. Or, at least, that's what I tell myself.

"Little by little, progress was made. One report had the phrase 'Desmodontinae Sanguis Sānctus' in it, which apparently referred to a type of bat, but otherwise, there was never any contextual information on the case. By the time we got to the fifth wave of volunteers, we were seeing increasing white blood cell counts. The breakthrough seemed to be tied to volunteers with O-negative blood types. Which made the steady stream of volunteers all the more surprising, seeing how only 7% of the population has that type."

Tina heard Miles shifting uncomfortably at the mention of O-negative. It was the first movement she had registered from him. She had his attention.

"With this breakthrough, I expected the case to conclude. I remember filling my report late one Thursday, heading home, and crashing. I woke up, went directly to work, and what did I find on my desk? Another manilla folder with a sticky note on it reading something like 'Sanders, Project E Phase 1.5. -E.S.'"

"The process was the same. The constant back and forth with Doctor Huynh (though always over encrypted email, never over the phone). Seemingly ceaseless waves of volunteers with O-negative blood. Though in this phase, the question was whether recipients of the enzyme could then transmit their white blood cell regeneration to other recipients. Specifics weren't included on how the transmission was conducted. The data was simply a scale from 1 (bad) to 5 (great). As the tests went on -- and we entered into our fourth week of the trial -- the results gradually improved. The median crept from being in the low-2s all the way to the mid-4s. We even saw a smattering of 5s. I assumed at that point that the study would be winding down. And it probably would've been, as far as I was concerned, if it wasn't for the power outage."

"Earlier this week?" Miles suggested.

Tina nodded. "Four days ago. Monday. I was working late. Again. Was probably pushing 8:00. I just wanted to get the data in so I could wrap up this weird trial and go back to my normal day-to-day. As I was inputting the data, I heard above me a loud scraping noise, followed by a long hiss. And then the lights died."

"Sounds about right," Miles said. "I was here late as well, catching up on some reading."

"Revelations?" Tina asked. When Miles failed to respond, she added. "I have no idea why my head went there. That was the only book in the Bible I could think of in the moment."

Miles chuckled. "No… I would not classify that as light reading. The Book of Jonah, for an upcoming homily."

"The whale…" Tina said, recollecting the only thing she knew about that story.

"Yep… Well, wait." Miles stared off. "As I recall, I *meant* to read Jonah in preparation for an upcoming homily. But instead, I procrastinated. Opened up *The Fellowship of the Rings instead.* Comfort reading." Miles shook his head guiltily. "I'm not sure why I said that…"

Tina shrugged. "Memory can be funny like that. So where was I?" She asked despite knowing precisely where. "Oh right… For a minute, I sat in my cubicle in total darkness. As far as I knew, I was the only one on my floor still there. I recall being startled by the 'click' as the generators kicked on. I started my computer back up, and it was only when I logged in that I realized that I was doing so in vain. Since we had over twenty offices worldwide, and God knows how many doctors, our system operated in the cloud. The outage kicked us off the internet and our building was notoriously slow to reconnect. Sometimes it took as long as half an hour. My file popped up where I left it - Project Enoch, Phase 1.5, Study QS54TY.2 Results." Tina read the file name out of her notebook, then covered up the specificity. "Sad that I can remember the code, but I suppose that's what I get for being married to my job. Anyway, I groaned and put my head down on the computer while I considered whether I should just call it a night.

"That's when I heard a strange noise. The cheerful 'bah-bing' when a report is filed in the system. I must've hit the Enter button when I put my head down on the keyboard. There was no way the internet would be back up this quickly. I checked the taskbar, and sure enough, no connection. *Maybe it was a glitch?* I returned to the data entry screen, deleted the gibberish I had accidentally submitted, reset it to N/A, and hit enter.

"'Data Recorded.'

"I pulled up the browser and tried to pull up a site.

"'No Connection.'

"The file wasn't in the cloud.

"I pulled up my messages. An email drafted to a co-worker who I may or may not have a crush on was sitting in my queue. Drafts were stored offline, and required a connection to be sent. The message was innocuous, seeing if she wanted to catch a Bulls game sometime. *Now's as good of a time as any*, I thought and hit send.

"'Message not sent. No connection.' My initial relief was soon replaced by confusion. So I pulled up another message in my queue. A request for preliminary results on the new sample to the doctors in Louisiana for the Enoch file. I clicked 'send.'

"'Message received.'

"Checking the connection once again, I tried to make sense of it. I clicked around. I couldn't access anything, other than materials connected to the file. All of those were live. Could even access the meta-data of the messages in my outbox. And sure enough, each message was being sent and received.

"But not where I thought.

"The I.P. addresses showed up in the code. Usually, these were hidden. I quickly took a picture.

"The messages weren't being sent to Louisiana. The IP addresses of the sender (me) and the receiver (the doctors) had the same root. Both were being sent right here in North Carolina.

"The bars of the internet clicked on.

"'Connection Restored.'

"I conducted some IP lookup tests. I plugged in the sender's address. Sure enough, those were being sent from my office, Wakestone Tower. I looked up the receiver address.

"Wakestone Tower.

"*That can't be right*, I thought. *I must've copied over my IP address by mistake.* But no, I checked and checked again. About one of every twenty messages was tagged with a location a few miles north, but every other one was downtown Durham. Wakestone Tower. About forty floors above me, if I was reading it right. The trials weren't being done in Louisiana. They were being done at the top of the tower. Where Jacob Wakestone works."

Tina stopped. She stole a glance at the flagged page in her notebook that outlined her plan. At this point, it branched in multiple directions, based on Miles' response.

"So you think that they're doing something illegal? Unethical?"

"Absolutely," Tina responded. "Why cover it up otherwise? With the deregulation of the past decade, CROs have been given tremendous leeway. Particularly in North Carolina, due to the sway of the pharmaceutical lobby. *Particularly* with Wakestone, who is hailed as the savior of Durham. Something sketchy is going on up there. Something much sketchier than what Wakestone and other billionaires have been legally allowed to do previously."

Father Miles let out a long, slow exhale. "Tina, I know how you feel. I truly do. But this is not on you. Whatever is being done in that tower is not your fault. And although I appreciate your confession, I am not the one you need to be talking to right now. It's the police you need, not a priest."

"Well... you're half-right," Tina responded with a shy smile. "I know that it's not my fault. I certainly have regrets. About what I did for that company and what I did for that trial. But that's not the sin I'm confessing." She glanced down at her notebook, picked a path, closed her notebook, and proceeded. "I'm sorry, but I've lied to you."

"What?"

"I don't want your forgiveness. I want your help."

2

Contrition

Father Miles stared through the partition before recognizing that doing so was considered bad form, particularly when the confessional booth was so poorly constructed that it provided very little privacy, as was the case at Saint Térèse's. Despite this, Miles couldn't help but gape at Tina. He saw a white woman, presumably in her 30's with thick, wavy, dirty-blonde hair pulled into a bun. Her outfit suggested she had come directly from work, despite it being late Friday evening.

"You want my help?" he asked as he adjusted his clerical collar. "What do you mean?"

"Well Father," Tina began, "First, I do want to say that I am truly sorry for misleading you. I figured that I needed to introduce you to the dilemma before I asked for your help." She reflected as she uncreased a dogeared corner in her notebook. "But I have a tendency to over-plan, so perhaps I should have been more direct."

"Was your story true?"

"Yes. Every word. Some questionable experiments are being conducted on innocent victims in Wakestone Tower. And at this point, you're the only one that can help me shut them down."

"How about your boss? Or the police?" Miles asked.

Tina nervously cracked her knuckles, sighed, and said "Have you heard of Armelle a Moute?"

"Ummm... I don't think so. Though the name sounds vaguely familiar."

"She was plucked out of Duke's Fuqua School of Business and placed in Wakestone's Research and Development department. She has this wonderfully unique and beautiful mind that enables her to dive into a pile of seemingly disjointed research and identify the common threads."

"Sounds useful," Miles commented.

"Yes and no," Tina responded. "She also had this wonderfully unique and beautiful yet sometimes unwelcomed ability to enthusiastically share what she researched, regardless of how that information might be received. Case in point, while working on one project, she stumbled upon a needlessly convoluted financial system for our trials. As she untangled this web of accounts, she noticed that some of them were tied to a religious non-profit that Wakestone partners with. She felt obligated to share this misstep, but she's far from a reckless person, so she collected a multitude of evidence through all the proper channels and presented them to her boss. Ten minutes later, she was on the way out the door with her possessions in a cardboard box."

"That's cold."

"Oh, it gets colder. She brought the evidence to the IRS. And to the police. And to the mayor. Got nothing but 'we'll be sure to look into it' in return. The Wakestones own this city. They have for over a century. You look up and you see the skyline that they constructed. You look down and you see how their influence has seeped its way into the soil."

Miles didn't argue the point. "And this Ms. a Moute…?"

"She landed on her feet." Tina smiled. "Was impressive, really. Completely pivoted and opened a lovely bookstore up in one of the few neighborhoods in Durham that Wakestone hasn't yet gentrified. So it worked out alright for her. But it might not for the next person."

Miles held up his hands in acquiescence. "Okay, I understand. I am not condoning you going outside of the proper channels, but I understand. That still doesn't answer the question of why you need a priest."

"A priest can get to places that others cannot." When Miles didn't respond, Tina awkwardly added, "I mean in Wakestone Tower, not like Heaven. You see, the Tower is sixty floors tall. Yet the elevator only goes up to floor 57. You need special access to reach the top three floors. A staircase monitored by private security 24/7 stands at the bottom of the stairs that connects the 57th floor to the top three. We know the 60th floor is Jacob Wakestone's penthouse and office. But the

58th and 59th? No one knows. I'm betting that's where the experiments are being conducted. But I can't get there. I'd be surprised if that empty-suit Sinclair can even get there."

"But you think a priest could?"

"I know so." She folded up a piece of paper and slipped it through the partition. Miles hesitated but then retrieved it.

"Huh. Wakestone Trials is seeking a priest? To—let me get this right —'shepherd the company to the promised land.' Odd."

Tina sighed. "Wakestone Trials has always had a… complicated relationship with religion. You can't find a single external document that doesn't have a cross on it somewhere along with references to their blessings. It's difficult to pinpoint where precisely the company ends and their religious non-profit begins." Tina pointed to the paper. "And did you notice the clearance?"

Miles squinted. "Diamond-level security clearance. That means…"

"58th and 59th floor. For whatever reason, Wakestone wants this person close."

"Okay, I'm following you. I get why you need a priest. But why me?"

Tina ruffled her suit. This is where she thought she might lose him. "Well… the religious non-profit they partner with? The one I've mentioned a couple of times now…" she trailed off. At this point in her outlined plan in the notebook, a giant question mark was circled. Surrounding that was a myriad of scribbled notes, each hastily crossed out. Her eyes were drawn to one line that read, "Is there a possibility of redemption?" Her mind trailed off and another line occurred to her: "Or is it merely an enticing invention?"

"Yes…" Miles said, interrupting her as she was about to record her rhyming couplet in the notebook.

Tina shook her head, chastised herself for the poetic distraction, and cleared her throat, yet the words still came out muffled. "It's the ARC."

Miles dropped the paper. "Did you say the ARC? The Apostolic Rejuvenation Convention?!?" He picked up the paper and shoved it back at Tina. It hung between them, wedged into one of the slats in the partition. "No. I'm out. No way."

Tina left the paper teetering in the latticed partition like a see-saw. "I'm sorry. I know. You know that I know, don't you? But don't you get it? That's why it has to be you."

"No. They used me."

Tina caught her breath, rethought her approach, and allowed him to take the lead. "How so?"

"The Hermeneutics of Genesis 1-11." Miles spat out the title of the paper with venom as he rubbed the back of his neck. "When I was out of the seminary, working as a Jesuit in a parish outside of D.C., Archbishop Johnson appointed me that position paper. He didn't tell me much, just that I was supposed to present multiple viewpoints on how to interpret the events of the first two movements of Genesis through a Jesuitical lens. So I did. My focus was dispelling the false dichotomy that these sections must be read either literally or figuratively. I stressed how the ancient Hebrews didn't think in this type of binary. How their word for 'truth' didn't mean 'real' but rather trustworthy. Therefore, I structured my piece around that, focusing on the fundamental *truths* in these early chapters rather than getting caught up in irrelevant questions such as the age of the earth or the age of Adam. It was the type of analytical theology that attracted me to the Jesuits. I was encouraged to ask questions. To seek answers. And not just within the Bible. In my piece, I pulled in Octavia Butler. I pulled in Hamlet. I pulled in *myself*." Miles remembered. It hurt. He pressed on. "That spoke to me."

Tina's mind lept back to when she was a senior in high school and her brother Robinson was a sophomore. As usual, he had procrastinated on an assignment. An essay on Hamlet. She had helped him write it. She didn't recall how it turned out, but she remembered him loving a particular line. She recited it to Father Miles. "To thine own self, be true…"

"Exactly!" Miles said excitedly. "If we are each the image of God, then shouldn't we expect to see ourselves in the Bible?" He tapped his heart with his tawny-beige hand. "Shouldn't we expect to bring elements of ourselves into our faith?" He stretched his arm forward and brushed his fingertips down the door of the confessional booth. "And I felt like in doing so, I approached a truth that was just out of reach." His visage fell and he stared at the ground. His eyes focused on his lavender-colored socks. Perhaps his bishop would disapprove of this pop of color. The rules of the vestment were nebulous when it came to what was underneath. But in his banished state, he didn't think it would matter. "To be honest, I feel as though what I produced would have been a useful text. I still have the outline in an old leather journal somewhere back there." Miles nudged his head to the left towards the back of the church and let the conversation stall out.

Tina knew this was where he wanted the story to end, but she needed to push him a little more. "But that's not what was published, was it?"

"No. It was not. What I was grasping for was yanked away from me. And what was left was…" He trailed off and rubbed his temples. "A week later the Archbishop called me into his office in St. Matthew's Cathedral. But when I entered, it was a different man sitting at his desk. A man who looked like he belonged more on a football field than in a church. His boxy, massive frame was accentuated by his bushy red beard, which faded into closely cropped hair. Disconcertingly, this austere image was offset by the massive smile spread across his face."

Miles stared off and recalled the interaction, in spite of himself.

"I remember him holding up my piece. He complimented my analysis, but then jovially asked me to elaborate on the process. But before I could even respond, he plowed on, explaining that bridging the gap between science and religion was the goal of the ARC. 'To connect the Word of God to the masses,' or something like that. He said that making my points more 'explicit' would help to do so. He gave me a week and informed me to drop it off at the ARC's headquarters on… Connecticut Avene, I think? Or maybe Rhode Island Ave? One of the two, I don't quite remember. But I can tell you with certainty the name he gave: Saul Ferris."

Miles rubbed the back of his neck as he looked upwards.

"And with that, he dismissed me by pulling out his laptop, as if it was his office."

Tina empathetically asked, "What did you think of that?"

"I tried not to, I suppose," Miles responded. "There was a kernel of truth in what he was saying, so I amended my paper, focusing primarily on the Flood, since there is the most research surrounding that section. I posited potential historical floods that the text may be alluding to, providing multiple entry points into Genesis 6. A week later, I stopped by The ARC's headquarters, a classically beautiful building that looks like it was transported directly from Rome. When I arrived, I was told at the front desk that Mr. Ferris instructed me to leave the paper with them. So I did. I'm trying to recall if I truly believed in that draft. I might have."

"You say 'draft,'" Tina pointed out. "Was that not the final piece?"

"No, it was not. A manilla envelope with the piece showed up in my mailbox the next day with the requested revisions. Tweaking some phrases. Modifying some emphasis."

"And what did you do with that?" Tina asked.

"I compromised. Not all at once. But little by little, draft after draft. Until the result was… unrecognizable. Like you said, a job is a job. I tried my best to maintain my Jesuitical approach, but I don't know how much of it remained in that final draft that I submitted. I certainly know that none of it was in what I saw published (and what I have seen republished over the years). Some of my words were in there, but none of my message. Whereas I tried to break down the false binary of society and theology by bringing what we know of the world around us into the Bible, they flipped it, rigidly forcing their pharisaic view of the Bible onto the world. My historical analysis of ancient Babylon was twisted to justify xenophobic foreign policy. My sociological analysis of the creation of Eve was corrupted to justify gatekeeping women from positions of authority. My poetic analysis of the phrases used when describing longevity in figures such as Enoch was---" he halted in thought. Tina finished his point.

"Used to justify questionable scientific studies."

"Yes," Miles replied. "I suppose so. "There was no Hamlet in that piece. There was no Butler in it. There was no *me* in it." He looked down at his hands. "Or at least nothing true. They used my name. My likeness. Filtering their oppressive views through the figure of a young, multi-racial priest apparently lent them some 'credibility.'" Miles glared at the ground, tugging his black pant legs over the top of his black shoes. "A part of me was left in those discarded drafts. I'm not sure if I have really dove into theological texts since. As I think about it, I don't even think I've even read any Shakespeare or Butler since."

There was no need for Tina to push. She gave Miles a minute to process.

"My piece… it was used not for truth, but for power. Within a year *my* words were weaponized to condone bigotry and neglect. Every time a politician needs clerical cover to ostracize a group, I see my words on an ARC letterhead."

"Or to justify questionable scientific experiments," Tina repeated.

"Great. Sure. I guess that too. Didn't even realize my words had infiltrated another industry." Miles sighed. "So that's it then? You chose me because I'm in this small parish at the edge of town. You figure my flock isn't aware of my connections. You expose me if I don't comply?" He gestured to the Wakestone Trials paper hanging between them. "This is extortion then? I'm the right person for the job due to my cowardice?"

"No," Tina said kindly yet emphatically. "Though you did hit upon something. This *is* because you're in this small parish. Your report made a lot of people a lot of money. Not just outside the church. I noticed that the financial donations collected by the Archdiocese of D.C. tripled after your piece. I would imagine that many opportunities opened up after ARC published your work." She gave him a moment to refute her claim. He did not. She pushed her point. "Am I wrong?"

Miles looked in the other direction. Through the slats of the confessional booth, he could see the neighborhood cat, Naomi, walking down the nave.

"No," he acquiesced.

"And yet, here you are. In Durham. You turned down money. You turned down prestige. You turned down power. That wasn't cowardice, it was courage. It was a step toward righting your wrongs. This isn't extortion, this is penance. Finish what you started." She closed her notebook and looked across the partition. "What do you say?"

Miles sighed. "Ideo firmiter propono, adiuvante gratia tua, de cetero me non peccaturum peccandique occasiones proximas fugiturum."

"Ummm… and what does that mean?"

He retrieved the paper from the partition. "It means 'let's get to work.'"

3

Holy Water

Miles was thirty minutes early on his first day at Wakestone Trials. Having barely slept, he pulled himself out of bed before the sun was up and figured he might as well head out. On his way in, he reviewed the details Tina had been feeding him the past week.

"Everything up to floor 57 we know about. We got the schematics, we can monitor the network. But floors 58-60 are a dead spot. There's definitely one access point - the elevator stops at 57, but there are private security stationed there guarding a stairway, presumably connecting the top three floors. With your clearance, that's how you'll get in. But my source on 57 has never actually seen Jacob Wakestone get to his office on the 60th floor through there, so be on the lookout for another entryway."

Miles was to be the eyes and ears. "We don't know what we don't know yet," Tina told him.

Eyes and ears Miles repeated to himself on his drive in. He thought of Jesus flipping tables in the marketplace and yearned to do the same. Tina suspected as much in their planning sessions. "Patience. You'll get your chance to make things right. But we need to stick to the plan."

Miles found himself playing their conversations on a loop while waiting in the parking garage. He acknowledged how fruitless that was, and decided to head in early.

Wakestone Tower was located on Foster Street, part of a neighborhood just north of downtown Durham that the Wakestone family was credited with revitalizing. Due to a city ordinance, no other building could surpass 30 stories, which resulted in Wakestone Tower looming large over the region. The building never failed to take Miles' breath away, though he wasn't certain if that was due to awe or anxiety. He strained his neck looking to the top, and spotted window washers outside the 59th floor. They appeared to be nothing more than tiny dots.

On his way into the building, Miles passed a neglected unhoused man and wished he could give him a gift card to the local food hall, but he was told to bring nothing other than his vestment to the job. He left the man instead with a trite "God be with you." As Miles walked away, he noticed a card in the man's collection plate with the name "Wakestone Trials" on it.

Immediately upon entering the tower, Miles was greeted by an enthusiastic young woman.

"Father Miles! How nice to see you this early. Right this way." She gestured toward a metal detector. "Security precautions," she explained. His car keys, which he placed in a bin next to the detector, were immediately scooped up. "You can retrieve these on your way out in a couple hours.

Upon exiting the detector, the young woman escorted him to the elevator, held the door open for him, and followed him in. Miles watched her press "57", the highest number available.

Filling the silence on the ride up, the woman introduced herself. "I'm Lindsey Lewis, by the way. I'll be assisting you with your morning shifts. Will Tuesdays and Thursdays from 7-9 work for you moving forward?"

Miles nodded. "Yes, yes. Our deacon can cover the mornings, so this fits in nicely. How long have you worked for Wakestone Trials?"

"Oh, actually, this is an internship. My father works for the ARC, so he was able to set this up for me. He was one of the ones who took the Nazarite Vow recently; You might've seen it on the news." She pulled at her hair anxiously, then changed the subject. "Hopefully it helps with grad schools."

"I'm sure it will. And what does your father do for ARC?"

"He works in the…" Lindsey began but then stopped herself, and restarted. "Oh, you know, this and that." She then faced forward and didn't say another word for the rest of the ride.

Eyes and Ears. Miles told himself. *Patience.*

When the elevator doors opened on the 57th floor, Lindsey said

"Right this way, Father." She led him down a nondescript hallway, through a maze of cubicles, until they reached a set of double doors. She handed him a badge. "Just through there."

Miles pressed the badge against the sensor and the doors swung open. As he walked through, he noticed that Lindsey stayed back. Waiting for him was a pair of uniformed security guards. Their garb was vaguely militaristic. Some type of weapon seemed to be attached to their belt, but Miles couldn't make out what. Miles wondered spitefully what Wakestone-funded legislation allowed his staff to carry such a thing. Without a word, they pressed their badge against another sensor, which opened up another set of doors and walked through them. Miles followed them into a dimly lit stairwell. When they reached the 58th floor, the guards approached the exit. Pretending not to notice, Miles rounded the corner and began to walk to 59 before a hand grasped him on the shoulder and yanked him back.

"This way, Father."

"Of course," Miles replied. "My apologies." He made a mental note that the stairway stopped at 59. The 60th floor was not accessible that way.

The guards opened the door for him. What he saw was unlike any office floor he had ever seen. An expansive corridor stretched from the doorway he crossed through to the end of the building. The far wall was comprised entirely of glass. But it was an odd glass. Slightly opaque. It cast a diffused light onto a desk where a man sat. He was not illuminated since the light was behind him, but something about his silhouette seemed familiar.

Miles walked down that long, empty corridor towards the large man at the desk. He attempted to set aside his feeling of unease by inspecting the rooms that lay to either side of the hallway. Each was marked by a spartan door. No windows. No signs. Just a bronze keyhole for each. As Miles walked down the hall, he noticed in the floor a set of scratch marks, at least a foot long and at least an inch deep, that the fresh coat of polish failed to cover up.

A voice shook him out of his inspection.

"Ahh Miles, the great Jesuitical scholar! It's been too long! So nice to see you again!"

Miles squinted at the large man across the hall. Eventually, he recognized him. Saul Ferris. The Director of the Apostolic Rejuvenation Convention. But his closely cropped hair had been replaced with long red locks, reaching down his back. "Saul?"

"Indeed," Saul responded, as he rose from his chair. "I see you noticing the hair. The Nazarite Vow. Are you familiar with it?"

Miles grimaced. In the Bible, this vow was taken by those who sought to consecrate themselves to the Lord. It was signaled by a refusal to cut hair, touch blood, drink alcohol, and other prohibitions. Those that took it were meant to be set apart from the temptations of society, fighting to preserve the sanctity of God. Miles wondered how a man like Saul would apply these ideas. But remembering his mission, Miles set these thoughts aside, and responded, "Certainly, Romans 12."

Paying no attention to Miles' lead, Saul continued as he approached with a smile. "Yes, yes, I encourage all those on the ARC council to take it. Along with our followers at the Apostle Tier, of course." Saul squared up Miles. "You are a listener to The ARC Weekly, I pray?"

Miles sought a deflection that was accurate yet not dishonest. "I have… missed the last few episodes, I suppose."

"Heavens!" Saul put on a theatrical face of indignation, before swapping in a beaming smile. "I won't hold that against you. I do, however, highly recommend tuning in. Our devoted Nazarites have made it the highest-rated biblical podcast, you know!" Saul extended his hand.

Miles hesitated, only for a moment, before he remembered *Eyes and Ears*, and shook the hand of the man who derailed his life. As he did so, he felt a sharp pinch. He pulled his hand away to see a thin trickle of blood oozing.

"My apologies. Must have been my ring. Pesky thing. Have been meaning to get that fixed." Ferris immediately removed the ring on his right hand and pocketed it. When he pulled his hand out of his pocket, it was holding a walkie-talkie. Speaking into it, he said, "We are ready." A man immediately emerged out of one of the nondescript doors along the walkway with a camera around his neck.

"Big smiles, Father," Ferris said as he wrapped an arm around his shoulder. "You are now the public face and heart of this dynamic partnership between Wakestone Trials and The ARC." The camera clicked in rapid succession before Miles could fake a smile. "We are, after all His emissaries."

"God's or Wakestone's?" Miles asked, but his response was only a showy smile by Saul as the flashes of the camera popped.

After a minute, Saul dismissed the photographers by saying "That should do," and guided Miles into a chair at the table.

"What am I to be doing this morning?" Miles asked tentatively.

"Oh, you've already done so much!" Saul said with a smile. "But as long as we have you here..." Saul rummaged under the desk. "Oh, how should I put this?" He placed a small tub of water on the table. "I suppose my colleague Emerson would call it an experiment?" He set a mason jar of salt next to the water. "How do you feel about making some holy water?"

It was clear this was not really a question.

4

Holy Blood

That evening, Tina met up with Miles at Baldwin's Books, Armelle a Moute's bookstore cafe. It was Tina's first time in the shop. She had always meant to visit, but something always held her back.

"Whoa," she muttered, as they crossed the threshold. Such a beautiful and accommodating space, she thought. Or *spaces*, to be more accurate, as the shelves and stacks of books carved out separate nooks, each thoughtfully designed: some were public, inviting conversation, while others were private, inviting contemplation. Each dripped of intentionality, from the lighting, to the furniture, to the sounds, to the scents. Tina and Miles wandered through the literary labyrinth, appreciating Armelle's fastidious design, before finding a quiet and comfortable corner of the store where they could catch up.

Whatever tranquility Armelle's space had provided was soon washed away by Miles' account of his first day at Wakestone Trials.

"I'm not entirely certain what I expected," Tina said, as an employee reached behind her to retrieve the empty green tea, a dabble of agave syrup lingering at the bottom of the mug. Tina waited for privacy before continuing. "But it wasn't photo-ops and holy water."

"Same. Sorry I couldn't be of more use."

"Nonsense, Father. We now know the specifics of one entry point and that there is another one hidden somewhere in those top three floors." Tina jotted these facts down in her notebook, but her pen hovered over the paper when she considered what else they learned.

"And I suppose we know that holy water is somehow involved with the experiments."

"And what does that tell us?"

Tina sighed as she cracked her knuckles. "No clue. But it at least gives us a starting point. You get some rest, and I'll do some research on Project Enoch."

Miles nodded, stood up, and took out his wallet to cover his coffee before Tina waved him off. She gestured to the twenty on the table. "It's the least I can do. Considering…" she added heavily.

As Miles exited, Tina gifted herself a moment for some self-pity. She had forsaken just about every relationship for her career. She didn't remember the last time she went on a date. Was it Evelynn? She hadn't had a conversation longer than five minutes with her brother since he left for spring training. February? The closest connection she had seemed to be with a priest, and she was an atheist!

"Okay, that's enough," she said quietly. "Let's get to work." She looked around Baldwin's Books, planning her next steps. She recalled reading a piece in The Indy about how Armelle had leased the building from the city under the condition that she covered the renovations. With surgical precision, Armelle managed to transform the space into a cozy shop without losing its historical charm. It respected the past while looking forward. And, as she understood it, it seemed to be doing quite well. While the ground floor targeted typical readers, the second floor operated as a resource for students at nearby NCCU or Duke. Apparently, some of the best zoological texts in the country were located here, which was just what Tina sought when she had selected this meeting place for Miles.

She rounded up a spiral staircase and was greeted by a wooden sign featuring a James Baldwin quote: "You think your pain and your heartbreak are unprecedented in the history of the world, but then you read." She passed underneath it and placed her notebook in a comfortable arm-chair set aside a minimalist desk. She stepped away to scan the bookshelves, before reconsidering. She retrieved her notebook off the chair, clutched it to her side, and returned to the stacks, weaving through the reference books that graced the upstairs of the bookstore. In trying to recall the classification system for non-fiction, she suddenly regretted her decision to conduct her research offline.

Okay, okay… Bats? Desmodontinae? How do I find this? she asked herself. As if in response, a tall woman with rich mahogany-colored skin and tightly cropped curls approached. "May I help you?"

Instinctively, Tina declined, but then she identified the voice as belonging to her former coworker, Armelle a Moute. As Tina looked at Armelle, a flood of thoughts and feeling surprised her, as did her response: "Yes, you might." Tina then justified this acceptance, thinking that Armelle had just as much reason to despise Wakestone Trials as she did.

When Armelle turned around, a look of recognition spread across her face. "Christina Sanders. I hardly recognized you outside The Tower. I haven't seen you since I left." Somehow this woman who had been so sorely wronged spoke without an ounce of bitterness in her voice. "How are you?"

"Good, good." She tried to think of some new life development to share, but other than partnering up with a seemingly depressed priest in an attempt to take down a multinational corporation, she didn't really have much. So she presented her request instead. "I'm working on a project. A clinical trial involving bats." *Technically true*, she thought. "And I was hoping to find some research for it."

"Of course! What in particular are you looking for?" Armelle asked as she grabbed the collar of her blue and gray striped cardigan with each hand and pulled it snuggly together.

"Desmodontinae Sanguis Sānctus. The Holy Blood Bat. Diet consisting primarily of blood, which is a trait called..." she checked her leather notebook, "...hematophagy. That's about all I know, but I'm hoping to learn more."

Armelle tilted her head to the side, and cut straight to what Tina didn't say. "Why here? Why not the research portal at Wakestone Trials?"

"Oh, you know," Tina said, stalling for an excuse, "those systems only pull in research that has made it through about ten layers of vetting. Useful to ensure you're getting valid and reliable reports, but sometimes it's nice to look into some more... outside the box."

Armelle nodded and walked away, assuming Tina would follow, which she did. They wove through a maze of stacks before ending up in an aisle toward the back corner. As Armelle walked past books, she let her hand gently brush over the bindings. "Here," she announced as she plucked a pair of books. "Can't be certain, of course, but these should suit your purposes." She pointed with one to a reading nook in the corner illuminated by a stylish bronze lamp emitting a soft light. "There's a small table by the window at the end of this stack."

"Thank you, Armelle."

Tina thought she saw the flicker of a smile on Armelle's face before she retreated downstairs.

Tina brought the books over to the table and placed her notebook next to them. It wasn't much of a lead, but it was a start. All the names in the research study were fake, so there was a decent chance that the name of the bats was just a cipher as well. But when Miles mentioned that his name was attached to a study on cellular regeneration in bats, she thought it was worth investigating.

The Desmodontinae Sanguis Sānctus, she learned, lived deep in caves in Costa Rica and survived on a diet consisting primarily of blood. More than survived, they thrived, with an average lifespan pushing 60, nearly twice that of typical bats. Researchers chalked that up to a peculiar rate of white blood cell regeneration.

Tina excitedly scribbled the notes down when she heard a soft clearing of the throat and looked up to see Armelle standing there with a cup of tea. "Another cup of green tea? Teaspoon of agave syrup and an ounce of almond milk?"

"That's— yes, exactly," Tina responded gratefully. "Much appreciated."

Armelle placed the tea on a coaster, stepped back, cocked her head to the side, then adjusted the string of the tea bag so that it ran perpendicular to the handle of the mug. With that squared away, she asked Tina, "Learn anything noteworthy?"

"Yes, actually," Tina responded. She looked up to see Armelle's rapt attention, which brought a blush to Tina's cheeks, which promptly spread to Armelle's. Tina summarized her research as a distraction. "There is a monastery deep in the jungles of Costa Rica that has chosen to study this species of bats. They're the ones who gave it the name 'The Holy Blood Bat' in response to some of its... peculiar attributes. Local legend says they were descended from the now-extinct Jerusalem Bats. They say the bats fed on the body of Christ when he was in the tomb, and that blood is what was passed down through generations until they somehow ended up in Central America, and that it's Jesus' blood that contributes to the long life."

"Fascinating!" Armelle replied. She had an endearing capacity for being fascinated by just about any topic. People didn't always hold Armelle's interest, Tina recalled, but noteworthy information always did. "How ironic that a bat in the Desmodontinae family would be considered holy!"

"Why do you say that?"

"Have you not come across their common name yet?" Armelle asked. "Oh you've been working through the graduate school text. Here, look at this one." Armelle pulled aside the second book and began flipping through it. Tina regretted not starting with that one as she saw it was full of useful diagrams and translations for the myriad of Latin. "Here you go."

Tina looked down at the page she laid before her, with a horrifying picture of a pale bat with beady eyes and sharp teeth. At the top of the page, it read "Desmodontinae - Vampire Bats."

5

I Have Seen Him

"Right this way, Father," the intern Lindsey said as the elevator door opened on the 57th floor. Miles stepped out, but Lindsey stayed behind. As was the case the previous day, security ushered him to the stairwell that only led to floors 58 and 59. Miles had tried in vain to spot some potential path to the 60th floor. *Eyes and ears,* he had said to himself.

When the guards opened the door to the 58th floor, Miles walked into the same room he had previously seen. The same set of locked, windowless doors to either side of the walkway. The same table sat at the end of the corridor. Yet instead of bottles waiting to be filled with holy water, there was only a single telephone. Sitting at the table was a man he had not met before, swiping at his phone.

"Good mor…" Miles began, before being cut off by the man.

"Emerson Sinclair. Wakestone Trials," he said as an introduction. Sinclair pushed back his chair and buttoned his expertly tailored gray suit as he prepared to rise, but something on his phone caught his attention. He remained seated and stated dryly, "Mr. Ferris won't be joining you, unless the situation calls for it. You understand." Whereas Saul Ferris was all smiles, this man seemed incapable of smiling.

"Nice to meet you." Miles approached the table and commented, "No holy water today?" Miles noticed that Emerson's skin was the shade of bronze that can only come from an expensive bottle of self-tanner.

26

"Oh no no," Sinclair replied dismissively as he pushed back his slicked-back hair. "That experiment was very much unsuccessful. Unsurprisingly."

"How so?"

For the first time, Sinclair raised his eyes from his phone and locked them onto Miles. He slid the phone into his suit coat pocket. He replied by quoting "How impossible it is for us to understand his decisions and his ways!"

"What's that supposed to mean?"

"You tell me. I heard Saul say it. From one of your books, I gather."

Miles sighed, "Romans 11. Yes, I know. But I'm not asking to know the mind of God, but rather my purpose here."

"Aren't we all?" Sinclair replied curtly. "And I will gladly tell you. Today, you are going to try another experiment. You see, some members of our… community… have been sick. Wakestone Trials has spared no expense, including funds coming directly from Jacob Wakestone's own pockets, to explore every possible scientific remedy. Your role, as a spiritual adviser to the corporation, is to complement those with spiritual solutions. Hence the holy water. Hence today's work: A confession."

"A confession?"

"Yes, yes. These patients were chosen for their antibodies, not their sanctity. But perhaps that's entirely the problem." Emerson rolled his eyes. "Or so they tell me. Perhaps after this, we can return to actual science."

Miles looked around and gestured to the compartments alongside the corridor. "In one of those rooms?"

"No, I'm afraid an in-person confession at this juncture wouldn't' be… feasible. We're going to have the penitent patient call in. Unorthodox, I know."

Miles began to prod for more information but then remembered: *Eyes and ears.* "Very well."

Sinclair pressed a button and the phone switched to speaker. "Katrina, are you there?"

A scratchy voice, lower than Miles expected, responded. "Yes… I mean, yes, sir."

"As we rehearsed."

Miles heard Katrina clear her throat, which then resulted in a dry cough. Once composed, she proceeded. "Forgive me, Father, for I have sinned. This is my first confession."

"May the Lord help you to confess your sins."

Silence.

"Katrina, are you okay?" Miles asked.

"She is perfectly fine," Sinclair answered on her behalf. "Simply in need of some penance, aren't you, Kat?"

"Yes. That. I've lied. I've cheated. I've stolen. I've sold stuff. I've used stuff."

"I understand," Miles stated.

"It didn't start like that. I didn't start like that. Few years back when I was a sophomore, I got clipped by a car on 60 on my way to work at Food Lion. Car took off. I dragged myself to Duke General. No insurance, so I left with a bill and a bunch of pills. Couldn't really handle either."

"Did you have any support at home? A guardian?"

"Had a mom. But that support kinda only went one way there."

"Oh," Miles said.

"I'm trying, Father." Miles heard through the phone a noise that was one part sigh one part groan. "It's hard."

Miles opened his mouth, about to remind her that "blessed be the poor." But he didn't suppose she felt so blessed. "I am sorry you have found yourself in this situation, Katrina. I truly am. We are fallen people in a fallen world, and sometimes it is those that need the most love who are burdened with the most suffering."

"I really am trying, Father. I was going to the meetings. I have been working more jobs than I can count. Some honest, some not. The honest ones pay regularly, but poorly. The others are the opposite. So when I saw the description of the clinical trials, I..."

"Katrina..." Sinclair cut her off.

"Sorrysorrysorry" she responded quickly and passionately, which then led to another coughing spell.

"Why don't we push this along, Father?" Sinclair suggested.

"Of course," Miles said to Sinclair, then turned back to the phone. "Katrina, are you Catholic?"

"Well...." she hesitated.

"Have you been baptized?"

A sad, scary laugh erupted on the other side of the phone, which soon turned into a mixture of breathless coughs with interjections of "sorry."

"What is your point, Father?" Sinclair asked.

"Confessions are a sacrament reserved for Catholics. God's love, of course, is offered freely to everyone, but the ritual we're ostensibly engaging in depends on the status of who is on the other side of the confessional booth. Unless the person is in mortal danger. Then it can be offered to non-Catholics." Miles turned back to the phone and began, "Katrina, would you say that you are-"

Sinclair reacted immediately, his hand pouncing on the mute button, and his eyes glaring at Miles. "Enough. Just say the prayer. Heal her. Or don't. It honestly does not matter to me either way. But do not forget your place."

Miles locked eyes for a moment, then nodded. Sinclair lifted his hand. Miles spoke to Katrina. "My child, you are clearly in pain. I can feel that. And so can our heavenly Father. He will be a stronghold for the oppressed, A stronghold in times of trouble. He may not be able to take away your pain, but he can give you rest. And I promise you, though it may not feel like it, there are worse things in the world than the pain you're feeling."

"Yes, I know," Katrina said sadly. "I have seen *him*."

With that, the line went dead. Sinclair had ended the call. "That will do, Father. You may leave."

6

Interlude: One Year Prior

The car pulled over on the side of West Geer Street and rolled down the window.

The young woman gestured to her backpack. "What are you looking for? Anything you want, I got."

A man with slicked-back hair stared back at her for a beat, eliciting a clarification from the young woman.

"Not that. I'm not selling that."

He shook his head sadly, uncertain about this approach but unwilling to contradict orders. He straightened his tie and countered: "The question, actually, is what are *you* looking for?"

The young woman scoffed. "Ugh. You're one of those zealots to convert poor, fallen women? That's even worse."

"That is not our goal. Not my goal. To answer both of your questions, what I am looking for is participants for a clinical trial. What *you* are looking for is money. I am offering far better pay than whatever you could get for that..." the man trailed off, waving his hand dismissively at her backpack.

"This sounds sketchy," she said. Yet she didn't walk away.

"Think of it as targeted recruitment. Rather than casting a wide net for participants that may or may not meet our requirements, we have dug through our database to identify previous participants that would be a good fit."

"And what makes you think that's me?"

"Type O- blood. Strong red blood cell count. And a... motivated participant."

"I'm not feeling too motivated right now." She ran her arm through her frayed black hair. "I'm good with what I've got, thanks."

"No? So your application to donate plasma was *not* rejected twice in the same week? My mistake." After she didn't respond, the man twisted the knife a bit further. "So you did *not* get saddled with your mother's medical bills after she passed? Fair enough..." the man began to roll up his window and shifted the car into drive.

"Wait..." the words escaped her lips quietly, but the man in the suit was listening closely. He placed the car into park, but kept his hand on the shifter.

"We are offering $1,000 per week for this study. That could do you some good, no?"

The young woman stood there, scratching her arm, considering.

The man held out a business card with the name "Wakestone Trials" atop it. "Stop by tomorrow. Hand this to the front desk and they'll escort you to the 59th floor for details."

He drove off before she could respond.

7

We Can Do Good

Tina sat at her desk on the 28th floor at Wakestone Trials, staring blankly at her screen. She tried to focus. She tried to work. But she couldn't. Not when forty floors above, Miles was doing real work. In the previous shift, they had him creating holy water, which was a curious (if indecipherable) clue into the minds of their adversaries. What would he be doing today? And, conversely, what would she be doing today? She wondered who would bear the stabs of each click of her mouse.

Not helping, she said to herself as she pulled her unruly curls into a messy bun and opened up her notebook. Five minutes later, she got in the elevator, trying not to notice the numbers stopping at 57, and rode up to 40. The doors opened to the executive level. *If I'm right,* Tina thought, *she should be around here somewhere…*

After a few turns, Tina inconspicuously bumped into a tall, strong woman wearing a sharp suit, with naturally bronzed skin and dirty-blonde hair pulled back into a tight bun without a single strand out of place.

"Sorry, sorry," Tina said, looking at the ground as she collected her possessions.

"Forget it," the woman said coldly before recognition dawned. "Wait. Christina?"

"Oh, Rebecca," Tina said with surprise.

"Oh, Tina! It's been too long!" she said genuinely. "How are you?"

"Good. Fine." Tina delivered the lines without credibility, hoping that Rebecca's savior complex would supersede her professional obligations.

Rebecca stared at Tina. "I know that tone. I know you." This was once true. Tina had started at Wakestone around the same time as her. For years, they both were at Tina's current position as Project Manager. During that stretch, they were quite close. Or as close as Tina would get to a co-worker. After good days at the office, they would meet up for a celebratory drink at The Sphinx. After bad days at the office, they would meet up for a consolatory drink at Alley 42. But when Rebecca got promoted, and then promoted again, they drifted apart. The good days and bad would pass by without that connection afterward. "Tina. How are you really?"

Tina held back a smile but lost the lead when Rebecca cut her off.

"Actually, no don't answer that. Not yet. You look like you could use a coffee. Let's grab a mocha. On me."

The two got into the elevator. Tina reached for the button with a 1 on it, when Rebecca stated "40. Please." Tina shrugged and obliged. The elevator ride passed in the uniquely awkward silence that can only be shared by two people who would have filled it genially in the past.

When the doors opened, Rebecca confidently led the way and Tina followed. After pushing open a set of double doors, they stepped onto a terrace with the type of furniture that was so simple they could only be unimaginably expensive. While they waited to be seated, Rebecca looked over the railing at the city below and Tina looked at the executive offices above. After being politely summoned by the hostess, they sat down at a table in the corner. From here, they could see the left field wall of the Durham Bulls' stadium. A waitress came by and Rebecca asked for a pair of coffees with a dash of almond milk in each. She smiled at Tina, proud of herself for remembering Tina's coffee order. Tina didn't have the heart to tell her she had transitioned into a tea drinker over the years.

"Now, I'll ask again," Rebecca said. "But I don't want a bullshit answer this time. How are you?"

Tina let out a sigh. "I've been better. I'm just wondering what I'm doing with my life. It seems I just dump my soul into these projects that only serve the rich and powerful, at the expense of the people we're supposedly there to help."

Rebecca nodded. "Well, first, I notice that when I ask how you're doing, you speak only of work. That doesn't sound too healthy."

Tina responded, half-teasingly, yet truthfully, "Are you suggesting that since we've last talked you've become any less married to your job than me?"

Rebecca laughed. "Fair enough. But I would guess that my marriage is a little more rewarding than yours, no?"

"That... might be true."

"And do you know how I got there? To this strong, fulfilling marriage with Wakestone Trials?"

"How's that?"

"The art of compromise," she said as their coffees arrived. Rebecca took a sip, then winced. "Ugh. Almond milk. The gesture wasn't worth the taste." She pushed the coffee aside. "But anyways, compromise. The center of any healthy relationship. You give where you can, so you can get what you want. And what do you want, Tina?"

Tina thought for a moment as she sipped her coffee. "To do good, I suppose."

"Easy! We can do good. We *do* do good. Hold on, just one second." Rebecca pulled out her tablet and scanned through a list of files. "Where is it..." she said to herself. "Ah yes. Here. Look at this." She flipped the tablet around gracefully and laid it in front of Tina.

Tina inspected what appeared to be a report for the C-Level. There was a line graph, trending upwards, passing over a set benchmark about two-thirds of the way through. Tina thought out loud. "By the code in the corner, I'm guessing this is Leukemia patients. Seems like it's a medicine meant to overcome the side effects of chemotherapy. Particularly nerve damage. Peripheral neuropathy, I believe is the term?"

Rebecca sighed. "You always were the smart one. But yes, you are spot-on. This is promising, Tina. This is saving lives. And this is us."

Tina nodded. "Fair. Absolutely. But what about those other cases you swiped by to find that one? Were those saving lives?"

"Saving lives? Some, probably." She then pointed to the top floors of Wakestone Tower. "Others are saving money for those above." Rebecca held her palms up, conceding the point. "But we need those to get opportunities like this." She tapped on the screen. "Compromise. Tina, I know you. Ever the perfectionist. You find yourself on a race and you're mapping out every twist. Every turn. But sometimes you gotta slow down and decide which races are worth it."

"True true. And I think I do have a race worth running. Only..." Tina trailed off. Some bullshit was still needed.

Rebecca perked up. "Only what?"

"Only I could use some help."

"Tina!" Rebecca expressed with fake shock. "I don't know if I've ever heard you say those words before!"

With a genuine smile on her lips, Tina responded. "I want to oversee more trials like *that* one," she said, gesturing at Rebecca's tablet. "I'm good at what I do. You know it. I want access to the most esteemed doctors, working on the most impactful trials. But Emerson Sinclair just drowns me in a never-ceasing flood of overpriced pharmaceuticals..." Tina trailed off at the end, hoping Rebecca would take the bait.

She did.

"Consider it done. By quitting time today, you'll be working in my department. Probably before your quitting time, because I'm guessing you still work way too late."

Tina grinned. "Oh, Rebecca! Thank you!"

"Don't mention it," Rebecca replied. "I truly feel that partnering on some of your cases will be mutually beneficial."

The rest of their coffee break was spent in polite chit-chat, catching up. Rebecca asked about Tina's ex Stephanie, who she was fond of, but they had broken up with over two years ago. Tina asked about Rebecca's terrier Rox, only to be reminded that he was actually a boxer named Terry. They parted with a smile, and Tina headed back down to the 28th floor while Rebecca went up to the 50th.

Sure enough, by 5:00, Tina received an email notifying her that she had a new manager, one who reported to Rebecca. Along with that message was unprecedented access to the log of doctors contributing to Wakestone Trials. Tina spent the next two hours scouring it, jotting down in her notebook the names and details of any that worked on blood disorders.

We can do good, she said to herself as she packed up and headed home. As she exited Wakestone Tower and turned onto Foster Street, she noticed someone hurriedly approaching her from the corner of her eye. Before she knew whether she should be reaching for spare change or her mace, she recognized the excitable figure of Armelle a Moute.

"I've been waiting for you! Here, I got you a green tea, sorry if it's cold." She handed her a cup. Tina took a sip and noticed that Armelle recalled her preference: Spoonful of agave syrup with a splash of almond milk.

Armelle continued, "You work late. I've been across the street at

McClanahan's. They had an incredible pear cider, it came from an orchard…" Armelle carried on in this fashion, which drew a smile out of Tina. "But anyways, you were looking into the Desmodontinae Sanguis Sānctus. The Holy Blood Bat. Well, it turns out there's a bat sanctuary run out of Wakestone Tech in Fayetteville that specializes in that species. They had the largest collection of them outside of Central America."

Tina perked up. "Had?"

"Well, that's just it. I did some inquiring. All their Holy Blood Bats disappeared a month ago."

8

Belly of the Beast

The time between Miles leaving Wakestone Tower and arriving at Saint Thérèse's Catholic Church in Durham was a blur. Miles' thoughts spiraled, thinking of the awful things being done to Katrina, the young woman he talked to on the phone earlier. With each mental gyration, his anger burned stronger and blurred out all other thoughts. So much so that he failed to process his lack of preparation for the Thursday night mass until he saw the message from Tina pop up on his phone: "Interesting shift. Headed to a bat sanctuary tomorrow. Let's find time after to catch up. Hope the service goes well."

The service. Oh...

Miles struggled to recall the passage that the homily was supposed to be based on. He flipped through his notes.

The Book of Jonah.

Of course, he thought to himself.

He tried reciting the prayer from Jonah 2 as he put on the vestment, but each time anger over the treatment of the patients and his inability to help them crowded out the words. He couldn't get through the prayer, never mind plan what he was going to say about it.

It's fine, it's fine... I've delivered this homily each year. I can practically recite it from memory.

Before he knew it, he was in the pulpit, delivering a version of the same message he had given countless times at this point in the liturgical calendar.

"…Jonah was asked to travel to Nineveh, so that he could steer them away from their wickedness. But Jonah chose a different path, and boarded a boat heading in the opposite direction…"

Miles' hands clasped his Bible like a vice.

"…Perhaps he was afraid of the Ninevites. Or perhaps he simply didn't want to contribute to the salvation of those he hated…"

His church felt small. Claustrophobic.

"…It was at the point when Jonah was thrown overboard by the sailors, drowning in the chaotic waters…"

The words of Katrina rang in his head. *I have seen him.*

"Then he found himself suddenly in the belly of the beast…"

His eyes scanned the small, under-funded parish where he had been exiled.

"…Swallowed by the great sea monster…"

Suddenly, the church doors opened, and in walked a man with a sleek gray suit and slicked-back hair. Miles recognized him instantly as Emerson Sinclair.

The bile, the anger, the hatred filled his body, his mind, his soul.

"The one foreshadowed in Genesis 1…"

He tore his eyes off Emerson and looked upwards, noting how much shabbier this church was from the one stolen from him in D.C.

"Mysteriously featured in Job and ominously shown in Revelations…"

His vision clouded.

"The tannin—"

The word halted him.

"The tannin?" he asked himself as he noticed that the vaulted ceilings, as small as they were, actually featured quite impeccable craftsmanship. He then looked to the side of the church, into his office. He could see through the window the silhouette of the church cat, Naomi.

"I had this… leather notebook at Georgetown where I collected my research. I can picture it… the leather had grayed. A patina. But it had this… what was it? Lavender… yes, a lavender cross embossed on it. It was filled with notes. There was a page… multiple… on that word 'tannin.' As I recall, we first see it in Genesis I, when God created the world. Or, perhaps, I should say creates order. He separates the chaotic waters below (the depths of the ocean) from the chaotic waters above (the sky). He pulls up the land and carves out a peaceful garden from the perilous wilderness. Spaces of order pulled out of spaces of disorder. And in each of these disordered zones, there are dangerous monsters. A number of interrelated terms are used for them: The tannin, the leviathan, the behemoth, the snake. But they're all linguistically and thematically linked. Creatures that corrupt the order. That de-create."

"The tannin." Miles tilted his head askew and took in Emerson as he repeated the phrase. "Yet none of those words are used for the sea monster that devours Jonah. No…" Miles rubbed the back of his neck. "The monster is not the tannin. Jonah is. The chaos is in him when he rejects the call to save his enemy. Because, I suppose, he wants to hurt those who have hurt others. Who have hurt him. Yes, there are monsters in the depths, but there are monsters in each of us as well. And perhaps when we find the darkness blocking out the light, when we find that monstrous force boiling up, we would be well served to remember the words of Jonah, when he was in the belly of the beast (and when the beast was within him):"

Miles closed his eyes and recited Jonah's prayer.

"I called to the Lord out of my distress, and he answered me;

Out of the belly of Sheol I cried, and you heard my voice.

You cast me into the deep, into the heart of the seas, and the flood surrounded me;

All your waves and your billows passed over me.

Then I said, I am driven away from your sight;

How shall I look again upon your holy temple?

The waters closed in over me; the deep surrounded me;

Weeds were wrapped around my head at the roots of the mountains.

I went down to the land whose bars closed upon me forever;

Yet you brought up my life from the Pit, O Lord my God.

As my life was ebbing away, I remembered the Lord,

And my prayer came to you, into your holy temple.

Those who worship vain idols forsake their true loyalty.

But I with the voice of thanksgiving will sacrifice to you;

What I have vowed I will pay.

Deliverance belongs to the Lord."

Miles looked up and took in the faces in front of him. He felt his breath fill his lungs, but his exhale caught his throat, resulting in a desperate cough, as he landed on Emerson's gaze. His memory turned towards another page in that forgotten lavender notebook which detailed what happened to the Ninevites in the years following Jonah's reluctant intervention. How within a generation, they returned to the same murderous and monstrous ways. The tannin returned, stronger than ever.

"Amen?" Miles asked his parish.

9

The Batman

Rebecca Canteel, Tina's new boss, was shocked when she got the call.

"You want to take the day off?"

"That's right," Tina responded. "Is that a problem? I have plenty of days banked."

"Oh, it's not a problem at all. And 'plenty' is an understatement. I just never thought I'd hear those words coming from you. Are you feeling alright?"

"Yeah, I'm fine. Just some tasks I need to take care of so that everything is squared away when I start working under you."

"You're taking off work to do other work, aren't you?"

Tina couldn't help but smile. "Something like that, yeah."

"Anything interesting?" Rebecca pushed.

Tina briefly considered telling her but decided against it. "Not particularly, just following up on a few things. On the road now, in fact. We'll catch up on Monday?"

"Sure thing, Tina."

Although the sun was just coming up, Tina was already just twenty minutes outside of Fayetteville, where the Southeast Bat Sanctuary was located. As she wrapped up the nearly two-hour drive, Tina reviewed the details Armelle a Moute had provided her as they walked around the American Tobacco campus together the day before.

"The Sanctuary seems to be a pretty fascinating place!" Armelle had said with genuine excitement as she flipped the opening flap of her chai up and down, matching the rhythm of her steps. If Armelle had someone else to open the shop, she probably would've tagged along. "It houses the largest collection of bats in North America. Just about every species you can think of: Otopteropus, Old World Fruit Bats, Bauerus, Bulldog Bats…"

"And Desmodontinae Sanguis Sānctus - The Holy Blood Bat, I assume?" Tina politely interjected, knowing that Armelle would continue listing bats until she ran out of breath otherwise.

"Yes! Well, no. They used to. Then about a month ago, they all disappeared. Without a trace. Italo Contreras, who runs the Sanctuary, was saying that he's been hounding the authorities, but there haven't been any leads. Which is hardly a surprise." The last line drew a rare hint of bitterness from Armelle.

"How many Vampire Bats did they have?"

"A couple dozen."

"How does one steal that many bats without being noticed?"

"Well, that's the mystery. In theory, there's ample security since the Sanctuary is housed on the campus of a sizeable university. In terms of people and cameras. Yet that security falling under the umbrella of Wakestone raises questions. As does the power outage that occurred on the night of the disappearance, despite no inclement weather." Armelle finished off her tea and asked again for the third time if Tina wanted another cup before continuing. "The next morning, the bats were gone with no footage to check. The security guards said they didn't see anything suspicious."

"Was anything else taken? Money, supplies, other bats?" Tina had asked as they completed their second lap around the American Tobacco Campus, passing by another construction site, as a bank of condos overlooking the Durham Bull's stadium was being erected.

"Just the Vampire Bats, along with the folders of research on them."

"Hmmm… Well, maybe I'll get more out of Dr. Contreras or the guards in person."

"Contreras, hopefully. But not the guards. Italo told me over the phone that the pair of guards assigned to the Sanctuary had left their positions just days later. When he sent their last paycheck to the forwarded address, it got bounced back. Who leaves without arranging for their check?"

"I suppose someone who is cashing a bigger check elsewhere?"

Tina recalled these words as she took exit 210 and drove through

Fayetteville. As graduates, her parents had taken her and Robinson to the campus for homecoming each year. But that was then. In the years since Wakestone had purchased, rebranded, and refocused the university, it had become unrecognizable. That school was gone. Just like her parents.

She pulled into a parking spot outside the Sanctuary and noticed an elderly man with russet-brown skin, wearing thick glasses, maroon chinos, and a loud yet stylish bowtie. He waited patiently outside the entrance.

"Mr. Contreras?" Tina asked.

"Please please," he said amicably, "Call me Italo."

"And you can call me Tina. Thank you so much for taking the time to talk to me, Italo."

"I'm just happy someone will listen to me about the Desmodontinae Sanguis Sānctus. Seems like everyone just wants me to get over it."

Tina followed him inside the sanctuary. From the outside, it looked like just another college brownstone. But when she crossed the threshold it was as if she was transported into a cave deep in the heart of Central America. The walkway was illuminated by a thin LED strip to guide them. Apart from that, there was little light in the habitat. As she peaked over the railing, she was surprised to not see a floor, but rather a deep pit that extended the reach of the light. She heard the faint sound of running water and flapping wings.

"This place is incredible!"

"Thank you, Tina. It is my life's work. Bats are truly majestic creatures. They have so much to offer the field of science. Yet when you coop them up in cruel enclosures, you lose the opportunity to observe them authentically. Scientifically. Humanely. By reconstructing their habitats, we're able to glean a tremendous amount."

Tina smiled to herself, thinking about how much Armelle would have loved this. She took out her notebook to scribble down key points, so she could report back.

"And the Desmodontinae Sanguis Sānctus? What had you been learning from them?"

Even in the dim light, Tina could see Italo's face light up. "Much! Such fascinating creatures. Come right this way!" He slowly led her to a railing overlooking an empty enclosure. She looked down and saw only darkness in the enclosure.

"I can't really see anything..."

"Precisely, Tina! Nowhere have we found a creature who lives as deep in the caves as the Sanguis Sānctus. It took over a year to construct their habitat so as to properly replicate the caves of Costa Rica. These creatures are remarkable. Being so remote, they're quite small, under 60 grams—although their weight and strength can nearly double when they're engorged with blood. And their skin! It is so pale that it is nearly translucent due to the lack of light. We often envision bats as so much larger and bolder, thanks in no small part to movies using flying foxes to paint a more noteworthy image."

Italo went on to share some trivia about bats used in various films. As interesting as it was, Tina politely steered him back on track.

"And what research was being conducted with them here at the University?"

"A pair of studies, actually. One with the Anthropology Department, another ostensibly for the Medical School."

Tina interjected. "Ostensibly?"

Italo sized up Tina while he polished his glasses on a fabric he pulled from his pocket before responding. "One has to always consider where Wakestone Tech stops and Wakestone Trials begins."

"And you don't like the Wakestones?"

Italo peered over the edge into the darkness. "I wouldn't say that. After all, if it wasn't for their… philanthropy, this sanctuary wouldn't exist. Sadly, in today's climate, research simply does not get done without the backing of some corporate interest. I understood the contract when I signed up to remain after the transition. And yet…"

"I understand." Tina briefly considered altering her plan in order to tug at the thread Italo had exposed but then rejected the idea. "Anyways, you said two departments were researching the Desmodontinae?"

"Yes, yes," Italo said as he returned his gaze to Tina. "The Anthropology study was based on an idea called 'Reciprocal Altruism.' It turns out that a stronger, well-fed Vampire Bat will sometimes share food with a hungry member of their group. The hungry bat will beg for food, and the more powerful one will regurgitate blood into its mouth." If Italo had any idea how gross this sounded, he didn't reveal it, as he continued as enthusiastically as ever. "This altruism is key to their survival. You see, it is extraordinarily difficult to rely on a diet consisting solely of blood. Particularly for the Sanguis Sānctus, which resides in such a remote setting. A bat can go two, maybe three nights, without blood, but any more than that and they will perish. Therefore strong social bonds are essential. And these don't just consist of family members, as we typically see in animals. No, these colonies mix relatives and non-relatives throughout, all in a complex power structure based on who is able to provide the blood. The Anthropology Department was studying just precisely how these dynamics played out in the wild."

"Interesting," Tina acknowledged. "Although I'm not sure I would describe that relationship as 'altruistic.' Sounds more contractual."

"What relationships aren't?" Italo asked.

Unwilling to reflect on her own relationships, Tina pressed on. "Fair enough. And the medical study?"

"Ah yes, lots of interest in that one. Or, at least, there was. You see Desmodontinae — and the Holy Blood Bat, in particular — have a unique protein in their saliva that has been found to enhance the recovery of stroke patients. The rate of regeneration of stem cells increases with this protein. It aids in rebuilding neuroplasticity."

"How is this transmitted to patients?"

"Well, that's the tricky part. In the wild, it occurs through bites. A bat bites their prey, the saliva mixes with the blood, and an anticoagulant enzyme named Draculin is pulled into the bloodstream. The Medical School had been trying to figure out how to simulate this process in the lab, but with little luck."

Tina's thoughts went to the clinical trial. *Could that be what was being studied? If so, why not just continue to do so through the proper channels?*

"Thank you. This is really helpful."

Tina could feel Italo's eyes turn toward her. "Helpful how?"

She opened her mouth to provide a non-committal response but decided that she had enough data to hasten her recruitment. "Italo, I think these bats were stolen, not lost. You have studied these bats to help people. But those behind this? I think they're using them to hurt people. I want to stop them."

"I was hoping you would say that. I agree. The authorities assure me that the front door was left open overnight—something I would never do—and that the bats simply flew out of the enclosure into a night illuminated by a waxing moon—something *they* would never do." He accentuated his point by tapping on the railing. With nothing to see in the bats' enclosure, they retraced their steps to the entrance. As he was holding the door open for Tina, he asked, "How can I help?"

Tina squinted as the morning light shone into her eyes. Italo was both more prepared and more stylish as he had placed a pair of rimless sunglasses on his face. After her sight adjusted, Tina responded, "Well, you already have, quite a bit. And I sincerely thank you for that. I just wish your research wasn't stolen. Can I help you access anything that might be buried in your computer somewhere?"

Italo peered at her over the tops of his glasses. "You presume that because I have my AARP card I don't know how to use a computer? Who do you think programmed the adaptive lighting program for the enclosure?" Tina's embarrassment passed when she saw the playful grin on his face.

"Think nothing of it," he said while handing her a flash drive. "It's encrypted, but the instructions on the Readme file will get you in. It's protected with two-factor authentication, so just send me a message before you access it and I'll let you in." He handed her his card.

"Thank you, Italo. I'll do everything I can to get your bats back." She pocketed the flash drive. "If something pops up, can I contact you?"

Italo held his head askew while taking in the sign at the entrance to his building: The Southeastern Bat Sanctuary | Wakestone Tech. "Please do." He turned and faced Tina. "Truly, please do. I fear that the terms of my contract here are no longer to my benefit. Perhaps they never were."

"I know the feeling." As Tina turned to leave, she thought of one more question. "All the people who you spoke to, none of them pushed for any information?"

"Not really." Italo paused, then reconsidered. "Well, there was one who asked many of the same questions as you had. Only this was a week before the disappearance. And his questions struck me as odd, seeing as he claimed to be from the University, so it seemed as though he would have had access to those answers already. Feeling suspicious, I deflected as much as possible."

"Do you recall what he looked like?"

"I did not get a great look at him, as he insisted on discussing matters inside the sanctuary. But I did notice that he was a tall and slender man, with slicked-back hair and a rather bland, though undoubtedly expensive, suit."

Tina sighed. "Emerson Sinclair."

10

Take Me Out to the Ballgame

Miles picked up his phone and heard Tina's voice.

"Hey."

"Hey."

An awkward pause lingered, as neither quite knew how to tell the other about what they encountered earlier that day.

"We need to meet," Tina said, eventually.

"Yes, agreed," Miles replied. He then thought of Sinclair showing up at his service. "Where?"

Tina's mind jumped to Armelle's bookshop. She felt safe there. Too safe? An alternative occurred to her. "Let's meet at the DBAP at six. The crowd will give us cover."

"The DBAP?"

"How long have you lived in Durham?" Tina said teasingly. "Where the Durham Bulls play. Ya know, the baseball team? I'll meet you outside the gate by the fountain."

"Ahh right right," Miles replied. He realized that he had never actually seen a game there, a fact that his eight-year-old self would have chastised him for.

A few hours later, Miles walked down Blackwell Street on his way to the stadium. He marveled, not for the first time, at how much the Durham skyline had exploded in the past ten years. As he approached the home plate entrance, he was nudged out of this architectural reverie by a tap on his shoulder.

Miles smiled apologetically. "Sorry, was distracted."

Tina nodded but mistook his admiration. "It really is an impressive stadium. I've lost count of how many I've been to, but this remains my favorite. The Wakestones receive the credit for Durham's supposed revitalization, but the city building this in '95 laid much of the foundation."

Miles shifted his focus from the skyline to the ballpark. "It truly is beautiful." Something about an urban structure blending into a pastoral field appealed to him. "Anyway, thanks for the tickets." Entering the impressive stadium through the condensed gate brought Miles' mind back to Jonah being swallowed up by the whale. He wondered where he would be spit out and what he would be expected to do when he landed.

"To be honest, I didn't actually pay for them," Tina said as they wove through the concourse, which was illuminated by periodic beams of light coming from the tunnels that led to the field.

"Who did?"

"He did," Tina said as they turned into section 107. At the bottom of the stairs was a lean outfielder playing catch along the third-base line. Miles noticed how gracefully and gratefully the athlete composed himself as he cycled through tossing the ball, taking swings, and signing autographs. He appeared to be genuinely thrilled to be doing all three in this minor-league park. Whether it was performative or not, he couldn't tell. He wondered if it mattered.

"And he is?" Miles asked.

Tina cocked her head and looked at him with surprise. "He is Robinson Sanders. He's a three-time all-star center fielder for the Tampa Bay Rays. Pretty famous. And he's also my brother. You really don't know him?"

Miles shrugged.

"That's actually kind of gratifying."

It was at this moment that Robinson caught sight of his sister. Somehow his smile became even more infectious.

"Mi Llave!" he shouted with glee and a rusty Spanish accent.

Tina shot Miles a stare, signaling that he should not ask for clarification. Robinson held out his hand to help Tina and Miles over the wall onto the field. Before his sister even hit the ground, she was enveloped in a giant hug. Miles noticed that, at first, Tina stood there awkwardly, but slowly she reciprocated the hug, and it was actually her that held on longer.

"I missed you, Robby."

"I know! It's been a long season. I haven't seen you nearly enough. But here we are!" He then noticed Miles and extended his hand to shake. "Who's your friend, Llave?"

Tina took a moment, wondering what the appropriate title would be for Miles, but then shrugged and accepted her brother's designation. "This is Miles."

"Nice to meet you, Miles."

Miles, still shaking his hand for some reason, opened his mouth to say something but was uncertain what exactly to say. Robinson mercifully sensed this and intervened. "And what do you do?"

"I'm a priest, actually. Saint Térèse's." Miles instinctively reached towards his collar before remembering that he wasn't wearing it. He pointed to the east. "Off of Fern."

Robinson looked at his sister and laughed, not unkindly. "Ahhhh sis… you are an enigma." He then turned back to Miles. "To be clear, I think being a priest is wonderful. Perhaps the noblest job one can have. Certainly more so than hitting a ball with a stick! I am just amused by my sister. She's the most intelligent person I've ever met, and that's saying something, considering how many PhDs are now in our front office. Her friends tended to be her books. Her jobs. But when she does make friends, she picks some unique, fascinating people." He returned his focus to his sister. "A priest is a new one, though."

Tina blushed, so Miles filled the silence. "I didn't know there were a lot of PhDs working for the Bulls."

Robinson shrugged, "There might be, but I was referring to their parent club: The Rays. I'm down here rehabbing. Strained my oblique a few weeks ago, and it's taken a bit longer than I hoped to get my swing back." His smile faded, but then quickly returned. "Guess that's what happens when you hit 30. Or .230."

Tina, knowing how hard the injuries had been on him, jumped in. "Just takes a little longer, but you'll be back in center, hitting lead-off by the playoffs."

Robinson returned a self-conscious smile, wondering if any part of that sentence after the 'but' was true. Changing the subject, he turned to Miles and said, "They were able to get you great seats. Front row, about halfway up the third-base line. You a baseball fan, Miles?"

Miles looked around the stadium. So many kids were elated to be there. So many adults as well. "I was. Growing up. Through high school. I loved the sport. My family was from Montreal, so I was an

Expos fan. My room was covered in Andre Dawson posters."

"What changed?"

"The Expos moved, and I got old, I guess."

Robinson shot him his most charming smile and replied, "You never get too old to enjoy the things you love." A whistle from the manager grabbed his attention. He turned to Tina, "Gotta run. We'll meet up after the game for a drink, yes?"

"Of course," she replied and held out her arms. Robinson gave her a quick hug, said "It was great meeting you" to Miles, and meandered over to the dugout.

Tina and Miles settled into their seats. They made idle chit-chat, waiting to share their distressing days until they received privacy from a full crowd and courage from an empty beer. Tina spoke about the nice parts of having a brother like Robinson. Miles spoke about the nice parts of being an only child.

By the second inning, the stadium was loud, but they still avoided talking about what they came to discuss. In the bottom half of the inning, an athletic 20-year-old outfielder for the Bulls hit a towering homerun that cleared the stadium entirely, which drew a comment of "That one might have hit one of Wakestone's buildings" from the announcer. Tina muttered, "Which one?" before accepting that it was time to talk.

"Okay," she said. "You first?"

Miles rubbed the back of his neck, not knowing where to begin. Then suddenly, it all came out.

The pain he heard in Katrina's voice.

The controlling manner in which Emerson Sinclair monitored the call.

The ominous comment of "I have seen *him*" when Miles mentioned evil.

As he told the story, he found the anger bubbling back up inside of him. This boiled to the surface when he revealed that Emerson Sinclair appeared at his church. He felt furious at all those at Wakestone Trials and the ARC for unleashing this injustice, and furious at himself for being so utterly powerless to stop it. To give himself a moment, he excused himself after telling the story. He retreated inside the cavernous stadium, walking through the tunnels under the grandstand as the anger infested him. Realizing that his absence was perhaps concerning, he reluctantly headed back to his seat. On the way, he grabbed a pair of giant pretzels. Taking a bite, he couldn't help feeling a little better. He savored the taste as he stepped out of the tunnel and saw, as if for the first time, the field in front of him. The lush green grass faded into the beautiful blue sky. The crack of the bat as a ball was shot up the middle for a single. For a moment, Miles felt like he was a kid again.

"Okay," Miles said to himself and returned to his seat. "I'm sorry," he said to Tina.

"No one should ever apologize when they're handing someone a soft pretzel," Tina responded.

"So, what did you learn?"

Tina took a giant bite of the pretzel to buy herself a moment. And because it was delicious. She swallowed down her food as well as her anxiety, and launched into her story, telling Miles about the peculiar bats with their taste for blood and their medicinal benefits.

How they disappeared.

How it was meant to look like an accident, but clearly wasn't.

How Emerson Sinclair was almost certainly behind it.

She felt herself perseverating on this threat but forced herself to conclude it as her brother stepped to the plate. He conducted his pre-at-bat ritual of tightening his batting gloves and crossing himself. He caught the eye of his sister and shot her a smile. The first ball thrown to him was a curveball, breaking just off the plate. When he was first in Durham, as he rapidly worked his way through the Rays' farm system, he would have swung at this pitch, and as ill-advised as it would have been, he probably would have somehow sent it off the left-field wall. But as he got older, he developed a better eye, and he watched it drop out of the zone for ball one. The next pitch was up and in; called a questionable strike. The third pitch was an elevated four-seamer. The type of pitch that the Robinson Sanders of old feasted on. But his bat speed wasn't quite what it used to be, and he was slightly behind. He made late contact, launching the ball right toward Miles and Tina, who instinctively ducked out of the way, despite the net being there to protect them. When they looked up, they saw that Robinson had broken his bat on the swing. What remained looked more like a weapon than a baseball bat.

The fear from the foul ball combined with the wooden stake in Robinson's hand unleashed a flood of thoughts that Miles and Tina were trying to hold back.

The experiment.

The blood.

The holy water.
The victim.
The bats.
"Do you want to say it or should I?" Tina asked.
"I don't think I can," Miles replied.
Tina sighed, composed herself, and responded, "I think Wakestone is attempting to turn himself into a vampire."

11

A Splintered Fragment

"Vampires?!?" Armelle asked.

Following the game, Miles and Tina agreed to process their theory, then meet up again the next night. When Miles asked for a location, "Armelle's" escaped Tina's lips, followed by refutation and regret. Yet Miles encouraged her.

"I find when my head is clouded, it's useful to listen to my heart."

"And what does your heart tell you?" Tina asked.

"Nothing good, to be honest! But yours seems to be telling you to trust Armelle, so I'll borrow your faith and your trust."

When they knocked on the doors at the recently closed Baldwin's Books, Armelle answered the door, her hands tucked in the sleeves of her cardigan, and eagerly invited them in. After ensuring that everyone was comfortable, Armelle stepped back with a curt "Be right back." Miles and Tina selected a table set aside for research on the second floor hidden in a maze of bookshelves that at least lent them the illusion of safety. Shortly afterward, Armelle returned with a platter containing four mugs. She handed Tina a cup of green tea, complete with the agave syrup and splash of almond milk, before presenting Miles with options. They sipped their drinks and bluntly revealed their theory to Armelle, expecting her to be horrified by this revelation. Or possibly embarrassed for them for believing it. But instead, she seemed excited. "Vampires?!?" was her response. "Tell me everything!"

Tina relayed the story as Miles walked around the bookstore, ensuring no one was listening in. He was feeling paranoid after Emerson Sinclair popped up at the Southeast Bats Sanctuary followed by the Thursday night mass at Saint Thérèse's. He weaved his way through the aisles of books on the first floor, before heading back upstairs to rejoin Tina and Armelle.

"Well, what do you think?" Tina asked.

Without a word, Armelle got up from the table and disappeared amongst the shelves.

Miles shrugged. "To be honest, that seems like a reasonable response to what we just suggested."

Tina smiled, sensing what Armelle was up to. Sure enough, she returned a minute later with a book tucked under her arm. She opened it up and scanned through the pages until she found the passage she was looking for. She smiled and read to them: "Just as speech is invention about objects and ideas, so myth is invention about truth. Inevitably the myths woven by us, though they contain error, will also reflect a splintered fragment of the true light."

"Who said that?" Tina asked.

"Tolkien," Miles answered.

Armelle smiled, nodded, and pointed to the cover of the book. It was a biography of J.R.R. Tolkien. "Myths about vampires have generated independently in different cultures at different times. We're most familiar with the vampire stories stemming from Eastern Europe leading to Bram Stoker's work. But there's also the Baobhan Sith in Scotland. The Yara-ma-yha-who in Australia. The Manananggal in the Philippines. Logically, each of these must be rooted in *some* scientific truths. Some disorders or diseases that yield the type of symptoms that we associate with vampirism. Furthermore, it makes intuitive sense that a man with access to limitless wealth and to the best doctors in the world would investigate that for his own gain." Having worked out those ideas verbally, Armelle nodded to herself in acceptance. "Yes, vampires. I think so."

Tina smiled while Miles pondered the next steps. "So... what do we do?"

"First off: who knows about this?" Armelle responded.

"I think just us," said Tina. "My brother would have laughed me out of the restaurant, so I didn't get into it with him last night."

"And your boss?" Miles asked. "Do you think she suspects anything?"

"Rebecca? I don't think so. She gave me the green light to collect the most accomplished research doctors for future cases, which should give me cover to track down sources that we might be able to turn to. But I can't imagine that she would have done that if she was involved."

Armelle cocked her head to the side and stared at Tina for a moment, before turning to Miles. "And you?"

"Me? No one. Just my cat."

Armelle and Tina looked at him inquisitively.

"Her name is Naomi," Miles added sheepishly.

"You need friends," Armelle stated bluntly. "Well, you have us at least."

Tina jumped in before Miles' face could turn any redder. "Alright, so our bizarre secret is probably safe. Though I don't like Sinclair popping up as often as he has, so let's cover our tracks."

Miles nodded and looked over the intricate cover of the Tolkien biography. His mind traveled to *The Lord of the Rings*. He considered how Frodo must have felt, knowing that there was something dangerous out there, spreading. How he undoubtedly wanted to hide in the Shire in hopes that the darkness wouldn't reach there. Yet, despite the beauty and comfort of his home (or perhaps precisely because of it) he left, in an attempt to thwart the evil that seemed so much larger than him. Miles reflected on this and asked his question again. "So, what do we do?"

Armelle nodded. "I propose we divide up tasks, then meet back here in one week, next Saturday, to report back.

Tina took out her notebook, scribbled out a plan, inspected it, then shared it with the group. "There's a research study in the queue on blood disorders. I think I can become the case manager of that one. In doing so, I can make connections with a few doctors that we can pull in, when the time is right."

"That's a good idea," Miles replied.

"Agreed," Armelle said as she left the table, returning shortly with a manilla folder that she handed to Miles.

"Blueprints of Wakestone Tower," she stated. "Architectural designs need to be filed upon construction, and updated for any renovations. The Wakestone Tower ones are conveniently obscured through dummy corporations and mislabelled file names, but they're there. Somewhere. I've been able to track down a few, but there's more."

Miles looked up, not quite sure what she was suggesting. Armelle continued. "There has to be some way to get to the 59th and 60th floor. We know Jacob Wakestone is there. The patients too." She looked down at the folder. "Possibly. I'm not sure. Seems like he would have been forced to transition to a larger space for the later trials, based on Tina's notes. But we know it at least started there." She nodded towards Miles. "And you're the only one who can get anywhere close. Use the blueprints and your access to figure it out."

"I can do that. I think." Miles held the folder tightly, before looking up at Armelle. "And you?"

"Well, I'll keep digging into the blueprints. There's something there I'm not quite grasping. But even more importantly…" Armelle trailed off as the biggest smile they had ever seen from her spread across her face. She gestured at the bookshelves around her. "I'm going to read every book about vampires that's ever been written!"

12

Access Granted

"Who goes first?" Armelle asked. She, Tina, and Miles sat around a table upstairs at Baldwin's Books. It had been one week since they had all acknowledged that their enemy, Jacob Wakestone, was attempting to become a vampire. Or potentially already was one. And it had been one week since they had assigned each other tasks for how to take him down. After checking the perimeter, they sat down at a table too big for the three of them, but too small for the pile of books Armelle had collected.

"I'll start" Tina offered reluctantly. She opened up her notebook. "So, my goal was to find doctors who can help us. And I found a lead."

"That's great news, Tina!" Miles offered.

"Maybe. Maybe not," Tina responded. "When I began digging on Monday, I found that while I did have expanded access to our database, I didn't quite have all the cases. So I went to my new supervisor, Rebecca, to ask for a manager profile."

"Any luck?" Armelle asked.

"Yes and no. She stared at me for a beat too long, and then casually asked 'Why do you need it?' I responded with something along the lines of, 'As we discussed, I'm hoping to leverage our incentives to recruit some of the most renowned doctors into our most cutting-edge trials. To do some good. I currently have access to any of the cases that either I have managed, or you have supervised, but that's still just a fraction of the ones our company has covered. Full access will help ensure no one is slipping through the cracks.'

"Later that afternoon I saw Emerson Sinclair pop into her office. About an hour later, he left, shooting me a curious glance on his way by, and Rebecca stopped by. Normally she's quite chatty, but she just poked her head in, said 'Access granted' and left."

"That's…" Miles started.

"Exactly," said Tina. "But full access is full access. I'm not sure how long I can play this out, so I've been digging through the files with each spare moment I've got. Not only did I receive details on every doctor that has ever worked at Wakestone Trials, but I believe I'm able to generate badges to operate the elevators." She held up her hands in a stopping motion. "But don't get too excited, we also have to figure out a way to gain access codes. Getting up the elevator does us little good if an alarm is triggered."

Tina was distracted by a quiet, painful groan from Miles. She gave him a moment to speak up, but when he didn't take it, she continued. "But we're of course not there yet. Mostly I've been focusing on any cases involving blood transfusions."

"Any patterns?" asked Armelle.

"At first, no. There were certainly a fair number of intriguing trials, but I couldn't find anything that connected them. One involving how blood transfusions can unlock epigenetic shifts by a doctor in Brazil; another involving the impact Type-O blood has on pain receptors; another on how bat saliva can improve the brain regeneration of stroke survivors."

Armelle interjected: "Wait. When was that one? That last one."

"Four years ago. In August."

"Which…" Armelle started as she flipped through her notes, "would be right around the time that Jacob Wakestone stepped back from day-to-day management of Wakestone Trials."

Tina smiled. "That was exactly my thought too. At the time, it was quite a shock. About six months later, he had returned with little more than a memo saying that he had been on a sabbatical. But we saw much less of him moving forward."

"Interesting," Miles added. "What did you learn about that trial?"

"Well, that's what was so peculiar. Not much. It was led by a doctor out of Duke named Maria Ivanov. Seems to be a well-respected doctor. Published all over the place. And prior to this study, she worked on several trials with us. But then after this stroke study, nothing."

"Seems odd. It was unsuccessful then?"

"Quite the opposite. Wildly successful. A medicine was on the market about a year later that is now used by nearly two-thirds of stroke patients to help them regain their mental faculties."

"That doesn't make sense," Armelle pointed out. "Wakestone Trials pays better than any competing Contract Research Organization. Why would they let a doctor like that get away?"

"That was my question as well. It occurred to me then that our system can be a little persnickety with names that have been translated from different alphabets. 'Ivanov' can be translated over as Ivanof, Ivanoff, Ivanow, and so on. Same with 'Maria.' But each doctor also has a corresponding ID number, so I instead searched for that. And sure enough, hits all over the place. That epigenetic shift trial. The Type-O blood trial. And even the white blood cell regeneration trial that brought us all together."

Armelle cut right to the chase: "Were they listed under different spellings of Maria or Ivanov?"

Tina smiled. "Great question. No. The epigenetic shift trial was supposedly run by George Schlosser. The Type-O blood one by Michelle Johnson. Our white blood cell case by Bảo Huynh."

"But Maria Ivanov is real, right?" Miles asked.

"That was my question as well. Thankfully, with Duke being a few miles down I-60, I was able to check. She teaches a pre-med class on Wednesdays and Fridays. So I popped in. And sure enough, there she was. Older woman. Maybe 60s? Very austere, in looks and personality. Dressed all in grey." Tina paused and considered. "Well, except for a childish and colorful beaded bracelet. Anyways, the next day…"

Armelle cut in, "What was she teaching?"

"Oh, well something about cadavers. I was only there a few minutes, but she was lecturing on common misconceptions about decomposing bodies. How the belly might swell, hair continues to grow, and so on."

"Did she mention Johannes Fluckinger?" Armelle asked abruptly.

Taken aback, Tina responded, "No. I don't think so. Who's that?"

Armelle closed her eyes and recited from memory, "An 18th-century Regiment Medical Officer from Serbia. Medveda, I believe. Villagers there suspected that something like 17 people had been killed by vampire attacks." She pulled out her notes to confirm, nodded, and continued. "The townspeople dug up the body of Arnold Paole, who was purportedly attacked by a vampire in Turkey years earlier, and noticed that his stomach was swollen, that his hair had grown, as well as his nails. They drove a stake through his heart. Later, scientists stressed that these signs were typical of decomposing bodies. The Empress of Austria even sent physicians on a tour around the countryside to disprove these superstitions."

Tina slowly sipped her green tea as she processed the history Armelle had shared. "She did seem a little agitated when she was lecturing. As if the 'superstitious folk' she was referring to were a little closer than the 18th century."

"Did you get a chance to ask her about it?" Miles asked.

"Well… no. I had to get back to the office. I intended to return for her Friday class and ask her then."

"You say 'you intended,'" Armelle pointed out. "So you didn't go yesterday?"

"I did," Tina responded. "But she wasn't there. Ivanov's Teaching Assistant greeted the class and said that *she* would be covering the rest of the semester. So I headed back. And who did I see in the parking lot waiting there, leaning on my car, his eyes locked on me with his beady stare?"

Miles and Armelle both groaned and muttered "Sinclair" simultaneously.

"Yep. Emerson Sinclair. He asked me, 'What brings you to Duke?' Having constructed a cover story previously, I responded, 'Rebecca and I are recruiting doctors for a potential study on a new medicine for stroke patients. Considering Doctor Ivanov's previous work with us, she seemed like a natural fit.' 'Funny,' he said, 'she hadn't mentioned that when we met.' I pointed out that she didn't report to him, which seemed to set him in his place. He opened his mouth a few times, before rethinking. Then a hint of a rare smile crept on his face as he said cryptically 'I can do all things through *He* who strengthens me.'"

Miles' head fell into his hands.

"I'm sorry," Tina said. "I pushed things too far. They're onto us, and it's my fault."

Miles looked up. "No, not at all. You did great. I wasn't upset because of you. But because of myself. 'I can do all things through He who strengthens me' - That line came from me. From the previous night's mass."

13

He Who Strengthens Me

"What do you mean that line came from you?" Tina asked Miles.

"It came from the Bible. Philippians." Armelle interjected.

Miles cocked his head at Armelle, not expecting a Muslim to recognize a new testament passage. She gave no reply, so he responded. "Well, yes, it came from the Apostle Paul. But I said it to Emerson the day before he said it to you."

He paused and jerked his head to one side, working out a crick in his neck. "I suppose I should take a step back and start earlier that week. I found myself unable to sleep Monday night, thinking over my shift the next day. Just perseverating on it. Running my head in circles. I found myself turning to the blueprints Armelle gave me, and that helped."

Armelle, who loved maps (or just about any topic), grinned ear to ear. Miles didn't have the heart to inform her that he found them helpful since their tedious nature put him to sleep.

"I inspected every square centimeter of the 58th through 60th floors. But I couldn't find any hint of where the elevator might have been connecting it to the lower floors. I just… needed to find a way to get up there. To get to him... To get to her… Eventually, I dozed off, the stack of blueprints under my head like a pillow. When I woke up, the pages were all ruffled. The page on top was now the layout of the 11th floor. As I began shuffling the papers back in order, I noticed something: There was a second elevator on that floor. Labeled 'K.' I checked all the floors underneath. Each had the same shaft for the elevator, down to Floor 0, where the kitchen was found."

Armelle cut in, "What about the floors above?"

"Exactly," Miles replied. The elevator wasn't labeled on any floor above 20. Yet, oddly enough, each floor had something fitting the same dimensions in that spot. On one, it was a storage closet, on another a server room, and so on. Leading all the way up through the 58th, 59th, and 60th floors."

"You found it! The way to Jacob Wakestone! To the prisoners!" Tina exclaimed.

"Well…" Armelle began.

Miles continued. "I think so. But I wanted to confirm. And… well… that's where I screwed up."

Miles paused, avoiding eye contact by scanning Armelle's shop. Each time he did so he felt positive that there would be some villainous force just waiting to pop out behind a bookshelf. He swallowed down his anxiety and continued.

"I had my shift at Wakestone Tower the next day. A new task awaited me. As I arrived, I found on the desk a pad of paper, a pen, and a note curtly reading 'Article on the benefits of the corporate/ religious partnership between Wakestone Trials & ARC. With biblical sources.' The initials S.F. were underneath this demand. Saul Ferris. I got to work. Writing a well-reasoned piece on biblical analysis can be tricky, but even harder is writing a piece that is bad enough to be unusable, but not so bad that it draws attention. Tougher still since my attention constantly drifted to the door four pods down on the left."

"The elevator?" Tina asked.

Miles nodded. "I believe so. According to the blueprints, it's about 30 feet in from the door. Before my shift, I measured my gait and estimated it would be about 14 steps off of the main entrance. As I was being escorted out at the end of my shift, I paused in front of that pod to kneel and tie my purposefully untied shoes. When I stood, I pretended to brace myself against the shaft. The noise… there was an echo. I think there was an echo."

"An elevator shaft," Armelle pointed out. "What did you notice about the door?"

"No keyhole. Looks like it can only be accessed through a badge. I didn't have a chance to check to see if mine would work with my escorts next to me."

"Nor should you have," Armelle stated dryly. "That almost certainly would've triggered a security alert."

Miles covered up his blush by taking a sip of his black decaf coffee that Armelle had waiting for him when they arrived. "When I hit the lobby, the intern was there to show me out. Before the exit, I halted, held my stomach, and said I had to use the bathroom. I find when you signal there are digestive problems, people don't usually push for further information. I stayed in the stall for a few minutes, banking on the intern not being invested enough in a non-paying job to stick around. Sure enough, when I exited, she was gone. Blending in with the employees headed to and from lunch, I made my way to the stairs, and headed down to floor 0."

"What did you find?" Tina asked. She looked excited. Armelle looked nervous.

"A kitchen," Miles responded. "Typical commercial kitchen. With what looked to be a typical service elevator tucked to the side, precisely where the blueprints said it would be. I tried my badge only to find a red light signaling that my access was insufficient."

Miles smiled apologetically. Armelle shook her head.

"But..." Miles eagerly added, in an attempt to defend an action that he knew was indefensible. "This did teach us something! If that was a normal service elevator, there's no reason why I wouldn't be able to access it with Diamond-Level Clearance."

Tina smiled. "That's our ticket!" Then her excitement waned as she added, "We just need to somehow get a badge that will get us in..."

"That was instructive," Armelle stated, "But about the badge..."

Miles sighed.

Tina jumped in, "Was that not actually the end? Or was there an issue with you trying your badge?"

Miles' shoulders dropped. "Both. Figuring that I had learned as much as I could, I returned to the stairwell. As I was opening the door, I heard the screech behind me of the elevator opening. I next heard the familiar, slimy voice of Emerson Sinclair saying '...the patient has stagnated. The rate of change has plateaued. We need to repeat Phase I with patients that are in better health. There are just too many variables that could be affecting her white blood cell count.'

"And, in response, I heard the equally familiar slow, deep voice of Saul Ferris saying 'As usual, your faith is misplaced and under-developed. She was not from the chosen line. You will not be selecting the next round of patients. You will be using our new recruits from the coast. And we will be proceeding with Phase II.'

"I then heard a sound I had never heard before: Emerson pleading. 'Please. Use your head. I just worry that…' Saul then dismissively cut him off with the verse 'Don't worry about anything. Instead, pray about everything.' That apparently was his way of ending the conversation, because the next thing I heard was the elevator door closing shut. Saul must have left, because then there was only the sound of Emerson swearing and knocking over what seemed to be a shelf full of glasses. I used the cacophony of shattered glasses as cover to escape up the stairs."

Baldwin's Books was still as the three of them processed this interaction. Finally, Armelle spoke up, "And Thursday?"

Miles nodded. "The shift began as normal. When I entered, I found a draft of my analysis marked up, with a note affixed to it reading 'Needs work. Add in some Solomon. -S.J.' Sensing that I may have pushed things too far on Tuesday, I buckled down and focused on the letter. I pulled in some details from King Solomon working with developers to build the Temple for God, trying to string this assignment out as long as I could. Knowing that we three were meeting just three days away, I decided not to push my luck by trying to get back to the basement again. So I left with the intern as normal. But as I exited Wakestone Tower I found someone waiting for me: Emerson Sinclair.

"Without giving me a moment, he asked 'Not headed to the ground floor after today's shift?' My mouth opened to respond, but no words came out. 'I'll walk you to your car, Father,' he responded and headed to the garage. 'Your badge was pinged on the ground floor on Tuesday. Now, why would someone like you be there?' he asked.

"'A parishioner of ours works there,' I lied in response. 'At Sunday's mass, he had said that he saw me in the Tower and told me to swing by.'

"'Is that so?' he asked suspiciously. 'And his name?'

"I tried to deflect: 'To be honest, I'm not quite sure. I'm better with faces than with names. Something with a J. James? Jones? Johnson? But I recognized him when I saw him.'"

Tina kindly shot a half-smile to Miles. "That was smart to not give a name. But even still he'll be able to check the crew and see if any of them attend your church. Chances are…"

Miles nodded. "I know. We're about out of time. Which horrified me. Particularly as we entered the dimly lit parking garage. But then I realized that our time being about up with this charade was liberating as well. And that emboldened me. A bit too much, perhaps.

"He had paused outside my car, which apparently he recognized. He looked me in the eyes. 'I have heard that your work for us has been… unsatisfactory of late. Perhaps if you cannot accomplish the tasks given to you, we should find another priest. So I think it would be in your best interest if you focus on your work, and minimize the fraternizing. Can you do that, Father?'

"His words were cold and sharp, but they were just that: words. If he was going to do something to me, he would've already done so. Even the threat of the dark parking garage was a shallow one, as there were ample witnesses around us at this time of day. I shot him my most winning smile, and referenced a line just a few lines down from the one Saul had threatened him with: 'I can do all things through he who strengthens me.' Not giving him a chance to answer, I got in my car and drove away. And I felt good about it too, until just now. Hearing that he tracked you down the next day and threw my words at you. He's onto us. Both of us. And knows we're working together."

Miles sighed. "He's a snake. A poisonous one. I don't know why he hasn't struck yet, and I don't know how much time we have left. We have to act. We gotta get in that elevator and get to that 60th floor. We can figure out the alarm later."

Armelle shook her head. "You're right in that we have to get to the elevator. But we're taking it down, not up."

14

Two Histories

Armelle a Moute organized her stack of books, either unaware or unconcerned that Father Miles and Tina were eagerly awaiting her report. Of particular significance was why Armelle insisted they would not be taking the newly discovered elevator in Wakestone Tower up to the protected 60th floor, where corporate mogul and suspected vampire Jacob Wakestone dwelled. Armelle waited to speak until she had just the right books in just the right order set neatly in front of her. Once each text was placed squarely on top of each other, bindings aligned to the left, she pulled her arms into the sleeves of her wool cardigan, pulled it tight, and began her story.

"I started the week tracing back a pair of threads: The history of vampires and the history of the Wakestones. Yet as my research unfolded, I realized that these two threads were inextricably braided together. You can't follow one without crossing over the other."

Tina looked taken aback. "The history of the Wakestones? What's to discover? Their whole brand is their history. Wakestone Trials' logo is overlaid onto a map of the colonies. You don't even need to scroll down on their webpage to see them parading their proud heritage."

"Yes, of course, but what is that heritage? How much of it is nonfiction?" She tapped the book atop her pile, "And how much of it is fiction?" she tapped the book underneath. "Or, put another way, where are the Wakestones from?"

Miles, who only had a cursory understanding of the family,

sheepishly suggested, "Durham, for generations, right?"

Armelle waived him off. "Yes, yes, of course. But I mean originally. Where did the family emigrate from?"

Tina piped in: "Hungary, I believe."

"Correct," Armelle replied. "Yet does 'Wakestone' sound like a Hungarian name?"

Miles shrugged. "That's not so uncommon. My great-grandmother's name was originally 'Akinyi,' but when her family made their way to the States in the 20's it was changed to 'Akins.'"

Armelle nodded her head side-to-side, as she did when she was engrossed in a task. "A common enough tale for immigrants. Yet usually the original name isn't a fiercely guarded secret. The Wakestones have published literally hundreds of pages on their family history, and yet not once did they reveal their original name."

Armelle let this sink in for a moment before she took the first book off of her pile and placed it before her.

"And for good reason, since the name 'Ebredkő' serves as a sort of Rosetta Stone. It unlocks the mysteries of not only the Wakestones, but also vampires."

Tina couldn't help but smile at Armelle's professorial nature. This woman who Tina knew as an analyst had transformed herself into a historian in just a week.

Armelle pushed the book into the center of the table. "*A General History of Pirates*. 1724. Here's where we find the Wakestone's true name. The family makes it abundantly clear that they made their name and money on the seas with the Royal African Company before landing in the Carolinas. Yet there's no word of a Wakestone in any of the records for the trading company. There is, however, a peculiar story of a privateer named Ambrus Ebredkő."

Miles piped in. "Privateer? What's the difference between that and a pirate?"

Armelle tilted her head to the side as she considered the question. "Mostly just who is writing the history. One country's privateer is another country's pirate. Take, for instance, Ambrus Ebredkő. He was on the crew of a ship called The Ninnat. This ship was ostensibly an extension of The Royal African Company. Like the RAC, they transported goods to British colonies (most notably slaves from the western coast of Africa), but the speed of their ship made it perfect for raiding other boats. As long as those boats happened to be French or Spanish, the British government was more than happy to take its cut and finance future operations. But when that financing runs out, one typically ceases being a privateer and becomes a pirate. That's precisely what transpired with the Treaty of Utrecht in…" Armelle trailed off, her head bobbing side to side in contemplation. In time, she shrugged, admitted "Sorry, I don't have a memory for dates," then consulted her copious notes before continuing. "Ah, there it is: The Treat of Utrecht: 1713. That brought peace between England, France, and Spain. The Ninnat kept raiding, but now no longer with the explicit permission of the Queen."

Miles pointed to *A General History of Pirates*. "Presumably they got captured at some point, or you wouldn't have seen his name in there."

Armelle tilted her head to the side. "Sort of. The British did bring in The Ninnat a few years later, but it wouldn't be accurate to say they captured it. Rather they came across a ship floating aimlessly, only to find three crewmen: Ambrus Ebredkő and a pair of slaves. Everyone else was gone."

"Dead?" Miles asked.

"Disappeared."

"What happened?" Tina asked.

"No one could say. Or would say. The slaves were shipped to the colonies, and Ebredkő was shipped to London for questioning. But he wouldn't talk. Possibly couldn't talk. The records say that when asked about the boat, he slipped into convulsions. If the British had considered the enslaved survivors as worthy of questioning, they might have found their answer."

Armelle turned and carefully placed the next book atop the pile in the middle of the table. "*Speaking with Vampires: Rumor & History in Colonial Africa*. This text is a collection of folk tales passed down orally through slaves in the American South. It reveals that Northern Africa was one of the only regions of the world without stories of vampires, at least until the triangle trade began. Then suddenly they appear in their folklore. If our theory that the… we'll call it a virus, originates with a Costa Rican bat, then it makes sense. Ships on the slave route, including The Ninnat made frequent stops in Costa Rica. Perhaps one of those stops resulted in contact with one of the Holy Blood Bats. And perhaps that resulted in this." Armelle opened the book to a full-page illustration of an empty ship floating in a sea littered with bodies.

"Stories were passed down over generations of a mysterious ghost ship. One night, they said, the crew awoke to find a pair of bodies. One below deck, drained of blood, another on the deck who seemed to have passed in excruciating pain, but with no clear sign of demise. The next night there were more bodies. Some hidden below, some exposed above. The crew threw the bodies into the ocean, but each night, more came. Until, apparently, not a soul remained, and the ship floated off, never to be heard from again." Armelle closed the book. "Obviously this is absurd. How would this story have found its way into the oral tradition without survivors? Perhaps Ambrus Ebredkő, along with the two slaves mercilessly sent to the New World, were those survivors."

Tina and Miles shuddered at the thought. After a moment, Miles asked, "So what became of Ebredkő?"

"Well, that was the question, wasn't it? Following the Treaty, the British were obligated to punish all pirates, and they could not deny that Ebredkő, as a crewmate on The Ninnat was precisely that. Yet the typical hanging seemed harsh for a man who had already suffered so much (not to mention who had lined the royal coffers so extensively)." Armelle reopened *A General History of Pirates* and pointed to a passage. "So instead they sent him as an indentured servant to the Carolinas. We never see the name Ebredkő again. Yet it was in this same colony that the mythology of the wealthy, land-owning Wakestones arose. It is probably worth pointing out that 'Ebred' loosely translates to 'wake' and 'kő' means rock."

Tina and Miles each looked confused. Tina asked, "So the Wakestones weren't wealthy landowners as they suggest?" while Miles simultaneously asked, "How did a Hungarian man end up on a British ship in the first place?"

Armelle smiled and placed the next three books on her pile out on the table. Her ordering of the books had perfectly matched where Tina and Miles had directed the conversation.

"Let's start with Miles' question. Have either of you ever heard of the book *Carmilla*?" she asked while pointing to one of the two texts. Miles and Tina each shook their heads no. "That's a shame. It truly is a remarkable book. Written in 1872, 26 years before Bram Stoker's *Dracula*. It tells the story of a Hungarian town beset by vampires. A chief source of this novel was Dom Augustin Calmet's *Traite sur les Apparitions*, which was written in the 17th century." Armelle placed a hand on each of these books. "Calmet presented a report from a priest who learned of a town in Hungary tormented by vampires before an unknown traveler sets a trap in the cemetery and decapitates the perpetrator. It's retold in Chapter 13 in *Carmilla*. One of the people who is said to be killed by that vampire? A young mother named Ebredkő."

Miles slowly exhaled. "Ambrus' mother?"

"Impossible to say," Armelle replied. "But presumably some relation. It was also around this same time that The Royal African Company was seeking crew for their expanding business venture. You can imagine why Ambrus might want to relocate."

"And yet he ended up sailing directly into the source of the problem he fled from," Tina pointed out.

"Indeed." Armelle looked toward Tina. "So let's now turn to your question. The Wakestones paint themselves as wealthy landowners, running a 'compassionate' plantation, before transitioning into a small-town pharmacy in the early days of the 1900s. That pharmacy of course grew into the 'lovable' Wakestone Trials that we see today."

"And that's not true?" Miles asked.

"The pieces are mostly there, but each is twisted a bit to fit into the forced jigsaw puzzle of their narrative. They did seem to be tied to the plantation that was just to the south of us, but they worked on it rather than owned it. Perhaps over the years they climbed the ladder and served as foremen, but they certainly never owned the land. Nor did they seem to possess much wealth. At least, not till the 18th amendment."

"Prohibition?" Tina asked.

"That's right. Although that term is something of a misnomer. There were all sorts of types and uses of alcohol that were not prohibited by The Volstead Act, including for medicinal purposes. That left a giant loophole for anyone who wanted to open what ostensibly was a pharmacy but functionally served as a speak-easy. Not that it was an easy or safe venture, mind you. There were limits on how much liquor a pharmacy could prescribe, so those with ambition needed to supplement that business with alcohol obtained and sold through... slightly more unsavory routes. Those with wealth or a reputation had no need to risk either, but the Wakestones, having neither, undoubtedly saw it as an opportunity."

Tina shook her head in agreement. "That certainly makes sense. Wakestone Trials dates back to the 1920s but is vague about its origin. But how certain are you?"

Armelle pushed forward the third book. A pulpy novel entitled *Al Capone's Vampires*. She handled this dime novel in the same way as she did reputable historical tomes. "A fascinating novella. Al Capone's fearful reputation is well-known, but also well-puzzled over, considering he was barely 20 when he began taking over the midwest.

Just how did this child, with few connections or means, manage to intimidate some of the toughest people on the planet?"

"So he used vampires?" Miles asked.

Armelle tucked her hands into her cardigan. "Oh, who knows. But the novella does feature an army of vampires sent from North Carolina. Furthermore, we do know from testimony at Capone's trial that he made off-the-books payments to some Hungarian bootleggers."

"Wakestone's great-grandfather?" Tina suggested.

"Possibly," Armelle replied. "Furthermore, this story shows Capone eventually becoming infected with a diluted form of the illness, which left him with ever-declining health as he withered away in prison. A 'curse' they claim that the descendents of Capone inherited."

"Is that true?" Miles said.

Armelle's eyes looked upwards in contemplation. "Possibly. Neither his son nor grandson passed 50. Each died from heart issues." Armelle looked towards Tina, waiting for her to connect the dots.

Tina's eyes widened. "Jacob Wakestone's father and grandfather died young…"

Armelle stacked her books neatly, and placed them to the exact center of the table, leaving one in front of her. "It must be stated that this is all conjecture. Correlation, sure, but we can't say much about causation." She then tapped the last book in front of her. Although to call it a book would be an overstatement. It was a loose collection of faded diagrams, barely held together with a worn leather binding. "But this is no novel." Armelle opened it up and pointed to a map that showed a cross-section of the city of Durham. About two-thirds down the page was a faint line, which seemed to suggest the ground. Underneath that was a line, connecting three locations. Armelle stated dryly, "This was found buried in the city's Volstead Enforcement files. It doesn't appear to have been ever used. It was probably just created to elicit a bribe." She pointed to the location on the far left. "The original Wakestone Pharmacy. On Foster Street. Now the home of Wakestone Trials."

She pointed to a marked location on the far right. "Wakestone Manor. South of downtown. Before Prohibition, this was little more than a two-room shack. But by the time prohibition had been repealed with the 21st amendment, it had been expanded to a veritable mansion. It remains the heavily guarded home of Jacob Wakestone. And, based on Miles' testimony about the expanding trial, I would guess it's where the next wave of patients are being held."

She then pointed to the location marked in the middle. "This is where the liquor was imported, before being sent to the Pharmacy. It was an old tobacco warehouse that the Wakestones bought in 1922."

Armelle then traced the line connecting the three locations with her finger. "And here is the tunnel connecting the three locations. A tunnel that--if the circuitous route that the fiber lines recently installed took are any indication--still remains."

Miles pointed to the map. "We know getting to the top floors of the Tower is... problematic. And I can't imagine a home invasion of the richest man in the state is feasible. Is the warehouse still there?"

"Somewhat," Armelle replied. "As Geer Cemetery expanded, the city annexed the land. There are press clippings of the Wakestones fighting it. 'Governmental overreach' they claimed as the reason why they clung to a neglected, dilapidated warehouse. But we can now surmise that there was an entirely different basis. Unwilling to reveal that reason to the courts, they lost their appeal. The foundation of the warehouse remains the same, though it's been tidied up a bit and now serves as a storage area for the cemetery." Armelle smiled. "We get into the cemetery, and we can get anywhere.

Miles, thinking of Jacob Wakestone and all the evil he and his family had placed on this earth, exclaimed "To the Tower!"

Tina, thinking of the prisoners who she had let wither away, simultaneously exclaimed "To the Manor!"

15

More

After debating which destination they should focus on, Tina stayed at the table, working on the logistics of the plan. Page after page she scribbled, but she couldn't unlock it. They had a destination and access, but then what? They had no power. No plan.

Frustrated and distracted, Tina found herself doodling in the margins, then chastising herself for doing so.

"What's that?" Armelle asked as she approached the table.

Embarrassed, Tina quickly shut the notebook. "Nothing. It's dumb. It's not any kind of plan, I'll tell you that much."

Armelle sat next to her. "Oh, that's fine. We're still in the data-gathering phase. When it comes time to make a plan, I'll help you." She tapped on the notebook. "But what was that you were drawing?"

Tina kept her hand held tight on the notebook before reluctantly opening up to where she left off. She slid it over to Armelle and looked away. In the distance, Miles was pacing through the bookshelves, fighting his own internal battle.

A smile spread across Armelle's face as she took in Tina's doodle. It was an elaborate maze. And throughout it was the word "perfect" traveling through paths, reaching dead ends. Over and over. None of them found the center of the labyrinth.

"I love it!" Armelle exclaimed.

"It's pointless," Tina deflected.

"No, it's beautiful." Armelle looked at Tina and cocked her head to

73

the side. "You're creative."

"Oh, I don't know about that. I used to be, I suppose."

Armelle considered. "I don't think it works that way. It's in there. Just gotta let it out."

"What I should be doing," Tina stated, "is working on the plan."

"And how was that going?" Armelle asked bluntly.

When Tina didn't respond, Armelle got up from the chair and retrieved a knitted blanket that was tossed over a chair in a reading nook near the window. She looked down at the blanket and said, "When my brain latches onto something, I tend to hyper-focus. It can be wonderful. But at other times, it can be problematic. Draining and isolating. Particularly if I'm stuck on a problem. It's hard to let go." She rubbed her hand across the interlocking hexagons on the blanket. "I found that knitting helps. Coming up with a design, creating it, seeing the end product. Even if it's not perfect, it's mine. That can be comforting. And, ironically, in the process, my brain often stumbles upon an elegant solution to the problem I was stuck on."

Tina inspected the blanket. The shapes and colors repeated themselves in an intricate pattern that she couldn't quite decipher. "It's incredible."

"It's yours," Armelle said casually, before getting excited. "And this isn't just anecdotal. There's science supporting this idea. Focused and diffused mode. In fact, I was just reading about a fascinating study conducted by a prominent cognitive scientist. He collected—" Armelle stopped herself as she noticed Tina shift her attention from the blanket to her. "I'm sorry, I know it's exhausting. I'll stop."

"No, don't apologize for that," Tina said. "I love how much you love things. I could use more of that myself."

Armelle handed her the pencil. "So do it. Write more. Draw more. Make more."

"I will, thank you," Tina responded as she looked down at the center of the maze. She let the pencil lead her and said to Armelle, "Now, tell me about that study?"

16

Manor / Tower

Armelle pulled up to Geer Cemetery at high noon, with the sun shining down directly from above. As Tina slid out of the car along with Miles, she said to Armelle, "Circle around, but stay close. Hopefully, this doesn't take too long." Armelle nodded, opened her mouth to say something, but then drove away wordlessly.

Miles pulled out their map of the graveyard and scanned the horizon to get his bearings. They were at the corner of Camden and Avondale. He pointed to a path weaving through headstones. "There. That should take us to the warehouse. Or whatever it is now."

They followed the path, passing by what seemed to be more graves being dug than would have been expected, marked by cheap headstones featuring only a name, if that. Tina pulled her coat tight around her to ward off the uncommonly cold October day. As they turned a corner, they spotted an odd-looking structure that didn't quite seem to fit the aesthetic of the rest of the cemetery; whereas every other building was constructed out of a pale grey stone, a nondescript wooden structure stood in the middle of a rotary: The Wakestone's former warehouse, used during Prohibition for smuggling liquor. Armelle's research suggested it was never glamorous (intentionally so) and the city's ownership of it certainly did not improve its aesthetics.

They halted, about twenty yards away from the building. Miles looked at Tina, hoping she would initiate the next step, only to find she had done the same. Each nodded to the other, and they approached the former warehouse in unison. Armelle had assured them that it would not be in use at this time of day, but they paused in front of the door, unwilling to enter in case she was wrong.

"Isn't there some prayer or something you could say right now to grant us some extra luck?" Tina asked Miles. She had meant it to be a joke, but somehow it escaped her lips with a desperate sincerity.

Miles thought of the Dungeons & Dragons games he loved as a child. He remembered the anticipation of rolling a dice to determine how lucky you would be in a quest. "I don't think God really works that way." If there was anyone inside, they would have been immediately notified by the rusty creaking noise. Not sure if it was her sake or his own, Miles tried to recite a passage that sprung to his mind.

"The Lord bless you and keep you…"

Tina stepped through and Miles followed. The warehouse, being built to fend off prying eyes, had only a few tiny slits in the wall for windows, and those were covered up by rakes and other cemetery maintenance equipment, leaving Miles and Tina with the unsettling feeling of stepping into a nearly pitch-black room at high-noon.

"The Lord make His face shine upon you…"

They each pulled out flashlights. They scanned the floor, looking for some sign of a tunnel underneath, but the room was littered with everything needed to keep a cemetery looking pristine that mourners would not want to see when grieving by a grave.

"And be gracious to you…"

The two split apart, and piece by piece, uncovered the floor, shifting the equipment aside as they searched for the door.

"The Lord lift up His countenance upon you--"

Miles' prayer was cut off by Tina exclaiming with a mix of excitement and dread "I got it!"

Miles raced over and stared down at a dim outline of a rectangle in the floor. The only sign of it being a door was a small circular hole toward the base. Tina curled a finger around it and gave a pull, to no avail. Miles tried and was unable to lift it either.

"Probably a good sign, actually," Tina pointed out while inspecting various rakes. "Means that this hasn't been in use. With any luck, Wakestone has only been using the connections between the Manor and Tower and has neglected this spot." Satisfied with a skinny, metal rake she had found, she walked over to the door and shoved the handle of it in the hole. Miles grasped the other end of the rake with her, and the two of them pulled together, using it as a lever. After some effort, the door cracked open. The effort splintered the rake, creating a pointy fragment in each of their hands. Miles and Tina each looked down at their half of the rake. Tina dropped her piece on the ground. Miles touched the point, disappointed at how dulled it was. Nevertheless, he placed this stake in his back pocket.

Tina directed her flashlights on the opening and spotted an old metallic ladder leading down. The light faded out before they could see where it landed.

"Ready?" Tina asked.

"Nope. You?"

"Hell no," Tina responded, before quickly adding, "Sorry."

Miles smiled, and said, "Feels like an appropriate response to this situation we find ourselves in." He tucked the flashlight into his belt, stepped onto the ladder, and descended into the darkness. Tina followed. They couldn't have been on the ladder for more than a minute, but it felt like an eternity. At some point, Miles dropped his foot onto what he expected to be the next rung, only to feel the concrete floor of the tunnel. "Just a few more feet," he whispered to Tina, who landed shortly afterward.

Miles shone his flashlight to the left, while Tina directed hers to the right, and said kindly yet firmly, "Miles…"

He thought back on their debate from the previous night.

"We should go to the Tower," he had pleaded then. "That's where Jacob Wakestone is. We stop that snake, and we end this all." He expected Armelle and Tina to agree, but when he only saw uncertain glances, he pushed on. "Tina, we can get the access codes from the files Rebecca gave you. We can pick up the elevator from the kitchen on floor 0 and take it all the way to the 60th. He won't be expecting us. This is our chance. After all the evil he's done. After all the people he's hurt…"

Tina had looked over at Armelle and could see her formulating her analytical response in her head, before laying a gentle hand on Miles' shoulder. All she said was "Katrina." And that was all she had needed to say.

Katrina.

Each time he tried to sleep, he heard the pain in her voice. *I have seen him*. Miles did want to see Jacob Wakestone suffer. He wanted to *make* him suffer. But he had a chance to save Katrina. "You're right," he had said. "We should go to the manor."

As he stood in that lightless tunnel, he knew what path he *should* take.

But what did he know? He spent his life studiously deciphering the will of God. Yet for every answer he found in the Bible, he discovered three new questions. He tried to hide it from his parishioners and himself, but the older he got, the less certain he got. So perhaps his interpretation of God's will was off. He certainly did not doubt that what Wakestone was doing was wrong. Wouldn't God want him stopped? Wasn't the Old Testament full of commands to vanquish the enemies of the Lord? Perhaps this urge was placed in his gut by God. To look into Jacob Wakestone's eyes as he took his last breath. Perhaps--

Miles' spiraling thoughts were interrupted by a curse from Tina, as her flashlight flickered on and off. She hit it against her thigh, hoping to jostle it back into functioning. "Would love it if this plan wouldn't fall apart before it even started," she said to herself, as she hit the flashlight against her leg again. It flickered, temporarily blinding Miles. "Sorry," she said.

"No..." Miles replied. "Not at all." That word 'love' pulled him out of the whirlpool his brain was sucking him into. He remembered the words a professor had said in his first week at Georgetown. "It's really quite simple: Love God, Love each other. Leviticus 19 and Matthew 22."

Tina hit the flashlight again. It illuminated and pointed the way to the manor.

Miles followed, saying to himself "For Katrina."

Tina smacked the flashlight against her leg again. The light reignited and pointed the way.

"To the manor," Miles said, "For Katrina." But he wondered what would happen the next time the light went out.

17

He Is Coming

According to Armelle's blueprints, the walk through the tunnel from Geer Cemetery to Wakestone Manor was roughly three miles, which, she assured them, would take approximately one hour to walk. They walked in silence.

"All hours are not created equally," Tina whispered, after checking her watching certain that they should have arrived only to find that only twenty minutes had passed.

They continued, each step feeling like a mile.

At some point, Miles had bumped into Tina, who had stopped short.

"What's wrong?" Miles asked as he reached for the dulled stake in his back pocket.

Tina cracked her knuckles. "I thought I prepared myself," she said. "I expected to see things, hear things, feel things that were..." Her words trailed off into silence.

"But there's nothing," Miles responded.

"Exactly. I don't see anything. Hear anything. Feel anything." She scanned the tunnel with the flashlight. Nothing. "It's somehow... worse."

Miles nodded. "I understand."

Tina stepped forward, staring ahead into the void. "I don't remember much about church. We were one of those Easter and Christmas families, you know?"

Miles followed. "Sure, we have plenty of those. I always figured if I did my job better on Easter and Christmas, there would have been less."

"Each Christmas when they would pass the candles around before singing Silent Night, my brother and I would use them to light the corner of the programs on fire, extinguishing them at the last possible moment." Tina smiled at the memory. "That's probably the reason my parents didn't bring us more often, nothing to do with the pastor."

Miles considered. "That actually makes me feel better."

"What was that prayer they say every service?"

"The Lord's Prayer?"

"Maybe?" Tina replied. "Can you say it?"

Miles filled his lungs with the damp air circulating through the tunnel. "Our Father… who art in heaven… hallowed be thy name…"

Their pace quickened.

"Thy kingdom come… thy will be done… On earth, as it is in heaven…"

It gave Tina something to hear.

"Give us this day… our daily bread… and forgive us our trespasses as we forgive those who trespass against us…"

It gave Miles something to feel.

"Lead us not into temptation…"

Tina cut off Miles' prayer. "Do you hear that?"

Miles listened attentively. A subtle clicking sound.

They followed. It grew louder with each step, until Tina spotted a trapdoor in the ceiling above her, which seemed to be the origin of the sound.

Tina directed her flashlight at the ladder leading up to the door, then turned it off. Miles followed suit.

Tina recalled her plan. "Just reconnaissance. Gather intel. Return armed with knowledge…"

With that, Tina climbed the ladder, pausing at the top, with the door above her. With her left hand on the ladder, she pushed at the door with her right, pausing after it was raised an inch or so, as she considered what she would find above. Knowing it was irrational as she was doing it, she closed her eyes tight while she pushed the door open, softly folded it down, and pulled herself into the cellar of Wakestone Manor.

Upon opening her eyes, all she saw was a trail of parallel lights, dimly illuminating a path. As her eyes adjusted, she noticed that to either side of those lights was a set of cells that seemed to be generations old. Tina then looked up and identified the clicking sound that had led them there.

Bats.

They were fluttering in the dark recesses of the cellar ceilings. Before Tina could register her apprehension, she felt Miles tap her on the shoulder. He pointed behind them. A cracked door revealed a regal room, with candles revealing a luxurious sofa. Tina took a step in that direction to inspect it, when she heard a strained voice creak out three fearsome words: "He is coming."

Tina traced the voice to a nearby cell. There she saw a pale chalky face and an unevenly shaved head. But what struck them the most was the eyes. They were cold, and scared, and deep red.

"Katrina," she heard Miles say.

Then she heard it. She wondered how Katrina had heard it previously, because it was practically silent at first, but grew steadily louder. The sound of footsteps descending the stairs.

Miles froze. Tina pulled him by the arm into a cell next to Katrina's that had a partially open door. It was not until they crossed the threshold that Tina wondered if there would be a body (alive or dead) waiting for them. They scurried to the back corner of the cell, which was smothered in darkness. If there was anyone else there, they weren't making themselves known.

The footsteps got louder. The sound transitioned from a ringing, hollow noise to a dull, thump. The person approaching was no longer on the steps. They were coming toward them.

Closer.

Tina felt the vibrations of Miles' hand shaking next to her. She forcefully put her hand on his elbow to steady him.

Closer.

Then the steps stopped.

Something plastic hit the metal door. A mechanical clicking noise.

"please. no." A soft, painful pleading from Katrina.

Then the screeching sound of the door being pulled open.

Next, Tina heard a vaguely familiar voice. "It is that time, my child." It sounded proper yet horribly wrong. Smooth and eloquent yet with a faint raspiness. She had heard it somewhere. Or at least a version of it that was more polished.

Katrina's strained voice grew and echoed throughout the cellar. "Please... Nothing left."

The other voice responded dryly. "Doctor?"

Sounds of other footsteps barrelled down the steps. Some other rattling noise accompanied the steps as they entered Katrina's cell. A brief but seemingly futile struggle ensued. Then Tina and Miles saw the silhouette of three bodies pass by their cell toward the room at the end of the hall. A young woman, presumably Katrina, was pushed in a wheelchair by an older woman, followed by a tall, wiry man. Before they passed by, the dim floor lighting caught the colorful beaded bracelet on the older woman's wrist. Ivanov.

When they had passed by, Tina whispered to Miles, "Should we do something?"

But all she heard in response was Miles muttering to himself. "Our father... Our father, who who who... Our father who father who our... Our..."

Tina saw Miles clutching his stake like it was a rosary and shook away any heroic ideas of rescue. Even if Miles wasn't in the middle of a panic attack, what could they do?

"Hallowed be... Hallowed be thy name..."

The familiar voice could be heard at the end of the hall. "Three pints, Doctor? And then provide her with the replenishing fluids from the trials. You are confident she will complete the transition afterward?"

A stammering voice, that Tina recognized as belonging to Doctor Maria Ivanov, responded. "Confident? Yes. Well, no. Not exactly. This is uncharted... By that, I mean that the research is..."

The other voice cut her off forcefully. "We will discuss the results when I come to. Make it work."

If Katrina was speaking, she couldn't be heard over the screeching sound of some device being dragged across the floor and set up.

"Thy kingdom... thy will... thy beast..."

Tina put a hand atop Miles' and breathed in for a four count.

One... two... three... four.

Then out.

One... two... three... four.

Miles' breathing began to slow down to match Tina's rhythm. Until the horrifying sounds of Katrina's wails filled the cellar.

"Daily Bread... bread...beast... the belly... the beast..."

onetwo.onetwo.onetwo.

"I don't know if she can take anymore."

"Three. Pints."

"Trespasses... against us...trespasses...trespasses..."

onetwoonetwooneoneone.

It continued.

Katrina's screams.

Miles' halting prayers.

Tina's hyperventilating.

And then the screams stopped.

"Deliver us… from… from…"

One.. two..One… two…

Tina heard the rattling of the wheelchair being pushed back to the cell. As it passed by, Tina cracked her eyes open and saw a motionless Katrina collapsed in it, being pushed by Doctor Ivanov. There was no sign of the wiry man.

Katrina's cell door creaked open. "Disgusting…." The voice of the doctor. "Back in a few with the treatment." No sound of the door closing.

"Ebbing away… away…"

One… two… three… One… two… three…

Good enough, thought Tina. She pulled Miles to his feet. Looked him in his glazed-over eyes. "We can save her. We can do good."

Miles nodded absently. Tina led him to the exit of the cell. They turned the corner into Katrina's cell. Her body was in the wheelchair. Head slumped forward between her knees. Arms hanging lifelessly toward the ground. Blood dripping from her wrists onto the floor.

Seeing this pitiful sight pulled Miles out of his stupor. He silently yet quickly wheeled her out of the cell toward the door to the tunnel. Tina raced ahead and pulled up the door. As she did so, she caught the light of the room at the end of the hall in her peripheral vision. Now fully lit, she saw a room that looked as if it was transposed directly from Versailles. An intricate chandelier holding seven candles. A plush, red leather sofa with solid gold accents. And on that sofa, passed out, with thin tubes hooked up to his arms, was the man whose voice she had recognized earlier. The voice from quarterly company earnings calls (though it was more polished there). The face plastered atop their webpage (though it was rosier there).

Jacob Wakestone.

Vampire.

Tina's view of Wakestone was obscured by Miles approaching the room. Prepared to… do something, stake in hand, despite it being too dull to draw blood. Suddenly Tina heard footsteps from the floor above her, headed toward the stairs at the end of the hall.

"No!" she whispered to Miles as she grabbed his shoulder. "Do you want to die?" His eyes remained set on Wakestone.

"Do you want her to die?"

Miles halted. Looked at Wakestone. Then at Katrina. Then at Wakestone, whose leg started to twitch. Miles inhaled quickly, turned toward Katrina and tossed her over his shoulder in one motion, then descended the ladder. With each dampened thud of his feet against the rungs of the ladder, Tina heard Miles restarting the Lord's Prayer.

18

Cordially Invited

Tina followed Miles down the tunnel. She quietly yet quickly closed the trap door behind her before anyone could spot their retreat. Yet something did manage to follow them into the pitch-dark tunnel.

Miles didn't notice it. His eyes were locked on Tina as she landed on the floor of the tunnel. "I'm sorry. I froze. I couldn't... I just couldn't..."

Tina pointed above his head and said, "Catch that and we'll call it even."

Miles glanced up and saw one of the bats had escaped with them. He carefully leaned the unconscious Katrina against Tina, took off his jacket, and swung it over his head like a net. It took a couple of tries, but eventually, he captured the Holy Blood Bat. He handed it over to Tina and picked up Katrina, carefully placing her back over his shoulders.

Tina caught his attention with her flashlight. "Miles. It's okay. Really. If you were the type of person who wouldn't be affected by this type of thing, then you wouldn't be the right person for the job. We will defeat them. But we'll do it our way. The right way."

"Thank you."

"Now let's get back."

The first few minutes of the trek through the tunnel were anxiety-inducing, as Miles and Tina expected to hear the sound of the trapdoor open behind them at any moment. Thankfully, that did not happen, and after about a mile, they became slightly more at ease. That was only so reassuring since Miles did not have an inkling what to do once they rejoined Armelle. Or even if she would be there waiting for them, as they planned. Yet when they reached the midpoint of the tunnel and climbed the ladder into the storage shed in Geer Cemetery, there she was waiting for them.

"You made it. And you found her." Armelle cocked her head to one side as she saw the shaking, balled-up jacket in Tina's hand shaking. "And…?"

Tina eked out a half-smile. "And a bat."

Armelle held one finger up in the air, then disappeared into the pile of supplies stored in the warehouse. She returned holding a cage, presumably for rodents found roaming the cemetery. Tina placed the jacket into the cage, then quickly pulled her coat from it and locked the door.

Armelle inspected the small bat. "We should tell Dr. Contreras," Armelle said. "I'll call him first thing tomorrow."

Tina was about to suggest calling him now when they stepped outside of the hut into the darkness. The day had passed.

Katrina was still draped over Miles' shoulder like a sack of potatoes. Tina worried how that might appear if anyone spotted them. "Here, let's carry her between us." One arm slung over Miles' shoulder, the other over Tina's, head limp, Katrina was carried between them. "If anyone spots us, they'll hopefully just think she has had a little too much to drink at Fullsteam. Or, at worst, that we're pulling off a grave-robbing Weekend at Bernie's bit."

For the first time since they had entered the tunnel, Miles smiled. But that faded as he took in the sight of Katrina: Pale skin. Emaciated. Unevenly shaved hair. Slits covering her arms like tattoos, some fresh, some old. Surely they couldn't bring this possibly comatose patient infected with God-knows-what back to their apartments. Armelle and Tina, however, had considered several contingency plans based on what happened underneath and were prepared.

"Plan C?" Tina asked Armelle, who nodded her agreement.

"That being…" Miles asked.

"The Lemur Center," Armelle stated.

"What?" Miles asked as they walked toward her car, parked a block away.

"The Duke Lemur Center," Armelle added as if this clarified matters.

"Didn't someone shut that place down years ago?" Miles asked as they approached the car.

"Yes," Tina recalled as they slid Katrina into the back seat. "In fact, we did."

Armelle propped Katrina up to ensure her comfort. "Correct. Wakestone Trials bought them out and transferred the animals over for research. Yet they--we--weren't interested in every animal. Or able to move every animal. The former director was a classmate of mine and pops over weekly to check on them, make sure their feeding systems are operational, and so on. When he's out of town, he has asked me to help out. And, luckily for us, he's out of town till November."

"You lemur-sit?" Tina asked incredulously with a smile.

"From time to time," Armelle responded as if this was a perfectly normal thing to do. "When the center was running, it was quite impressive. The largest collection of lemurs outside of Madagascar itself. But now it's abandoned, other than a few spare lemurs who were left behind."

"So it's secluded," Tina said. "That is… useful."

"Correct," Armelle stated. "And then there's Rufus."

"Rufus?" Miles asked.

"Rufus," Armelle repeated, as she pulled the car into drive. "An aye-aye. Fascinating creature. Largest nocturnal primate. Has very specific needs, and Wakestone was unwilling to replicate its enclosure. So it's still there."

"Nocturnal…" Tina said, connecting the dots.

"Exactly," Armelle said as their car pulled onto 85. She gestured backward to the bat cage on Miles' lap. "That one is going to need a dark place" — then she pointed toward Katrina — "And I have a feeling that one will require the same."

As they drove, Tina and Miles caught Armelle up on the events in the cellar of Wakestone Manor. Armelle surprisingly paid particular attention to the tone of Doctor Ivanov. "She seemed agitated, you said?"

Tina looked to Miles to see if he read the situation as she had. "I think so. Yeah."

"Not tired, but irritated? Annoyed?"

"Hard to say, but I think so," Miles responded. Tina grunted in agreement.

"And you're positive no one followed you into the tunnel? Seems like that would have been the natural place to check once she noticed

Katrina was gone."

Tina considered this. "I suppose once we were a quarter mile or so away, we wouldn't have noticed if it had been opened. But no one seemed to follow us."

With that, the conversation turned to how Armelle had spent her time. Consulting her map of the tunnel, she traced it back to Wakestone Manor in search of any other possible outlets. There didn't appear to be any. Then, keeping as much distance as possible, she searched the area around the manor for anything of note. Doing so was harder than she imagined, however, as a ten-foot brick wall encircled the eight-acre property. The only entrance and exit being a gate monitored by a security guard off of Carver Street. After an hour or so, she circled back to Greer Cemetery and took an inventory of the material in the warehouse.

By the time each person had summarized their day, they were pulling into the entrance of the Duke Lemur Center. As Armelle wove the car through the grounds, they felt as if they were transported to a different continent. The forest around them gradually changed from the familiar deciduous trees of North Carolina to something more akin to the rainforests of Madagascar. After several winding turns, Armelle pulled in front of a large brick building. A decorative sign that must have been used when the Lemur Center led tours for the public informed them that this was the Kim Nash Center for Nocturnal Research.

They approached the building from the western entrance, which was covered with floor-to-ceiling windows. These provided them with a glimpse into the building, where they saw a lobby in front of a series of enclosures. As they entered the building, they noticed that the glass was darkened from the inside, preventing sunlight from disrupting the nocturnal animals on display.

"This side was for tours," Armelle explained. "Those enclosures should prove helpful for them," Armelle nodded toward the bat and the young woman before leading through a hallway that passed between a set of four rooms for lemurs on either side into what appeared to be a small dormitory, "And these rooms should be useful for us." They saw a kitchenette, common room, full bathroom, and set of five rooms on the eastern wall. Armelle elaborated, "Years back, The Lemur Center had an exchange program with the government of Madagascar. Researchers from the island would be housed here while studying."

Tina tried to express her appreciation for Armelle's research without indicating the anxiety at possibly being transplanted here.

Miles looked at Katrina and the bat. "Let's get them settled."

"Right," Armelle said as they retraced their steps to the western side of the Nash Center. The only one still in use is for Rufus the aye-aye." She tapped on the darkened glass of an adjoining room. "Perhaps this one on the end for Bruce?"

"Bruce?" Tina asked as he inspected the placard next to the enclosure.

"Needs a name, doesn't he?" Armelle responded matter-of-factly.

Tina read the sign on Rufus' room next door. Apparently aye-ayes were the swiss-army knife of the animal kingdom, with an unconventional assortment of attributes: The teeth of a rodent, the face of a bat, and an elongated, bony tapping finger found nowhere else else in nature. Technically lemurs, they bore little resemblance to the other species in the superfamily, be it in looks or longevity, as their lifespan was nearly twice as long. She found herself growing attached to these strange, unique creatures, which made her all the sadder to read that they were often hunted in their homeland as their unconventional appearance and nocturnal habits led to them being considered a bad omen. A curse.

When Tina looked away from the sign, she spotted Armelle glancing at Miles with a confused expression on her face. Miles stood frozen, Katrina propped up against him, looking into the open doors of the enclosure between Bruce and Rufus.

"Miles…" Tina began.

"When she wakes up… if she wakes up… she'll be trapped in a cell. No way to see out. That… that sounds like torture."

Armelle looked at Tina, hoping she had the appropriate response to set Miles at ease. Tina wasn't sure what to suggest.

Miles placed Katrina in the enclosure but left the door open. He dropped himself next to her and unrolled her sleeves to cover her scars. "I'm staying here for the night," he declared. "Get the lights on the way out, please?"

Armelled nodded. "Doctor Contreras might be able to glean what was going on based on an evaluation of Bruce. I'll let you know tomorrow."

Tina agreed. "I'll go through the database tomorrow from home and find a doctor that can help with Katrina." She glanced at Miles. "You going to be okay here?"

"I think so."

"Meet back here, first thing?" Armelle suggested.

Tina followed Armelle out of the building, extinguishing the lights on her way, and leaving Miles and Katrina in the darkness. Half an hour later, Armelle had dropped her off outside her apartment.

"Thank you," Tina said as she exited the car, locking eyes for a moment. "For everything."

"Of course," Armelle responded.

Tina's head was swimming with what she was thinking and feeling as she entered her building and took the elevator up to her unit on the 10th floor. These thoughts and feelings evaporated as she opened her door and saw an intricately decorated envelope that was slid under her door. She opened it up to see an invitation addressed to her:

"Christina Sanders,

Your attendance is requested at a banquet at The Blind Tiger on the evening of October 2nd starting at 9:00 P.M.

Sincerely,

Jacob Wakestone"

19

For a Moment

Miles paced back and forth in front of the three inhabited cells in the Nash Center. On one end was Rufus, a nocturnal aye-aye who slumbered in the corner. On the other was Bruce, the bat they had collected from Wakestone Manor; the sun was just beginning to rise, so he wasn't active either. In between those two rooms was Katrina, unconscious in her pitch-black cell. Miles looked back and forth across the three rooms for some time. He then shook his head and crossed the lobby where Tina had scattered papers across the large table in the center. He peaked over her shoulder onto the notebooks and noticed flowcharts and bullets and diagrams. Maybe an item or two was circled. A lot more were crossed out.

"Perhaps..." Miles began when he was cut off by a voice across the room.

"Nope."

Miles saw Armelle shaking her head without looking up from her book. Miles then registered the frustration in Tina's mad scribbling. He crossed the room and plopped himself down in a chair next to Armelle.

"I don't know what to do," he admitted.

Without looking up from her book, Armelle said, "Read."

Miles pulled the invitation for that evening that he had found in the offering plate at Saint Thérèse's that morning.

Armelle looked at him over her book. "Not that," she said as she tapped the bookshelf next to her. "From here. The previous workers left behind some decent titles." She held up her book for him to see. "I hadn't read this one in years."

Miles squinted. *The Silmarillion.* "So, are you a Tolkien fan?" he asked.

Armelle closed her book and looked towards the ceiling. Initially, Miles worried he had pestered her, but when she spoke he realized that she was considering the question. "Yes and no."

Miles waited for her to elucidate, which she eventually did.

"It is constructed to be a mythology for a culture that I'm not a part of." She took a sip of her tea and stared out the window next to her. Miles followed her gaze to the collection of Bismarck Palm trees that had been transplanted from Madagascar to provide the lemurs with a suitable environment. Armelle continued, "Though then again, maybe that applies more to my parents. They were the ones who actually lived in Cameroon. I grew up in a town named after a British princess." She looked in Miles' direction. "Hard to figure out which world you belong to sometimes."

For the first time, Miles realized that it was his Polish father who had initially introduced him to *The Hobbit.* It was something that they shared. Something his Jamaican mother had never joined them in.

"Quite true," he conceded.

Armelle tapped the book on her lap. "This didn't quite appeal to me the first time I read it, but I must admit that the world-building is exquisite."

Miles grimaced.

"Not for you?" Armelle asked. "Ironic."

"Why's that?"

"Well, isn't it essentially the Bible of Tolkien's universe?"

Miles smiled. "Sure. Doesn't mean either is easy to read!"

"But you do so anyways?"

"I try," Miles said, not sure which text she was referring to.

"What do you like about it?" Armelle asked.

"Tolkien? I read the Lord of the Rings series every year. I start Fellowship in early September and read the last few chapters of The Return of the King after the services are done on Christmas Day."

"Why?"

"It's reassuring, I suppose. I spend my life seeking God. Hoping He's there. Wondering if..." Miles rubbed his neck as he pivoted. "There's this term Tolkien came up with: Eucatastrophe-"

Armelle nodded. "Oh right. The sudden, joyous turn. The Eagles."

"Exactly," Miles said. "Everything is set right. By grace. It's reassuring to escape into a world where that happens. Where… what is the line Sam says? 'Everything sad becomes untrue.'"

Armelle adjusted her mug so that the handle was equidistant between her two hands. "But not everything. It always bothered me that the movies skipped The Scouring of the Shire."

"Same," Miles said. "It's painful, but you see that there are always lingering scars. That Eucatastrophe doesn't mean that everything is happy. That everyone makes it. Or that the good sticks around. But that, for a moment, everything is as it should be."

"For a moment," Armelle said as she reopened her book.

Miles felt himself sink into the chair. He closed his eyes. Smelled the cardamom wafting from Armelle's tea. Heard the gentle cooing of Rufus the aye-aye. "For a moment."

"And then what?" Armelle asked.

Miles rubbed the back of his neck and asked, "Do you want the Bible's answer or Gandalf's?"

"Oh Gandalf's, of course."

Miles closed his eyes and recalled the words from *Return of the King*. "It is not our part to master all the tides of the world, but to do what is in us for the succor of those years wherein we are set, uprooting the evil in the fields that we know, so that those who live after may have clean earth to till. What weather they shall have is not ours to rule."

The quote was punctuated by Tina slamming her notebook shut in frustration. "I'm going to work."

20

Plan, Practice, and Prepare

"Aren't you meeting Miles soon?" Armelle asked as Tina sat by the bed of Katrina.

"Well, yes." Tina checked her watch. 8 PM. "Half an hour," Tina admitted. She didn't need to check her watch. She had a ticking clock in her head all day. She had been uncertain about going to work (Armelle begged her to skip), but she still needed some files in the database. Hardly a minute went by that she didn't check over her shoulders, expecting someone or something to approach. No one had come. Yet that didn't set her heart at ease.

Armelle calculated the route in her head. "It's past rush hour, so you should be fine, but you will need to leave soon."

"Well, yes," Tina repeated.

Armelle looked at Tina for a moment, uncertain what was going on, before pulling a chair next to Tina.

"I don't like this," Tina stated.

"Me either," said Armelle. "I should be there too."

Tina looked toward Armelle with concern. "If he doesn't know about you, we need to keep it that way." She then looked at the young woman lying in the hospital cot across from them. "Plus, you need to be here to take care of her."

Armelle stared at Katrina for a moment. "I don't know what to do." Each of them had felt uneasy about watching over Katrina. They longed to save her, but that didn't mean they weren't afraid of her. Her pale skin and red eyes filled them with a sense of dread. She hadn't moved yet. What would she do when she woke? What should she need? What would she eat?

Tina nodded. "I know the feeling." She cracked her knuckles, one after the other. "I don't like this."

Armelle looked at Tina for a moment. "You're not really a 'show up without a plan' kind of girl, are you?"

"No!" Tina responded, at first out of frustration, then, despite herself, she laughed. "Not at all! Planning is what I do. My brother was the one who could just roll out of bed and be perfect. But me? I need to plan, and practice, and prepare."

"And how has that worked out for you?" Armelle asked.

"It got me a 4.0! It got me the top of my class in grad school! It got me a leadership position at the most prestigious clinical trials organization in the country!" This last one slipped out before Tina could recognize what she was saying.

Armelle inched her hand closer to Tina's, the sides of their hands touching. "And how has that worked out for you?"

"It should be enough, but it's not," Tina sighed. "It looks like everything is perfect, but it's not. And the more others thought of me as perfect, the more I realized just how far off I was." Tina looked up at Armelle. "Does that make sense?"

"Yes," Armelle answered.

Tina smiled. "Do you ever feel that way?"

"No," Armelle answered.

Tina's smile disappeared.

"I feel pretty much the opposite," Armelle stated. "Others look at me, and they see someone who is kind of… off. I don't say the right things. I don't like the right things. I don't feel the right things.. All my life I was made keenly aware of all the ways I was far from perfect. Yet all the while, I knew that I had something to give. That all my weird imperfections allowed me to see things that others don't see. To say things that others won't say. The problem wasn't that I was imperfect, but rather that the systems and structures that I was engaging in weren't perfect because they couldn't find a place for me."

"Like Wakestone Trials?" Tina asked.

Armelle shrugged. "That was just one of many places. So I made my own space where anyone could feel welcomed." Armelle dropped her head slightly. "I miss my shop."

Tina considered that Armelle did not need to be here. Wakestone didn't know about her. She could escape into her own perfect world. But she chose this one instead. Tina nudged her pinky over so it was interlocking with Armelle's. "Thank you for being here."

Armelle inched closer to Tina. "You don't need to be perfect. You just need to be you. And eventually, you find places that are perfect for you." She curled her pinky around Tina's. "You find people that are perfect for you."

They sat together in companionable silence.

"This is nice," Tina said, thinking instead *this is perfect*, before forcing herself to leave. To see Jacob Wakestone.

21

What are you going to do?

Tina and Miles met at the top of Central Park, about a block away from The Blind Tiger, where they were ominously invited to meet Jacob Wakestone. Thankfully neither Armelle nor Italo had received a summons. Armelle was on the Katrina shift and Italo would be up mid-week to analyze any changes to Bruce, the Holy Blood Bat. They hadn't yet decided what to reveal about Katrina.

Tina and Miles had taken separate cars, and parked at separate locations, following the advice of Armelle. They met outside an old tobacco warehouse that was in the process of being rehabilitated into expensive condos.

Tina spotted Miles across the lot.

"Anything to worry about?" she asked.

Miles stared at her. "I don't know how to answer that…"

"Fair enough. Anyone seem to follow you?"

"I don't think so," Miles said. "But the Jesuits didn't exactly train me for this sort of thing."

"I didn't notice anything either," Tina said. "Let's head over."

As they walked down Foster Street, they recalled the history of The Blind Tiger that Armelle had taught them. Originally constructed as a soda shop in 1902, it found itself gobbled up by the Wakestones in the 1930s as part of what they claimed was their burgeoning chain of pharmacies, but Miles and Tina now recognized it as another speakeasy for their illicit rum-running business. The website stressed that the venue was closed on Mondays for cleaning and maintenance, so Miles and Tina were surprised when they turned onto Jones Street to see The Blind Tiger bathed in light and overflowing with the sound of jazz. Their feeling of dread was soon joined by one of embarrassment as they noticed everyone inside was in formal wear. They sheepishly entered through the side, Miles wearing chinos and a button-down; Tina in a pair of jeans with a plaid sweater.

They were immediately engulfed by a swarm of people conversing about second homes, golf scores, and 401ks. Miles and Tina plodded through the room, ignored by the powerful socialites around them, but were unable to find Jacob Wakestone. They swam through a sea of guests and escaped through the other side only to find themselves on a sparsely populated dance floor. On the other end of the parquet floor sat a long rectangular table, with seats all on one side, overlooking the venue. In the center of that table was a slender yet muscular man in a perfectly-tailored charcoal-colored suit that complemented his skin, which had a grey hue to it. His hair parted nearly on the side, with not a single strand falling on his long forehead which led down to his cobalt-colored eyes.

Jacob Wakestone.

He stared directly at them. With a subtle nod of the head, he beckoned them to the table. As if under a spell, Tina and Miles approached. Whereas the guests to either side of him had beautifully plated dinners in front of them, Wakestone had only a glass of what appeared to be ruby-red wine, which he swirled around as Miles and Tina approached. The wine rose higher and higher with each revolution, touching the tip of the glass, but never splashing over. When Miles and Tina were in front of him, he gracefully placed the wine down in front of him. The tannins spun around the glass one or two more times before slowly crawling down the side of the glass. With a glance to either side, he dismissed the guests alongside him. They scrambled away like cockroaches when a lightswitch is flipped. Tina recognized some of them as prominent members of the community. As she watched them leave, she caught the eye of someone else in the crowd: Rebecca Canteel. Her boss. Her champion at Wakestone Trials. Tina noted that Rebecca refused to make eye contact. Tina was disappointed, but hardly surprised.

Someone had placed a pair of seats behind them. They sat and looked across the table at Jacob Wakestone.

He waited.

And stared.

And smiled.

It was then that Miles noticed that Wakestone's eyes weren't entirely blue. Surrounding the pupil was a small yet distinct halo of red fading into his irises. This unnerved Miles, who instinctively looked down at the table.

Unable to withstand the silence, Tina spoke up. "What are you going to do?"

Wakestone tilted his head to the side so as to observe them from a different angle.

"Whatever do you mean?" His delivery was smooth and polished. The type of voice one acquires after working with a P.R. firm from an early age. Yet a hint of raspiness laid underneath.

Miles felt the hatred boil over. "We know who you are! We know what you do!"

"Well, of course you do," Wakestone countered calmly. "There is not a person in this city who does not know of me. Or of what I can do. And, I hasten to add, as… insignificant as you may be, I know who you two are." He picked up his glass and extended his long index finger at them while holding it. "I know what you aim to do. Hence the invitation, to make perfectly clear the…" He paused here, searching for the right word. He stared into his glass, as if the answer could be found there, before continuing. "The disparity of our outreach."

Miles looked around in disbelief. "But you're a…"

"A what?" Wakestone shot back, firmly in control. Then, in a whisper, he commanded, "Say it."

Tina locked eyes. "A vampire." Each of them had previously wondered whether he had actually attained this state, but their doubts had withered away when they were in his presence.

A thin smile spread across Wakestone's face. "I am many things, my darling. But is that what concerns you? Is that where you think my might is derived?" A guttural laugh escaped his lips. "Hardly."

He pointed across the room to a rotund man who Tina recognized as the C.F.O of Wakestone Trials, then toward the Bishop of Raleigh. "With a word, I could derail your careers." He tilted his glass toward an elderly man in a three-piece suit conversing with a group of young women: The Wake County Sheriff. "With nothing more than a nod, I could have you locked away, never to see the light of day again." He then returned his glance to Tina and Miles. "And not only you. Make no mistake about it. But the livelihoods and wellbeing of everyone you care about." He turned toward Tina. "Say, your brother?" He turned toward Miles, a tight-lipped smile upon his face. "Or your…well, you don't really have anyone, do you?"

He took a slow sip from his glass, daring Tina and Miles to speak up. They did not.

"I am many things. I am a philanthropist. I am a beacon of the community. I am the face of Durham history. And yes, I am a patron of the sciences, at the edge of a medical breakthrough that will save millions. I am He who God has chosen to lead our people out of the wilderness."

He set the glass down and locked eyes. "You possess anxiety over my power to destroy you. Yet you think too small. In truth, I don't need these" — his smile opened up, revealing two elongated eye teeth extending over his lip — "when I have these" He waved his hand in an arc pointing toward the guests.

Miles spoke up. "We'll tell them. About what you are. About your experiments."

"Tell them what, my child? What I am? Perhaps what I'm… drinking?" Their disgust seemed to invigorate him and drew a spot of red to his pale cheeks. "What you call a vampire, I call the next stage of evolution. What you call my experiments, I call Phase One trials. What's more, every single action I have taken, everything I have done to myself (all of which serves the greater good of this community, mind you), has been completely legal. *That* is my true power." He waved his hand across the room, pointing to the entire venue. "You think your pitifully small amount of information is a weapon? No, my children. They do know. And they say nothing. They *do* nothing. All in hopes that the scraps that fall off my table might land in their outstretched, pleading hands. That is who I am."

Tina smiled. "Not that. We all know — everyone in this room, and more importantly outside of it — that you are a parasite. We'll tell them that you're a fraud."

Wakestone's eyes squinted. The red seemed to seep further into his irises.

Tina pushed on. "That the Wakestone legacy is nothing more than a family of hucksters. Pathetic alcohol pushers willing to do the dirty jobs that respectable families considered beneath them during prohibition." Veins raised along Wakestone's neck, spreading out like tributary rivers. "And now, a sad old man so afraid of death that he engages in pseudo-science that respectable scientists would rightfully consider beneath them."

Wakestone slammed his fist on the table, which splintered on impact, knocking over his glass. "LIES!" The entire room was silent. None of them dared look in his direction. None of them dared say a word. With a hiss, he quickly scanned the room. "Proceed," he spat out in a voice devoid of its usual charm. The band picked back up. The murmur of conversation reluctantly restarted. Jacob Wakestone's volume receded to its previous level, but there was an extra note of bitterness in it now.

"The Wakestones built this town. We earned every cent with our God-given intellect and ingenuity. Those that seek to rewrite history, to tear down the monuments of the great men such as my ancestors, will find that we will not easily be silenced. The history of this town *is* the history of the Wakestones. As will be the future. And this is because we have always been willing to lead where cowards stick to their precious and easy security. But not us." He looked them in their eyes. "Not me."

Wakestone collected himself, taking deep breaths. He picked up a napkin and soaked up the viscous liquid on the table. Inspected the damp rag, tossed it to the side, then licked the remaining drips off his hand.

Tina looked down at the solid oak table, now fractured in each direction. The bravery she possessed with her previous monologue was fading fast. She tried to find leverage by changing tracks. "But we have your…" she stalled out, not knowing how to refer to Katrina.

Wakestone's composure returned, and he shot back, "What exactly do you have? Have you thought this through? Are you referring to the woman you abducted — without her consent, mind you — from a scientific study she was legally enrolled in? The Durham Police Chief is here somewhere, would you like me to send her over so you can tell her what you have?"

He waited for Tina or Miles to respond. They did not. He continued. "In truth, I'm grateful. Phase II is looking much more promising, which leaves us with the arduous task of disposing of the previous… samples. You have taken one off our hands. One that, I assure you, will not last the week without her treatments."

Wakestone gave them a moment to let this sink in before proceeding. "You started by asking 'What are you going to do,' yes? Well, I will return the question: What are *you* going to do?"

Tina and Miles had no idea. They were speechless.

Jacob Wakestone smiled, his canines just barely sneaking out from underneath his lip. "Yes. Precisely. Go back to your lives. Check-in with your precious loved ones. Return to your jobs." He noted their surprise. "Oh yes, you worry about my wrath, but my mercy is just as powerful. Go back to your jobs—or don't—the paychecks will continue regardless. Just don't do anything to… jeopardize that security. For you now work for me." He traced his finger across the table, pulling a thread of the thick red drink along with it. "Do not forget that."

He dismissed them without a word by glancing behind him at a broad-shouldered man. In a moment, the table was full again of the powerful men and women of Durham.

Tina and Miles ceased to exist.

They slinked out of their chairs, through the exits, and back to their cars, all without registering what transpired.

Jacob Wakestone never did tell them what he was going to do.

22

Interlude: One month Prior

"How do you feel?" the doctor asked the young woman. She stepped backward out of the cell into the hallway of the office building to give her space.

"Sick."

"Noted. What else?"

The woman stood slowly, clenching her firsts. Closed, open, closed, open. "Strong." She fell back down, feeling dizzy. She held her head in her hands. "But weak."

The doctor approached, slowly, out of both respect and fear for the subject. She flashed a light in her eyes and watched her pupils rapidly dilate, then placed a finger on the subject's wrist while checking her watch. She spoke to someone at the end of the hall. "Type V has stabilized. The transfusion was successful." She fiddled with the beaded bracelet, rubbing her thumb over the brown one, and whispered to herself, "For Anne."

A strangely melodic voice responded, "Good."

But the subject was concerned. "The woman on the other end. Ava. Is she..."

The doctor grimaced. "Yes."

"No," the young woman said, softly at first, but then louder.

"No."

And louder still.

"NO."

In the flash of an eye, she pounced out of the cell. At the end of the hall, a tall man stood with his back to her, looking out the window at the city below. "You," she hissed and sprinted down the hall. A table stood between them, bolted to the ground. The woman ripped the table top off the iron legs and held it over her head, prepared to slam it over the head of the man in front of her, only to find him somehow already on the other side of the room. She flung it toward him as if it was nothing more than a toy block, but he gracefully stepped aside and let it pass by him. The table top hit the fuse box behind him, killing the lights in the building, which tripped the circuits and resulted in a brief local blackout.

"You may be quick, but I am quicker," he said. And suddenly he was right in front of her.

She reached for his throat, but he grabbed her arms and easily pinned them down by her sides.

"You may be strong, but I am stronger," he said.

He pulled her back toward her cell. She resisted fruitlessly, dragging her nails across the ground as she was tossed into her cell. The screams were stifled as the door locked her in, but not before he said "You may be smart, but I am smarter."

23

They Didn't Need To

No one followed Tina home.

She thought for sure someone would. Every headlight in her rear-view mirror petrified her. She changed lanes. She sped up. She slowed down. With each maneuver, she expected that the vehicle behind her would follow, but they never did. She took a circuitous route back to her apartment, taking abrupt turns without signaling, but it was pointless. No one followed her. They didn't need to.

Because they were already there.

As she passed by the doorman and entered the lobby, keys interlaced between her fingers, ready to serve as a knife as needed, she saw the slimy presence of Emerson Sinclair waiting for her. He was leaning against the wall, chatting with a neighbor of Tina's when he caught her eye. In his most charming voice (which was still quite cold), he bid adieu to the neighbor, then he turned his attention to Tina.

"Good evening, Christina."

Tina was having none of it. "What are you doing here?"

"Waiting for you, of course. I wanted to make sure you didn't do anything… regretful, following the function."

Tina made no effort to keep the scorn out of her voice. "Yeah? Like what?"

Sinclair shrugged. "Something that would jeopardize your future at Wakestone Trials. Something that would jeopardize the tremendous good we can do with our study. Nearly 800,000 have a stroke each year in the U.S. alone. Over an eighth of those die from it, including, if memory serves, your grandmother?"

He waited for an acknowledgment from Tina that never came, then continued. "This trial — which is of great interest to Jacob Wakestone himself, as you are well aware — can save countless lives. Blood substitution therapy has proven to be successful in cases such as these, particularly if we can maximize the chances of matching blood type. The work is truly revolutionary. It would behoove you — all of us, really — to not forget that."

Tina was in no mood for a morality lesson, particularly from this snake of a Wakestone Trials executive. "How did you even get in here?"

Sinclair casually scratched his chin. "Oh, the doorman is an... acquaintance of mine. I was able to help him out of a tough time, a while back. Speaking of which," he now made direct eye contact with Tina, "how is your brother doing? Shame, really..." On that ominous note, he abruptly left.

She rushed into the elevator. On the way, she dialed up her brother. No response. Wondering what Emerson was referring to, she searched his name and hit "news."

Former Tampa Bay Rays All-Star Robinson Sanders caught using a corked bat, suspended for the MLB playoffs.

Her heart ached. Baseball was everything to her brother, and now it was taken away from him. Even before this incident, she wasn't sure if his contract would be renewed. And now...

Something bothered her. Robinson was many things, but a cheater was not one of them. When he was working his way up through the minors, he saw countless teammates inflate their numbers by taking steroids, but he never joined them. He understood why they made that choice and withheld judgment, but he steadfastly refused to partake. Would he cheat now? His skills were fading, so it wasn't out of the question. But it just didn't sound like him.

And why did Emerson Sinclair bring it up? Sure, before this recent ordeal, Sinclair would only speak to her when he thought he could get baseball tickets out of it, but this visit was anything but social. Every word, every gesture seemed pre-determined to send a message. So why then mention Robby?

Tina checked the article: The news only broke half an hour ago. Perhaps Sinclair was browsing his phone while waiting for Tina. Or perhaps he knew before the journalist did.

Tina exited the elevator but froze as her hand hovered over her doorknob. What would she find? Would her home be ransacked to send a message? She entered and found everything exactly where it was supposed to be. They didn't enter her home.

They didn't need to.

24

Welcome to Saint Thérèse's

Miles gave a half-hearted wave to Tina as they split up outside The Blind Tiger after Wakestone's gathering. He got in his car and drove away, barely aware of his surroundings, his head fixating on the injustice of it all. He found himself repeating a line from Job:

Why do the wicked live, reach old age, and grow mighty in power?

Why does Jacob Wakestone prosper? A man who was unconditionally blessed at birth with untold wealth and power. A man who received this unwarranted gift not with righteousness, but rather greed and cruelty.

Why does Wakestone Trials prosper? A tower built on deception reaching into the heavens like Babel.

Why does the ARC prosper? An organization that twists the word of God to further their own ends.

Why do the wicked live, reach old age, and grow mighty in power?

And why does he wither away, crushed under the heel of each of these forces? Like Job, his thoughts turned into what he did (or did not do) to deserve all this. He thought of Daniel, bravely facing down Nebuchadnezzar with nothing more than his words. Of David toppling the Goliath with nothing more than a single stone. Of Moses sweeping the Pharaoh away with nothing more than his staff. And how he, when directly across from Jacob Wakestone, was simply washed away in a flood of anxiety. No words. No stones. No staff.

He thought of the courage that each of these possessed as they defiantly faced forces bigger than them.

He thought of the courage that he lacked. And the reservoir of faith that ought to have sourced this courage, but had long since dried up.

With this thought in his head, he found that he had not driven home, but rather to his church, Saint Thérèse's. He exited his car and entered the church in a haze.

He stood in the middle of the nave for a minute before taking a seat in the first row of pews. His hands rested on his knees. Every so often he lifted them as if to pray, but found that they repelled each other like a pair of similarly-charged magnets.

Then he heard a sound. A soft, scratching sound. And he saw a plump cat, chocolate brown with one yellow eye and one green eye. Naomi.

A year or two back, Miles had seen a scrawny cat meandering around the neighborhood. When Miles attempted to approach it, the cat dashed away. He thought nothing of it, until seeing that same cat appear the next day. Avoiding eye contact so as not to startle her, Miles purchased some milk and cat food at the market next door and set it down outside Saint Thérèse's. When he came into church the next day, he found each bowl empty, so he refilled them.

In a few days, the cat approached him. In a few weeks, the cat let him pet her (once or twice, followed by a gentle bite when she was done). In a few months, the cat would enter the church with Miles each morning.

One day, when she was snuggling up next to him in a pew as he was drafting his homily, he declared, "I'll call you Naomi." It had been a few years since he had moved down to North Carolina. During that stretch, he found each friend he had made in D.C. had drifted away. Too stuck in his own melancholy, he had yet to replace them with new acquaintances around Durham.

Miles recalled the story of Naomi and Ruth as he rubbed the cat's chin, trying hard to forget the unjustified and unstoppable power of Jacob Wakestone. The rhythmic purring soothed him and, for a moment, the whole mystery of life didn't seem quite so difficult. How to be present. How to love. How to be who God created him to be.

But only for a moment.

At the sound of the door opening, Naomi leaped off his leg and raced out of the church, splitting between the two men entering.

Saul Ferris, the director of the ARC, approached along with a sheepish young man with freckles, parted blonde hair, and thick glasses.

Saul spotted Miles and paused at the entrance, rubbing his long red beard as he chose his words carefully. "Ahh... Father Miles. I did not expect to see you here. May I introduce you to Father Michael?"

If Miles was anywhere else, he would have disregarded this man who had done more damage to his faith and livelihood than anyone else. But this was a church. *His* church. A place that should be welcoming to all. So he gritted his teeth and approached Saul and the young priest.

"Welcome to Saint Thérèse's."

"Thank you. Sir. Father." Michael's cheeks flushed red with embarrassment. "It will be a pleasure working with you."

Miles shot a glare to Saul, who returned a smile. "Well, Father Miles, as you know, we in the ARC pride ourselves on finding places for promising young priests such as Father Michael into parishes that would be... conducive to their development. The Arch-Bishop agreed that this would be the perfect place for him to hone his craft. We felt that this arrangement would be mutually beneficial for all parties. We need, after all, Nazarites spread throughout Babylon, don't we?"

This news hung in the air like a fog. Saul waved it away, and added, "Do not fret - it leads only to evil. For the wicked shall be cut off, but those who wait for the Lord shall inherit the land!"

As Saul recited this passage, he threw his large arm over the young priest next to him. Miles stared at them.

Saul elaborated, "Perhaps you did not catch it, but those are God's words, not mine. From--"

"Psalms," Miles replied curtly. "57."

Father Michael, uncomfortable with the silence, attempted to fill it. "Mr. Ferris was just telling me about your recent publication!"

Miles' eyebrows raised. "Oh was he?"

Saul smiled. "I took the liberty of tidying up your article on the benefits of the corporate-religious partnership between Wakestone Trials & ARC. Since you haven't had a chance to return to the office this past week, of course." Saul smiled as if he had done Miles a favor. "Think nothing of it. Was little more than some copy-editing. Fixing up a few grammatical issues, and finishing a few... incomplete arguments."

Father Michael eagerly added "He was saying that Senator Thompson will even be referencing it in a stump speech later this week! Congratulations!"

Internally, Miles cringed at what the Senator known for his xenophobia might do with this paper that somehow bore Miles' name. Externally, Miles attempted to not visualize his displeasure. It clearly was in vain, as a smile laced with schadenfreude spread across Saul's face.

"And what did you think of the piece?" Miles asked Father Michael.

"Oh, who am I to weigh in on such a thing? I take Mr. Ferris's word on the matter that the piece will have profound theological impacts on our society."

The bitter words slipped out of Miles' mouth before he could catch them. "Something tells me you'll do just fine working here."

Father Michael failed to pick up on the insincerity and beamed at the assumed compliment. "Thank you, sir!"

Saul placed his hand on Father Michael's back and steered him toward the rooms past the altar. "Let me finish showing you around."

They never asked for permission to enter Miles' office.

They didn't need to.

25

A Fall From You

"I'm so glad you came," Father Michael said to Armelle and Tina as they approached him after his Sunday morning service. It had been nearly a week since the events at the Blind Tiger. During that time, Armelle and Tina had grown closer. During that time, Miles had drifted apart.

"Of course," Tina said.

Armelle cut straight to the point. "Where is he? How is he?"

Since Tina and Armelle were so focused on Katrina, they had failed to notice Miles' declining state. Each day they worked with Italo Contreras trying to get Katrina up on her feet. No one had seen her move yet. The only sign that she was still alive was a barely beating heart rate of around 40 bpm and the disappearing butcher's blood that they left in her cell. While monitoring her signs, no one noticed that Miles was showing up less and less. When he was there, he rarely spoke. The only words they could recall him saying was "We can't keep on like this," which they had interpreted as advocating for taking shifts at the Nash Center cell, but in hindsight had perhaps meant something more.

"In the sacristy - The backroom," Father Michael had answered, as he took his glasses off, cleaned them against his clerical shirt, and placed them back on his freckled face. "And not great. Thank God for that cat of his. Naomi. That's about the only one he'll talk to. He was supposed to lead the service, but I couldn't find him." He rubbed his hand over his blonde-speckled stubble. "I wasn't prepared to lead it. I wasn't prepared for any of this."

Armelle leaned against Tina, knocking their shoulders together affectionately, then left to find Miles. Tina lingered for a moment. "It was a good sermon. Message. Speech? What do you call it?"

Father Michael smiled faintly. "A homily. Thank you."

She pressed on, "Is there any chance you've heard anything about my brother? Robinson Sanders?"

Father Michael looked confused. "No? Who… The baseball player? I don't… understand…"

Tina wondered how wrapped up in all this the young priest was. Her brother had been missing for a week now. She had called everyone in her family and everyone the Rays organization; they all assumed he had flown away in shame to some island after his suspension. It was true that Robinson loved escaping to remote locations in the off-season, but he always told those closest to him where he would be. Not this time. The only clue of his whereabouts was Emerson Sinclair's cryptic reference. Was Wakestone Trials and the ARC connected to his disappearance? And was Father Michael a part of it? If so, her next statement might doom her, but she couldn't just stop trying.

"My brother… I think… I think they have him. Wakestone Trials. And the ARC. Have you heard…" she trailed off.

The priest hung his head in shame. "No. I didn't realize… who they were. I guess I saw that some of their interpretations were… theologically problematic, but they offered me a way into a community. Here. And now…"

"Have they asked you to do anything? To tell them anything?"

"No," Father Michael shook his head. "Not yet."

"If they do, you know what to do," Tina said as her eyes drifted to the crucifix on the wall.

"Yes, I think I do," the young priest asserted as he again cleaned his glasses on his shirt.

With a nod, Tina departed, following Armelle into the sacristy. Miles wasn't there. But his clerical collar was lying on a table. The door to the back of the church was cracked. There they found Miles sitting on the curb facing the adjacent park, his hands on his knees. Naomi was weaving an infinity symbol around his legs.

"Where have you been?" Armelle asked.

Miles held down his hand for Naomi to rub up against. "Here. Trying to write a refutation of what the ARC has published in my name. But the words won't quite come."

Tina looked at the bible lying on the ground behind Miles. "Well, what does your book say? What words are in there?"

"My book?" Miles held up his hands. "It says, 'this world… is an unweeded garden that grows to seed.'"

Knowing that Armelle was raised as Muslim, Tina mouthed the word "Hamlet," but Armelle was ahead of her, who shot back at Miles, "There's nothing either good or bad, but thinking makes it so."

"Never engage in a Shakespeare battle with a bookseller, I suppose," Miles said.

Before Tina could redirect the conversation, Armelle replied, "There's only one person you're battling. And you're losing—" She was cut off by Tina tapping twice on her hand. Armelle noticed Miles' downcast head, blinked a few times, nodded her thanks to Tina for the cue, and softened her approach. "I know how thoughts can get stuck rattling around one's head. Truly, I do. Let me rewind and try a different Hamlet quote instead…" Armelle's head oscillated side by side as she searched for the line. "'We know what we are, but know not what we may be.' Look to who you may be. And that can start by looking to *where* you may be. You should be at the Lemur Center. We need you."

"Has she woken up?" he asked.

"Katrina? No." Armelle responded.

Tina jumped in. "But she will. And when she does, she'll need you."

"For what?"

"Your faith," Tina suggested, which drew a glare from Miles. Tina pressed on. "She has gone through a traumatic event. We might be able to help her scientifically, but she's going to need help spiritually as well."

"Well then, I definitely know I'm of no use if you need my faith. I don't have any."

Armelle replied, surprised and confused. "You don't believe?"

Miles stammered. "I'm… I don't… I'm not sure I ever did." He held up his hand to block the sun beaming down on him. Moved it to the side to let it through, then blocked it again. "Just as light can be… revelatory, illuminating things that were already there, so can darkness. And these last few weeks have revealed the shallowness, the emptiness of my faith."

Although not a believer herself, Tina was crushed to hear this. "But you *do* have faith. I've seen it! Each time you put on the uniform."

"Vestment," Armelle corrected.

Tina continued. "Each time you say a silent prayer before a meal. Each time you show up here."

Miles shook his head. "You have it backward. I don't do these things because I have faith. I have faith — sometimes — because I do those things. But it's not working. And I don't think it's really supposed to work that way. I think it's supposed to… just be there. When I need it."

Tina and Armelle looked at each other with uncertainty. Tina was raised as a Christian and Armelle as a Muslim, but neither considered themselves believers anymore. Yet Miles' declining faith felt different, somehow.

"Tell me about those times," Tina requested. "When it is there."

Naomi lept on Miles' lap. He rubbed under her chin, eliciting a soft purr. "Every so often. My mind stops racing. My breathing slows, and with each breath, I just feel… filled up. With an energy. A ruakh. In those moments, I can feel it. I can believe it. I can see it."

A car pulling into the back parking lot startled Naomi, who hopped off Miles' lap and ran inside the church.

"But now? I can't feel it. I can't believe it. I can't see it. I keep trying." Miles looked pleadingly into the eyes of Tina and then Armelle. "I really do. I put on the vestment, but they just feel like clothes. I say the prayers, but they just feel like words. I show up here, but it just feels like a building."

Miles patted his chest, again and again, successively quicker and harder. "The ruakh. The spirit. It's not there. Just a void. The only thing that fills it is the… the… anger. At what they have done. And the guilt, at what I cannot do."

A car door closed as Miles pointed past the church to the west. "That woman? Katrina? That poor woman? She's lying there. Dying. Or undying? And there is nothing I can do."

Miles hung his head in his hands. "I can't save her."

Footsteps approached from the parking lot.

"No, but I can," said Maria Ivanov, Jacob Wakestone's Doctor.

26

Am Become Death

"I can help," the mysterious Doctor Ivanov repeated, "bring me to her."

Miles and Armelle each looked at Tina, who nodded affirmatively to signal that this was, in fact, the doctor who had led the blood transfusion trials which had resulted in the current states of both Jacob Wakestone and Katrina. They took in the sight of the diminutive doctor, dressed all in drab grays except for a colorful beaded bracelet on her left arm.

"No," Tina responded coldly and firmly.

Doctor Ivanov, standing just outside Saint Thérèse's, scanned the faces of Miles, Armelle, and Tina, who were in the doorway, then directed her response to Miles. "So you choose her death then?"

"I have not chosen any of this," Miles answered. "But you have."

Doctor Ivanov waved away Miles' words as if they were a pesky fly.

Miles continued, his pulse beginning to race. "Why would we let you see her? So you can hurt her more?"

"Because I can save her."

Tina shot back, "But you're the one who did this to her!"

"That is precisely why I know I can save her. Where is she now? Is a doctor treating her? Have they been successful?"

None of them offered up the truth that she was being looked at by a bat scientist who hadn't the slightest clue what to do.

Doctor Ivanov pressed on. "What is her resting heart rate?"

"Tops out at around 55 bpm," Armelle responded, before clarifying. "An average of 40."

The doctor conducted some calculations in her head. "That's a 20% decrease. If this continues she'll be dead within a week." This prediction lined up with Jacob Wakestone's warning. Ivanov asked, "What is she drinking? How often?"

Armelle looked to Miles and Tina for permission to respond. They neither gave nor rejected it, so she said, "Chicken blood. About once a day."

"You need me." Ivanov shook her head in irritation. "*She* needs me."

Something about the doctor's delivery caught Miles' attention. "Why would you do this for us?"

Doctor Ivanov scoffed. "For you? Not at all. This is for… science."

"Yeah, and what else did you do for science?" Tina shot back.

Maria rolled her eyes. "Words words words… that's all you offer. I offer you the scientific understanding and experience that your words merely represent. You speak of science, but what are you using? You speak of salvation, but how are you saving her?"

No one answered, which only frustrated Maria more. "What do you want from me?"

"A sorry would be nice," Armelle pointed out.

"I'm more sorry than you could ever know." She fiddled with the colorful beaded bracelet on her wrist. "I owe quite a few people quite a bit. But not you. To that young woman, I owe my service. If you would kindly get out of my way, I can start working off my debt. And if not? Well, then you might want to ask yourselves what the cost of your precious words truly was."

No one had a response to this. Eventually, Tina asked, "Can we trust you?"

Ivanov was taken aback. "What a simple-minded question. No one and no thing can be fully trusted." She tugged on the loose-fitting gray peacoat that was wrapped around her skinny frame. "Can this jacket be trusted to keep me warm? Certainly. Can it be trusted to protect me from a mugging? Of course not."

Armelle sighed at her pedantry. "Fine, then why are you doing this for science?"

Tina added in, "Or for yourself."

The doctor looked inquisitively at Tina, as if the suggestion of selfish motives was purely absurd, then continued. "That narcissistic billionaire thought only of his own glory, but with the proper resources and support, advancements in this area could be monumental. This could be the biggest breakthrough since the discovery of penicillin!" Maria scanned their faces, then added with a note of pleading in her voice, "Think of all the lives that could be saved. How many children with blood disorders whose deaths could be prevented!"

Tina rolled her eyes at the doctor's conspicuous appeal to emotion.

Armelle thought of the monster that Jacob Wakestone was turning himself into. "Or perhaps the more apt analogy is the atomic bomb. And your name will be attached to it."

"Yes, yes," Maria said impatiently. "I am become Death, the destroyer of worlds and all that." She marched into the church and sat down next to the bookshelf, shaking her head as she inspected the texts included. "I don't know where this field of study will lead. But I know that for good or ill, it has my name attached to it. I want to direct it somewhere positive." She looked at Miles. "And I can start with *her*."

Miles rubbed the back of his neck and averted his gaze.

Ivanov tried one more time, pleadingly. "With the right space and resources, I know I can save this. I know I can save her."

Miles looked through the doorway to the altar of Saint Thérèse's, hoping some wave of wisdom would wash over him, revealing the right decision. Feeling none, he sighed and made the choice anyway. He mouthed the word "yes," at Tina.

She was skeptical, but looked toward Armelle, trusting her to deliver the analytical choice. Armelle shrugged, then nodded affirmatively. Tina sighed. "Would a Lemur Center qualify as the right space?"

27

For Science

"When did it start, you ask?" Doctor Ivanov repeated the question without shifting her attention off of Katrina onto Tina, Miles, or Armelle. "Well, that depends: For me or for Wakestone?" They had been pushing her for information all week, but the doctor rarely acknowledged them or their questions, instead placing all her focus on her research and her patient.

"For you," said Tina, while Miles said "For Wakestone," and Armelee said, "For science."

Doctor Ivanov considered the three options while she gradually turned the dial controlling the modified IV bag hooked up to Katrina. They were technically in the same cell in the Nash Center as before, but it barely resembled the room as it was four days earlier on October 8th when Ivanov had begun working with Katrina. What once resembled the rainforests of Madagascar, now was a fully functional laboratory (albeit a dimly lit one). In the center of that lab lay Katrina, hooked up to an IV drip that was placed into her a blood mixture that Maria had refused to specify. Cords ran from various points of Katrina's body into a computer which displayed an assortment of metrics on the screen. "I will take Ms. A Moutte's request because A) I believe it will address all your queries, and B) the science is much more important than myself or Jacob Wakestone (despite what his inflated ego might lead some to believe)." Tina rolled her eyes, not for the first time, at the haughtiness of the doctor. She had first heard the Doctor when she observed her class two weeks ago. She was disappointed to learn that she apparently always spoke as if she was addressing an audience of scrupulous students.

Doctor Ivanov walked over to one of the monitors and tapped the screen, where a horizontal bar chart was displayed. The chart was split in two, with one side labeled O- and the other V. Currently the O-segment covered 71% of the bar, with the V comprising the remaining 29%. Tina didn't quite understand what that signified (every time she asked, Ivanov huffed and shot back that she didn't have time for her pestering), but it appeared that the higher the O- portion was, the better. On Monday, the V was nearly 80%, and it had been gradually receding over the week as Ivanov worked (with the assistance of Italo Contreras, though Maria rarely acknowledged his contributions). This transition accelerated each day, with the O- percentage jumping from 50% to 60% that morning, before leveling off. This seemed to put Ivanov in a more approachable mood, which perhaps explained why she finally graced the others with an update.

"In rare circumstances, one's blood type can change. This phenomenon has been associated with rare life events: Bone marrow transplants, certain forms of cancer, unusual infections, etc. These cases have been observed, but never directed. Yet, of late, there have been a few studies that provided pathways forward for blood type changes."

She paused at this point to jot down the readings from the screen in her notebook before continuing.

"We'll start with the most... altruistic study. A team at the University of British Columbia has been making progress with converting Type A blood into O-negative by injecting bacterial enzymes into the guts of patients. These microbes eat the mucin (the sugar-protein combos lining the gut wall) and in doing so remove the A-defining antigens, thus converting the blood to O-negative."

Armelle noticed that the Doctor fluffed Katrina's pillow, which was curious because she had never witnessed her doing anything that was not medically necessary. In doing so, Ivanov's beaded bracelet popped out from her sleeve. The doctor quickly covered it up with her coat, then shined a light into Katrina's eyes and marked in her notebook the dilation of her pupils before elaborating. "This study caught my attention because patients with O-negative blood, of course, are universal donors, whereas patients with Type A blood account for nearly a third of the population. Approximately 17,000 liters of blood are required each day for transfusions; therefore, if we can create more

O-negative blood, that could save countless lives."

Miles rolled up the sleeves of his button-down shirt. "Fascinating. I can imagine. I have O-negative blood and have been told all my life how desperately needed it is."

Tina noticed that Ivanov briefly glanced up toward Miles, which was curious because it was the first time the doctor had registered anyone's presence with eye contact. Something that resembled concern splashed across her face before it was replaced with disgust as Ivanov spoke of Jacob Wakestone. "This study caught Wakestone's attention as well because he gets blood transfusions as frequently as others in his age bracket get botox."

Armelle, who had been investigating Wakestone's past, was intrigued. "For the blood disorder?"

Without looking up, Ivanov returned, "Point for Ravenclaw," which drew a chuckle from Miles who had devoured the Harry Potter series before he entered the seminary. "As Ms. A Moutte has apparently discovered, the Wakestones carry a hereditary blood disorder. No one quite knows the source of the Wakestone's generational wealth--"

Armelle interjected: "Rum-running during prohibition."

A giant smile spread across Ivanov's face. "Perfect. That is perfect. Thank you so much for that gift." She paused, savoring this piece of information, before continuing. "So, apparently all the fortunes they have amassed from the illicit alcohol sales have been insufficient to help the Wakestone males survive past their mid-50s. Jacob swore it was the result of interactions with vampires tainting their blood in the 20s, whereas I ascribe it to the epigenetic consequences of poor health decisions. Regardless of the source, this has manifested as a quick decline in middle age, often commencing with a stroke and culminating with a lethal cardiac arrest. In an attempt to offset this fate, Wakestone had been following some questionable science, which brings us to the second study."

Ivanov stood back, and analyzed the screen, before typing in a command in the computer controlling the various tubes connected to Katrina. The resulting beeps from the monitor and peaks in the line graph above the blood type chart seemed to satisfy the Doctor since when she resumed her updates she did so in a more enthusiastic manner.

"An absurd start-up in the Bay Area has been experimenting with injecting narcissistic millionaires with two and a half liters of plasma from younger patients. It was quite morally dubious, preying on young people in search of a quick buck, and — less tragically — preying on the pockets of over-compensated octogenarians; they promise their rich elderly clients 'rejuvenating' effects, and charge north of $10,000 for the procedure."

"Rejuvenating?" Tina asked.

Maria shrugged, focusing on Katrina. "That's merely their codeword for what the rich are actually chasing: Immortality."

Miles scoffed.

"My initial sentiments as well," Maria responded. "Yet when Wakestone approached me following his stroke with the attempt to replicate and advance their work, he presented their research notes, which cited some… captivating research. This brings me to the third study."

This transition was marked by a groan and a twist of the torso coming from Katrina, which drew a surprised gasp from Tina, Miles, and Armelle, but merely an expected nod from Doctor Ivanov, who dialed down the IV drip before continuing.

"Parabiosis. The blood transfusions for the wealthy were based on a parabiosis study dated in 2014 where a pair of mice were surgically attached, resulting in the sharing of blood circulation. A new study based on ancient studies, for scientists have experimented for centuries with adjoining two animals so that they each share blood circulation. What I posited was that this process could be completed without the grotesque attachment. Furthermore, that it could be exponentially more effective when merged with the research on blood type changes. Which leads to your study, Ms. Sanders."

"*My* study?!?" Tina asked incredulously, wondering how Maria could be shifting the blame onto her. Yet when the doctor resumed, she spoke of the clinical trial that pulled Tina, Miles, and Armelle together not with scorn but rather pride.

"Our study, I suppose. And although Wakestone Trials employed some questionable methods, the results were quite promising. With the aid of the bonding enzymes found in the Desmodontinae, we were indeed able to temporarily alter the blood type of a young donor and then embed the life-giving properties of that blood into the circulation of a diseased recipient through disconnected parabiosis. Do you realize what this means?" Maintaining her disaffected professorial approach, Ivanov answered her own question before her pupils could interject. "No longer must we fret over blood-type matching. No longer must we question whether a recipient's immune system might attack the red blood cells based on them being from an outside circulatory system. Millions of lives saved! And at practically no cost! Within a day, both the donor and the recipient's blood type and circulatory system have reverted to their original state."

"Then what happened with her?" Armelle asked, pointing toward Katrina.

This question set Ivanov on her heels. Despite Katrina's pulse being displayed on the screen (now pushing 60 bpm), she placed two fingers to her wrist to test it. "It wasn't enough for *him*. It should have been. Following the parabiosis period, there was no sign of the degenerative blood disorder. With monthly transfusions, Jacob Wakestone would live a long, healthy life, something males within his family haven't done for generations."

"Then what was the problem?" Tina asked.

"The parabiosis period. The 24 hours when his circulation system was adjoined with the donors. With hers," Ivanov gestured toward Katrina, "as she was the first successful donor. During that stretch, we registered some... well... rejuvenating effects. Enhanced strength, both physically (as measured by stamina and strength tests) and mentally (as measured by recall assessments), without taking an observable toll on the body. In fact, all these achievements occurred without the heart rate eclipsing 50 beats per minute. The result of this revolutionary transfusion is what appears to be a completely unique blood type, one Jacob Wakestone oh-so-poetically insisted be labeled 'V.'" She pointed to the V on the screen while shaking her head sadly.

Armelle tilted her head to the side. "Could this happen in nature? Outside of a lab?"

Ivanov raised an eyebrow. "You're referring to these historical vampires that Wakestone was always raving about?" She uncreased a wrinkle on Katrina's bedsheet. "I suppose if a Desmodontinae did bite someone with O- blood who was immunocompromised, something like this could occur. And they then could infect others afterward."

"And if someone with a different blood type was bitten?" Tina asked.

"Depending on the bacterial transfer, they might die, or they might —"

"End up with an inheritable blood disorder?" Armelle interjected.

Ivanov nodded. "I would imagine that if there was a transition, it would be an ephemeral one. That was what we found in our study. The physical effects remained, but the mental gains became... unstable over time. As for the donor, since they are not receiving the beneficial effects from the parabiosis, then the process is extremely... taxing."

Tina pushed suspiciously: "Define taxing."

Ivanov sighed. "Lethal. Wakestone drained and disposed of countless donors. He was reluctant to do so with Katrina, feeling as though they shared a special bond since she first empowered him with her blood. But so many others gave their lives for his vain pursuit of immortality. All of which was covered up by your creative paperwork, Ms. Sanders."

Tina hung her head and muttered, "I didn't know," while at the same time, Armelle leaped to her defense as she confronted Doctor Ivanov: "Shouldn't you say 'all of which was orchestrated by me'? You've got blood on your hands, Doctor!"

Armelle expected her to deflect or deny, but she acquiesced. "Yes, I do." She pressed a button on the side of Katrina's bed and slowly inclined the back of her bed roughly 30 degrees. "Wakestone became addicted to the feeling of the V blood coursing through his veins. No longer was I leading the study, but simply following his absurd orders." She held out her arms before she could be interrupted. "That is by no means an excuse. I could have escaped. I *did* escape. But too late, for one of his obscene demands actually worked."

Armelle piped in. "The V blood. He converted the blood of his donors to V before the parabiotic transfusion."

Ivanov was both impressed and saddened. "Correct, again."

Armelle pushed on. "But doing so would require a never-ending stream of donors. Each one relying on multiple donors with V blood underneath them."

Tina was aghast. "It's a pyramid scheme!"

Ivanov nodded. "It's Phase II. In the initial phase, there was at least the pretension of a legitimate study. The fatality rate was of course elevated and unethically covered up, but it still followed the basic tenants of a proper clinical trial. Phase II, however, focuses not on science but on ego. It is not the public that benefits from it, but solely the megalomaniac at the top of the pyramid."

An eerie silence crept over the Nash Center, punctuated only by the rhythmic beeps from Katrina's monitor and the cooing of lemurs outside the walls. If they hadn't been so engrossed by Ivanov's story, Miles, Tina, and Armelle might have noticed that Katrina was flexing her pale fingers.

"Yet, like a once-healthy host body that has been overtaken by cancerous cells, there is something here worth saving if we can only rid it of the parasitic elements preying on it. So I left. Five nights ago, I convinced Wakestone that he was ready to receive four liters in a single transfusion. I hinted that this may result in increased strength. Enough to play off his vanity. Enough to put him in a stupor that would last most of the next day. With him passed out, I collected all the data I could and fled. I contacted a trustworthy source at Wakestone Trials and described the figures I pretended not to notice taking the body of Katrina a week prior, and learned your identity." Here she gestured at Miles and Tina. "This research can still save countless lives." She looked down at Katrina. "Including hers."

Tina opened her mouth to ask about her contact at Wakestone Trials, but she was taken aback by the maternal look on Ivanov's face as she gazed into the flickering red eyes of Katrina. Witnessing this familial bond resulted in another question escaping Tina's lips: "While there, did you ever hear about my brother? Robinson Sanders? I think they have him. I think he's in trouble."

Ivanov looked Tina in the eyes. "Robinson Sanders? No, I'm sorry. The name sounds familiar, but not from there."

Tina sighed as Armelle compassionately reached for her hand. "So you haven't seen him?"

But then the pained, strained voice of Katrina responded: "I have."

28

But I Did

"And you're sure?" Tina asked again about the status of her brother. It was difficult to decipher the few words Katrina had spoken as she slipped in and out of consciousness, but the message had remained consistent.

"Enough," Ivanov impatiently responded, as she laid a hand on Katrina's shoulders, instructing her to rest with a glance at the cot. Katrina rubbed her hand over the stubble on her recently shaved head, then passed out on the bed in the room previously designated for mouse lemurs at the Nash Center. Ivanov then left the room. When Tina followed, the doctor followed up accusingly.

"Is your need for constant reassurance worth her health? She has told you countless times these past three days: There is an experimental lab somewhere around Wilmington, and she overheard Sinclair mention clearing a space for a 'Robinson' there. If she could tell you more, she would. Besides, don't you have a train to catch? Seems like you have more pressing matters to attend to."

Tina awkwardly scratched her left arm. She hadn't actually come here to confirm the whereabouts of her kidnapped brother, but rather to deliver a message. "Well, now that you bring it up, before heading to the station, I needed to talk to you about something."

"Oh?" Ivanov dryly responded as she jotted down notes in her notebook. The O- percentage of Katrina's blood had seemed to flatline at 80%; much better than it was previously, but Ivanov seemed frustrated by the lingering traces of V blood in Katrina's veins. Or, for that matter, the manifestation of that lingering V: Her throbbing veins were visible through her skin, which left her susceptible to UV rays, but also left her with increased strength (when she was conscious).

"Well, yes. I was just speaking with Dr. Contreras."

Ivanov raised her head to the ceiling and exhaled loudly. "The veterinarian?"

"You know perfectly well that he's not a Vet. Last I checked, he has more Ph.D.s than you, not to mention he's been published more often. He's one of the most respected doctors in evolutionary biology, so you should…" Tina cut herself off here as she could see Ivanov formulating her cutting response. "You know what? I'm sorry. Forget it. Just let him help, okay? He can help."

Ivanov was muttering something about "real science" when Tina saw through the tinted window that Rufus, the aye-aye, crept alongside Katrina and settled in the hook of her arm. In truth, the animal that more closely resembled a giant mutated rat than a lemur creeped her out, but his presence did present an alternative line of persuasion. Tina pushed on.

"For instance, have you figured out why one of the few phrases Katrina has muttered was used requesting the aye-aye? Or why Rufus' presence has directly correlated to her improving O- rates?" Doctor Ivanov confirmed that she had not with sullen silence, so Tina continued. "Seems like an area where someone like *Doctor* Contreras could help, no?"

Ivanov looked through the window at Rufus. When Contreras initially brought the aged aye-aye into Katrina's cell, she assumed it was for feeding purposes. The idea sickened her slightly but would have provided a useful data point on Katrina's dietary needs. In truth, she could not explain the bond between the two.

Tina was shocked to hear the doctor whisper the word "sorry," and was prepared to facetiously comment on it before realizing that Maria was talking to Katrina through the door.

Ivanov faced Tina and said, "Fine."

Tina smiled. "Thank you."

"He can get me a colony of the Desmodontinae," Maria stated.

"Probably. You should ask him," Tina delivered with a wink, knowing full well that Dr. Contreras was already in the process of obtaining them from a research center to the north.

She exited the Lemur Center building and hopped onto the bike she found on an online marketplace, which she road to Brightleaf Station, two miles to the east. She felt uncomfortable riding a bike, something she hadn't done in years, but Armelle insisted that their vehicles would be monitored. It was the same reason they were taking the train to the coast. As she got to the station, she noticed that Armelle had beaten her there. Tina approached, but Armelle was lost in thought, staring across the track, pulling the sleeve of her cardigan up and down repeatedly. Tina saddled up next to her and followed her gaze to an old brick bookstore called "Simone's Books and Records."

"Know the owner?" Tina inquired.

Armelle kept her eyes on the bookstore, but slipped her pinky around Tina's as she considered the question. "I did. But a few years ago, it was bought out by one of the big online stores. They kept the name, kept the veneer, but it's essentially just a front for the website."

Tina scowled, chastizing herself for previously patronizing the store with the pride of supporting a local business. "Which site owns it now?"

Armelle shrugged and looked down at the word 'bato' tattooed on her forearm, leading Tina to wonder if it was because Armelle didn't know the answer or if it was because Armelle knew the answer didn't matter. With that, Armelle took her eyes off the store, pivoted, and headed toward the platform. They approached the gate together and paid in cash for a pair of tickets to Wilmington.

"Here you go," the man at the counter said as he handed them their tickets. Tina was so focused on their plan (or lack thereof) that she didn't process the man's comment regarding the recent influx of traffic on the route.

As they boarded the train, Armelle skipped over the small talk and informed Tina about the history of the route they were on.

"I didn't actually realize it was funded by the Wakestones," Tina admitted, feeling uncomfortable with the realization that their enemy had laid the tracks beneath them. That their enemy had provided the infrastructure that their state relied on.

"Somewhat," Armelle said, as they pulled into the run-down stop in East Durham, near Saint Thérèse's. "Public-private partnership. What Wakestone invested he has more than recouped in tax write-offs."

Miles stepped onto the train, and locked eyes with Tina and Armelle, before scanning the rest of the crowded compartment. Picking up on his hesitation, they walked through the train until they found a secluded section.

Armelle sat next to Tina, and Miles across from him. Uncertain about what to say to Armelle, Tina addressed Miles. "Everything go okay at the church?"

Miles nodded. "You know, I think so? Michael... Father Michael, excuse me, will be handling the services tomorrow."

"And Naomi?" Armelle asked, inquiring about his adopted cat.

Miles smiled. "I had a list of instructions ready to hand over, but as I pulled into the parking lot, I saw that he had already left out a saucer of milk. And some expensive treats too. He'll spoil her." He considered what he was leaving behind, and what Father Michael was stepping into. "I have a feeling they'll do just fine."

"*They* will," Tina said, then anxiously began cracking her knuckles. Armelle instinctively wrapped her pinky around Tina's and the cracking stopped. They looked at each other, then awkwardly at Miles, and let go.

"It's okay," Miles said.

"It's just..." Tina stuttered. "We thought... or... I just wondered..."

"If you thought this was wrong, Armelle stated.

Miles noticed that though they were no longer holding hands, their knees were touching. "No, I think it's right."

"Why?" They both said in unison.

Miles sat down across from them and poured himself a glass of water from the pitcher on the table. "Do you want my theological answer or my personal answer?"

Tina said "Personal" while Armelle simultaneously said, "Theological."

Miles smiled. He opened his mouth, about to launch into a detailed account of biblical interpretation, touching on the translation of the Greek word Arsenokoitai, John's threefold test, and so on, but that analytical approach didn't leave his lips when he noticed that Tina — whose stress was palatable just minutes ago — was in a state of peace as she leaned on the shoulder of Armelle, then he restarted. "I could get into the theological distinctions. Questions of translations and cultural contexts and all that. But, I suppose I can't top the words of Jesus when he was being grilled on the application and interpretation of biblical laws. Citing Deuteronomy and Leviticus, he summed it up succinctly: Love God and love each other."

Armelle and Tina blushed. That was not a word they were using.

Tina and Armelle averted their eyes from each other awkwardly, yet their hands remained locked.

Miles held up his hands apologetically. "Sorry, strong word, but when I look at you, I see two people who care for each other. Who protect each other. Who put the others' needs above their own. A true covenant." He massaged his neck. "And when I see that, suddenly the world doesn't seem quite so dark. Suddenly I can see and feel and believe things that otherwise surpassed my grasp." He looked at them in the eyes. "And that feels right."

Armelle locked Tina's hands in hers. This brought a smile to Miles' face. Armelle noticed this and asked, "Does this make you a bad priest?"

"Armelle!" Tina scolded her softly.

Miles waved away her concern. "It's okay. Thank you, in fact. This is a question that's been rattling around my head recently." He paused and considered. "Little more than recently. But, to be honest, maybe it's irrelevant? Am I even a priest? Where is my vestment?" He gestured at his Oxford shirt. "Where is my church?" He gestured at the Wakestone-branded train car around him. "Where is my parish?"

Tina wanted to comfort him but wasn't sure how.

"You're my priest," Armelle stated. "For what it's worth."

Miles smiled.

Armelle felt the need to clarify. "Though I am a Muslim. Non-practicing, but still not a Christian. So maybe it doesn't count."

"It counts for quite a bit," Miles said, before giving them space. "I'm going to grab a coffee from the cafe car and catch up on some reading. Either of you want anything?"

"No, thank you," they both responded.

"Be back in thirty," he said. As he walked away, Tina noticed that he had a copy of *Hamlet* sticking out of his back pocket. When the door to the adjoining car had closed behind him, she turned to Armelle.

"What about your shop?" Tina asked.

Armelle dryly stated that it could manage a few days closed.

Tina stammered. "But… Wouldn't… This isn't…"

"Do you not want me here?"

Instinctively, Tina responded. "Of course! More than anything. But… it's not safe. This isn't your… Well, you didn't *need* to come…"

Armelle cut Tina off by brushing a strand of hair away from her face and then leaning in for a long kiss. Armelle pulled away, looked Tina in the eyes, and responded, "But I did."

29

Mi Llave

"Nothing?" Armelle asked.

"What do you mean?" Tina asked as she gripped her pen fiercely. It had hovered over the paper for two stops now, yet nothing came. When she looked up, she saw that Armelle was not accepting her attempt to play dumb. Tina sighed. "I used to be quite creative, you know. I loved to write. It was my way of processing. Connecting. I wrote poems. Sonnets, in particular." Tina considered it. "I think I actually appreciated the restraints if that makes sense? 14 lines. 10 syllables per line. ABAB CDCD EFEF GG. That probably sounds weird."

"I don't think that's weird."

Tina blushed. "But I haven't written one for years. Decades?" She looked out the window and watched the Piedmont region blur by them. "But since then, I only create clinical recaps. Nefarious ones, apparently. And now…"

Armelle sat next to her in empathetic silence. In time, Armelle jumped to the topic that Tina had wanted to write about.

"Tell me about him?"

"Mi llave…" Tina said to herself with a smile that quickly turned to a frown.

Armelle smiled. "My family's from Cameroon. We speak French, not Spanish. But based on your pronunciation, I would say you don't either. Where did that come from?"

"It means 'key.' Actually, 'my key.' It's my brother's nickname for me. To be honest, I've always hated it. Not sure why it jumped to my mind."

Armelle pressed on. "Why does he call you that?"

"Oh, it goes back a while. He must have been… a freshman in high school? Yeah, cause I was a junior. In the fall. I was hyper-focused on college admissions. Felt like I needed more extracurriculars so that I could get into Duke. Or McGill. So I joined the Robotics club."

Tina felt dizzied by the trees rushing past her and looked down at the small table between her seat and Armelle's to ground herself. She took a sip of her green tea and felt pulled back into the past.

"The club must have been late because it got out after his practice."

"Baseball?" Armelle assumed.

"Actually, no. Football. Wide receiver. He led the team in touchdowns as a freshman. Robby is one of those infuriating people who is effortlessly gifted at anything he tries." Tina paused, then corrected herself. "Well, no. Not actually. Rather he doesn't have to put in the effort to become completely engrossed in any activity. He just engulfs himself in everything he tries with a passion that allows him to become the best. Not in a competitive way, ya know? He just loves anything and everything."

Tina looked at Armelle, who held eye contact for a moment, smiled, then looked away. Tina reflected, "He actually reminds me of you in that way. I could give you a textbook on how cardboard boxes are made and you would know everything there is to know on the topic by the end of the day."

Armelle held her head askew. "Are you making fun of me?"

Tina chuckled. "Not at all. It's endearing."

Armelle exhaled in relief. "Good, because the process of making cardboard is genuinely fascinating! You see, you gotta use softwoods with long fibers. Like a pine or spruce." Armelle smiled self-consciously. "But I'll stop myself. Go on. He had football practice and you had Robotics."

"Right, so any other day I would have been home before him. I was involved in several clubs, but they all took place right after school. Robotics must've been closer to 4:00 or so and ended after football. I get home, and who's sitting on the front porch? Robby.

"'What are you doing outside?' I asked him. Sometimes it can get pretty chilly in Houston when the sun goes down. This must've been one of those days. He just shrugged. 'Where's your key?' I asked. And you know what he said?"

"No, what?"

"'Why do I need a key when I have you?' It suddenly occurred to me that Robinson relied on me every day to get into his own house."

"He didn't have a key?"

"Of course he had a key. And of course he had lost it. One after the other. No one can find themselves in the flow state quite like Robby. When he's working on something, nothing else in the world exists. Which is wonderful, and has earned him millions. But it becomes a little less wonderful when it's basic life skills, or basic relationships, that slip by."

Tina sighed. She spent her whole life looking forward. She wasn't used to looking backward. But she continued. "Every day that semester, I came home from Robotics to find Robby sitting on the front porch, waiting for me to let him in."

"Was he impatient about it?" Armelle asked.

"No. It almost would've been better if he was, you know? No matter how late I got home, he greeted me with a smile and an exclamation of 'Mi Llave!' (Spanish was his favorite subject - I suppose cause it helped him connect with some of his teammates.) And now that I'm recalling this, I remember testing him. Seeing how late I could be before he demanded I get home sooner. My mom and dad would have to close up the shop each night, so it was just me. I figured at some point he would either snap at me for being late or suck it up and ask our parents for a new key. But he never did. Always a pleasant smile and a jovial exclamation of 'Mi Llave!'"

"What did he do each day?"

Tina laughed at the thought. "Not his homework! Some days he'd be teaching the neighborhood kids how to throw or hit. Some days he'd be playing on the second-hand ukulele that he left on the porch for these moments. Some days he'd just be staring off. Do you know how hard I have to work for a moment of calm when meditating? And that's pretty much his base state." Tina shook her head. "Infuriating."

Armelle said, "I can see that bugging you."

"It did," Tina admitted. "And it was always *something* like this growing up, you know? I resented him for needing me so much as a kid." She took a sip from her green tea. "And then he got drafted by the Rays right out of high school. Second round pick. From that point on, the team surrounded him with people to do all that frontal lobe stuff for him. With that in place, the only way I would hear from him was if I initiated it. Particularly after our parents were gone. Of course, he was cheerful and zenful when we met. As if it hadn't been months since our last conversation. As if it wouldn't have been months longer if I wasn't the one to initiate the call. So then I resented him for not needing me at all as an adult."

Armelle considered this, nudged her shoulder against Tina's, and said, "Well, he needs you now."

Tina thought about this reversal and nodded. He did need her. Not only that, but he probably had needed her for a while now. While he was mired in a slump through the spring. While he was injured during the summer. While he was suspended in the Fall. He didn't reach out, of course. But neither did she. And he probably needed her to. She opened her mouth to share these thoughts with Armelle, but her words were covered up by the sound of shouting the next car over.

The car Miles was in.

30

What's the Difference?

Tina and Armelle rushed to the adjacent compartment and rapidly pressed the button to open the doors. As they waited for the door to slowly slide open, they heard a flurry of unfamiliar voices.

"please god no please god no please god no."

"You're lying! Give me the money."

"That's all we have! Most of the tickets were pre-paid! Like yours! Pleasegodpleasegodpleasegod…"

They heard the familiar voice of Miles. "Please, sir. Put the knife down. It's not too late."

Tina and Armelle burst through the door and saw Miles slowly approaching a man in ragged clothing shaking a knife at a train employee. Miles held his palms up and took small steps. The man pivoted, cycling between directing the knife at the employee and Miles, when he saw Tina and Armelle enter. They could feel his panic, his uncertainty about where to direct threats. Miles kept one hand faced openly toward the man, and shifted the other toward his friends, signaling them to halt.

"They're with me," Miles said quietly. "It's going to be okay."

"YOU DON'T KNOW THAT!"

"True. But what is it you need?" The man didn't answer, but just swung the knife around in a circle, vaguely threatening the four of them. Miles continued. "Money, yes?"

"Money. Yes. Need to get out."

Miles took another step. He was now within the reach of the man. "Okay." Miles gestured toward the train attendant with a tilt of his head. "He doesn't have any." Miles placed his hand on his own chest. "But I do. Let him go, and work with me."

Tina stepped forward, but Miles stopped her. "It's alright. He's not going to hurt me." Miles looked the man in the eyes. "Right?" When the man didn't respond, Miles took another step forward. The man shifted away from the train attendant, faced Miles, and shoved the knife up against his throat where his collar would be. The attendant scrambled out of the compartment.

Miles froze, held his hands up, and waited. The man pulled the knife back an inch, leaving a drop of blood on Miles' neck. Miles nodded toward the booth next to them. Careful not to move his jaw into the knife, Miles whispered, "Sit? Talk?" When the man neither objected nor condoned the request, Miles slowly slid into the seat. The man dropped into the seat across from him. The knife remained directed at Miles' head, but then swung toward Tina and Armelle as they approached.

Miles spoke up, "It's okay. They're going to sit in that booth over there." Tina and Armelle slipped into the referenced seats across the aisle.

The four stayed there, frozen in time, with the contrasting sound of the man's rapid breaths compared to Miles' long inhales and exhales. Eventually, the man's breathing slowed and began to match Miles'. When the rhythm of their breaths synced up, Miles asked him for his name.

"Dean."

"Dean, my name is Miles." His hands still in the air, he shifted them across the aisle, then slowly down onto the table. "That's Tina. And that's Armelle."

The man slid the knife down to the table but kept his hand on it.

"You need money," Miles spoke. "I get that. I'm going to take out my wallet and put it on the table. Is that okay?"

The man nodded quickly. Miles slid his wallet out and opened it up to show a set of 20s clipped in. Tina sighed, regretting selecting Miles to hold the money for the trip.

"Where are you headed, Dean?"

"The coast. Fort Fisher."

"Why's that?"

"I don't know. I was told to."

Armelle jumped in. "What's your blood type?"

The man spun toward her. "What? Why? Why would you ask that too?"

Tina protectively placed her hand on the table in front of Armelle. "Someone else asked you that question?"

The man shook his head. "Yeah. A man. And a woman. The ones who put me on this train."

Miles spoke up. "What do you mean by that?"

The man put down the knife for a second to scratch his arm before hurriedly picking it up. "I don't... I don't remember. Just a little. I was... I was having a hard time. They showed up and asked us who had O- blood. I was the only one there with it. They pulled me into another room. Told me they had a way for me to get more... to make some money. I didn't trust them. The guy... seemed... slimy. The woman, scared. I said no. The man said 'Such a shame' and called for someone. Then I see this strange wiry pale dude coming out of the shadows. Next thing I know, I'm on this train with a ticket and a notecard pinned to my coat."

The man was visibly exhausted after the story. Miles gave him a moment to regain his breath before asking him if he could see the note. The man glanced at the wallet. Miles took out the cash and slid it across the table. The man slid the notecard across in return. Miles looked at it, then handed it across the aisle to Tina and Armelle.

"Two addresses," Tina said. "One in Durham, one on Kure Beach." She looked up at Dean. "The Durham one..."

"Mine." He shook his head rapidly. "Well, the shelter."

Tina nodded sympathetically. "And the one on the coast...?"

When Dean failed to respond, Armelle pulled her phone out and plugged the address into Maps. "The old Aquarium. Before it reopened on the pier."

Tina nodded her head. "Right. About a decade ago. They had that big expansion."

"Expansion..." Miles began, "Who financed that?" But Armelle was ahead of him and had the answer pulled up on her phone before he finished the question.

"'A generous grant from the Wakestone Family,' it says."

Tina, Armelle, and Miles sat in silence. They had their destination. Dean anxiously held onto the knife in one hand, the money in the other. His eyes darted across the table when Miles' hand went inside his coat pocket.

"It's okay," Miles assured him, as he pulled out a small notebook and his phone. He placed them both on the table, then scribbled a name on a page, ripped it out, and slid it across the table. "We're about 20 minutes away from New Bern. An old friend of mine is a social worker there. His name is Terrance. He was... Is a good man." He tapped on the page, where the name was written, then on his phone. "I'm going to send him a message. He's going to meet you at the station. He'll take care of you. Is that okay?"

The man stared, then nodded. Miles pulled up Terrance's contact and quickly typed out a message to his old friend, the first one Miles had sent him in years.

The four of them sat in silence as the train pulled into New Bern station. Miles nodded toward the knife on the table. "You're not going to want to take that with you." Dean kept his hand atop the weapon. "You're not going to need it," Miles promised. The man gradually pulled his hand away and stood up, backing toward the door. Armelle grabbed the knife, which drew a suspicious glare from Dean. Armelle slid the knife into her bag and raised her hands. The doors opened and Dean slipped off of the train. Miles saw his Terrance greet him with a wave and walk away, but before doing so, Miles locked eyes and shot him a grateful nod of the head.

The train lingered at the station for a few more minutes longer. Eventually, the attendant burst into the compartment with a police officer alongside him.

"Where did he go? Are you okay?" The attendant pressed.

"We're okay," Armelle assured him.

The office asked, "Where did the man go?"

"He's getting help," Miles responded.

The officer sighed ruefully. "Did you at least get his name?"

Tina quickly answered before Armelle could tell him the truth. "No."

The officer grumbled and left the car. The attendant lingered, staring at them. "He deserves to be in prison," he said as the train left the station.

With that, Miles stared out the window, watching New Bern recede in the distance. He was startled out of this trance when Tina and Armelle sat in his booth across from him.

"Looked to me like you believed back there," Tina said.

"My parish in D.C. was... complicated. I have a bit of experience with that sort of situation." Miles watched New Bern retreat behind him. "That wasn't belief, that was just… habit."

"What's the difference?" Armelle asked.

31

Interlude - One Week Prior

"Why are you doing this to me?" The sinewy man shackled to the table pleaded, as the creatures scattered away from him, leaving a trail of blood behind them.

The righteous man with the long red hair and beard sighed, then responded condescendingly, "That's precisely the point. This is not about you."

A laugh escaped the lips of the man on the table, which soon gave way to a pained cough. "Sure feels personal."

"Oh I didn't say it wasn't personal," the righteous man replied. "It is always personal in this... this modern-day Babylon. The devil has curved your spines so that the only thing you can see is your own navel. You and the masses that follow you. They make an idol of you for playing a children's game. Tell me, do you think you are more deserving of acclaim than others? Than me? Than God?"

The half of the man's face that could move curled up into a smile. "Than others? No. Than God? Of course not. I'm aware of how fortunate I've been. But than you? Oh, most definitely."

"How trite. Truthfully, you do have value, to God and to others. Just not in the way that you think." The righteous man sat on the edge of the table that the younger man was chained to. "You are a powerful symbol. One of our generation's golden calves. While the selected few climb the Mountain to commune with God, the barbaric masses that have lost their way bow down to idols like you. They fill stadiums,

140

chanting your name, rather than His. They seek to know your words and your wishes, rather than His. Your rise has caught their attention." He locked eyes and a smile popped out from behind his beard. "And so shall your fall."

The man on the table averted his eyes.

"No witty remark this time?" The righteous man slid off the table and approached the bolted door on the other side of the room. "I said you have value to God and to others, but have only spoken of how God has a use for you. Aren't you curious about what your value is to others?"

The man on the table muttered, "Please... not again..." as the righteous man gently knocked with two knuckles on the door.

"Your value to others?" A button was pressed on the wall, and the man on the table was covered in a harsh white spotlight. "Sustenance." He pulled the bolt on the door through the brackets and a stream of pale creatures flooded in. Their movement was quick yet awkward as if they were in a movie where every other frame was dropped. They stopped at the perimeter of the light, and paced around it with their drooling jaws dropped and their unblinking red eyes fixed upon the man on the table.

"Please... no... I have nothing left..."

The righteous man pulled out a tablet and said under his breath, "The man who loves his life shall lose it," before flicking the switch on the wall. The light faded out and the creatures fell atop the man on the table.

The righteous man stood in the corner, glancing curiously at the dials on a monitor spiking. When one measure began blinking red, he hit the switch on the wall and the man on the table was again bathed in light. The righteous man took out a long flashlight, illuminating and clearing a blue-white path as he walked to the table. He quickly flashed it in the eyes of the surrounding creatures, causing them to shriek and retreat into the adjoining room.

"Now tell me, do you feel... chosen... now? Do you feel better than me now?"

The man on the table groaned. A quiet word escaped his lips. "Why?"

The righteous man cocked his head to the side, then pressed his index finger firmly into one of the man's many wounds. He held it up, showing the blood dripping down onto his hands. He placed his palm over his heart, leaving a bloody handprint on his shirt. "When the

LORD goes through the land to strike down the Egyptians, he will see the blood on the top and sides of the doorframe and will pass over that doorway, and he will not permit the destroyer to enter your houses and strike you down."

The righteous man walked to the other door in the room and opened it to expose the sound of circulating water. Before exiting, he looked back and said, "We chosen few will start a kingdom of priests. We will make the way straight. For many be called, but few chosen."

The man on the table lost his energy. His head slipped backward and fell against the table. "You're sick."

The righteous man shook his head sadly. "One who is often reproved, yet remains stubborn, will suddenly be broken beyond healing." He looked down at his watch, and a smile passed across his face. "I am not sick. What I am, is late. I have a train to catch. But don't you worry, my… associate will be ruling this little kingdom in my stead. He sadly is more a man of science than of faith, but one finds what allies one can when living in Sodom." The righteous man found this funny, and the last thing the man on the table heard before he lost consciousness was the sound of his laugh echoing around the empty tank he was trapped in.

32

You, however, will not

"Deep breath," Tina said quietly, perhaps to herself, perhaps to Armelle and Miles, who stood next to her. They stared at the side entrance to the seemingly abandoned aquarium.

Each of them was keenly aware of just how woefully unaware they were of what awaited them on the other side of those doors. This was simply not how Armelle functioned. It required a faith from Miles which he was currently lacking. Tina, ever the perfectionist, was no more comfortable with their utter lack of a plan. But she needed to save her brother. She needed to be there for him in a way that she had failed to do recently.

If only her feet would move.

But then she felt Armelle's pinky slip around hers. And Miles calmly placed his hand on her back. She took a deep breath and pushed on the double doors.

There was little light. Just one of the fluorescent bulbs still flickered, guiding a dim path through the corridor. They glimpsed empty tanks along the sides. Every so often they came across one partially full of water, but none held any animals.

There was little sound. Just the rhythm of their footsteps splashing the damp puddles as they headed toward a direction they randomly chose.

Tina held onto the flashlight, pointing it forward as they traveled.

Armelle held onto the knife they had taken from the man on the train, pointing it side to side aimlessly as if that would stop a vampire if they chose to attack.

Miles held onto nothing. His hand anxiously massaged the back of his neck.

They paused as the corridor ended in a hallway that split to either side. Tina looked to Miles for inspiration, but he stared forward blankly. She then looked toward Armelle, who held her head at an angle, directing her ear to the left. The pathway there led to what once was a grand staircase that elevated beyond their sight. Armelle shot the two others a curious glance and gestured with her hands to suggest that there might be footsteps that way. It occurred to Tina that this could be a reason to head in that direction or to do the exact opposite. Yet they had come this far, so she would see it through.

They walked up the stairs. With each one, they could more clearly hear the footsteps above them. They saw that the stairwell ended in a door with a faded mural of various sharks. Before they even reached the top stair, a voice called out to them.

"About time. Enter."

The voice of Emerson Sinclair.

They opened the door into an expansive room that once featured numerous tanks in front of a railing that overlooked the lobby of the old aquarium three stories down.

Tina's eyes were drawn to the center of the room, where a tabletop was placed on a small fish tank. Passed out on that table was her brother, Robinson. His wrists were shackled to the table. Sprouting out of his arms were several tubes. At first, Tina assumed it was IV bags that he was connected to, but then she realized that she had mistaken the direction; this setup was not meant to put fluids into him, but rather to take blood out of him. The bags at the end of each line resembled the bladder of a boxed wine, with a tap on the end for eager drinkers.

Armelle's eyes were drawn to the man next to the table. Her former colleague, Emerson Sinclair. He wore the same silvery-gray three-piece suit that he always seemed to sport. He was leaning against the table, recording figures down on a clipboard resting next to Robinson's leg, which hung limp over the side.

Miles' eyes were drawn to the gigantic circular tank behind the table, which stretched from the ceiling forty feet down to the lobby. Swimming throughout this tank were several hammerhead sharks that apparently did not make the trip to the new aquarium.

Emerson held up a finger instructing them to wait, jotted down some notes, then glanced up at the three of them in annoyance, as if they were barging into one of his C-suite meetings. He exhaled slowly, walked behind the tank that Robinson was on, and pulled out a pistol and an odd-looking flashlight. He followed Miles' eyes to the shark and casually gestured to it with the gun.

"Makes for a memorable backdrop for my video calls, don't you think?"

Tina fumed. "What are you talking about, you maniac? This is not an office, this is a crime scene!"

Sinclair sighed irritatedly. "This is why your career plateaued, Sanders. You have a solid grasp of the science, but simply lack a mind for business."

"You call this business?" Miles responded.

Sinclair glanced down at the table and shook his head. "Since nothing is preventing me from being candid with you three at the moment: No, not entirely. This is quite disconnected from the core aims of the organization. Yet, sometimes a company needs to placate those in charge with a few line items so as to not lose momentum on the work that truly matters." At this point, he directed the flashlight into Armelle's face, who instinctively winced before realizing that it was not a harsh fluorescent light on her face, but more akin to the light beaming from the mid-day sun. "Isn't that right, Ms. a Moute?"

Armelle, who had the knife tucked into her back waistband, looked at the chart on the table. "You think you are here because of your business acumen? You're here because you are the only one spineless enough to kowtow to all of Wakestone's irrational whims. You're not a man of business, you're just an empty suit." She pointed at the clipboard, which stood about fifteen feet in front of her. "Tell me - what important 'business notes' are you recording?"

Sinclair looked down at the clipboard and shook his head. "Truthfully? I was estimating how much of our budget has been wasted on this man-child. Wakestone loves his metaphors, and Saul loves his frivolous fantasies, but there comes a point when you have to cut your losses."

"So you'll let him go then?" Tina asked.

"Oh heavens no," Sinclair replied drily. "Doing so would only incur more costs once he was released." He paced past the table toward an interior door. He tapped on it with the flashlight while he continued, "I'm telling you this not because he'll be leaving these doors. Quite the opposite. Same with you."

Tina had enough of his smug attitude. "So you're going to kill us then? Go ahead and do it. Hearing your pompous proclamations is worse than being shot anyway."

Sinclair looked down at the gun in his hands, as if he had forgotten it was there. "Actually, I've been forbidden to kill you, or him for that matter. Saul and Wakestone claim you all have symbolic value, and me putting a bullet through your skulls — as tempting as that sounds at this moment — would be difficult to deny. But sometimes an employee has to save his supervisors from themselves. Such a shame that you arrived at the aquarium while I was out obtaining another shipment of blood from the hospital." He unlocked the door he stood next to. "And such a shame that Saul, that foolish shaman, left the door to the pen unlocked." Sinclair opened the door, stepped aside, and shone the flashlight on the ground in front of him. It emitted a bright UV light that resembled rays of sunlight. "My colleagues will get over it. Phase II has been successful, after all. They will recover." It was then that a herd of pale, emaciated, red-eyed figures poured out of the doors toward Armelle, Miles, Tina, and Robinson.

Sinclair showed them a rare smile. "You, however, will not."

Miles and Armelle froze, as the vampires rushed toward them, covering the ground in a frantic, staccato motion. Tina sprinted in their direction, stopping at the table of her incapacitated brother. She furiously clawed at the shackles as the vampires reached them. Tina closed her eyes tight, preparing herself for what came next. A moment later, she opened them in surprise after not feeling the expected teeth on her neck. She saw Miles swinging his fists, fighting off the vampires that were crowding around her. She saw Armelle hammering on the shackles with the knife, little by little severing the connection. For a moment, it looked like they might escape. But only for a moment, for the vampires continued out the door and huddled around them. Tina, Armelle, and Miles jumped on the table to temporarily achieve the high ground. They kicked out at the vampires swarming around them, but for every one that they fought off, two more took their place.

"I'm sorry," Tina tried to say as she unchained her brother, but it was drowned out by the screams of her friends and the hisses of the ravenous vampires. Armelle swung the knife around wildly, but it failed to thin out the herd, and she eventually dropped it after being struck. As Miles prepared for the end, he tried to recite a prayer, but no words came.

Yet, they were delivered nonetheless.

Somehow, the swarm of vampires thinned from the outside in.

Before they could identify the cause, they heard the angry voice of Sinclair exclaim, "Weren't we rid of you two?"

Tina followed his gaze to see two figures fighting off the vampires for them: Katrina and Doctor Ivanov. The doctor attempted to do so with a staff she must have found on the ground that she had split in two. But it was Katrina who was doing the bulk of the damage. She moved with agility and ferocity, tearing through the lines of vampires.

Just when it seemed as though Tina, Armelle, and Miles had an escape lined up, everything changed. Sinclair had traced a path for himself to the back of the table, near the ledge that dropped to the floor below, by shining the UV flashlight at nearby vampires. Katrina pounced at him, but he knocked her off the path by shining the light into her face. She covered her eyes, hissed, and fell to the ground. In spite of the pain, she crawled toward him, as he alternated between flashing the light at her and the nearby vampires. As he did so, Sinclair placed the gun that was in his other hand on the table and rifled through a pocket in his suitcoat for a small device.

"I've been meaning to test this out," he said with a snarl. If a little bit of light has this effect, I wonder what will happen when I do this?" He emphatically pressed a button on the device and the room was suddenly flooded by UV lights placed in the ceiling. The screams of countless vampires, including Katrina, filled the room.

Tina, Miles, and Armelle instinctively covered their ears. Katrina covered her eyes, but still pulled herself toward Sinclair. Ivanov, seeing the gun on the table lunged for it, while curiously shouting "You leave Anne alone" which drew a sad, knowing look from the defenseless Katrina. The much younger Sinclair kicked Ivanov in the ribs and grabbed the gun. She fell backward, smashing her head on the circular tank at the edge of the balcony. A thin trickle of water escaped out of the tank. It blended with the blood from Maria's wound, forming a pink river that cascaded down to the lobby three floors below.

With the flashlight momentarily taken off of Katrina, she sprung on top of Sinclair. In the struggle, Sinclair's gun was knocked from his hands, sliding under the old railing. Katrina, weakened from the UV lights, was quickly overpowered by Sinclair, who pulled her up by what little hair she had regrown since he had seen her last. He held her between himself and her friends.

The seven of them froze, forming a terrible tableau. Sinclair and

Katrina stood between the circular tank and the table. Within an arm's length was Armelle, who had raced after the gun, before it was knocked over the ledge in the commotion. A barely conscious Robinson had his arm draped over the shoulders of Tina. In front of the tank was Doctor Ivanov, sitting in a pool comprised of tank water, her own blood, and the colorful beads of her burst bracelet. When she stood up, she did so holding Armelle's knife. She slowly raised it toward Sinclair.

Sinclair swung his head between Ivanov on one side of him and Armelle on the other.

"Stay back, you two!" Sinclair shouted. He dragged a syringe across Katrina's neck, drawing a thin, watery maroon blood from her veins. "You know what's in this? The compounds from the bat saliva that will bond with her V-blood."

Doctor Ivanov looked toward the unarmed Armelle and said "Back off."

Armelle kept her eyes on Sinclair but took a step back toward Tina, Miles, and Robinson.

Yet Doctor Ivanov remained, pointing the knife at Sinclair.

Sinclair grunted. "Get back, you frail old hag. You take a step closer, and you'll get this in your neck right after her. I'm intrigued by what it would do to Katrina in her hybrid state, but I am quite confident that it will kill you in a matter of seconds."

Ivanov slowly pointed the knife down to her side. In doing so, she rotated her grip so that the tip was facing behind her.

"Smart move, doctor," Sinclair said as he took a step toward the door behind him. "And who would know better than you? You made this, after all." Whether he was referring to the compound or Katrina was unclear.

Ivanov looked sadly at Katrina. Without taking her eyes off of her young patient, she said to the others, "Save her." Then she forcefully swung her fist backward, jamming the knife into the crack in the multi-story tank behind her. A stream of water jetted out, knocking over the seven of them. Katrina laid unconscious between Sinclair and Armelle. Each of them lept toward her, Sinclair doing so with the syringe held in his fist. But before he could jam it into Katrina's neck, Doctor Ivanov wrapped her arms around him, planted her feet, and launched them both backward. Tina gasped as she saw the two disappear over the railing, falling out of sight. Tina raced after them and peered down at their lifeless bodies on the lobby floor forty feet below.

The floors were quickly filling with water. The UV lights above them flickered and shorted out, which elicited a moan from the surrounding vampires as they slowly regained consciousness, Katrina among them.

"Maria?" She asked. But all that was left of her was the scattered beads of her bracelet.

Armelle looked toward Tina, who was waiting for some signs of life from Ivanov, yet the doctor was floating face-down next to Sinclair, as hammerhead sharks circled them. Tina shook her head sadly.

"I'm sorry," Armelle said as she attempted to pick up Katrina, who shoved Armelle aside so that she could collect the colorful beads before rising.

Miles looked at the vampires around them. "We have to go." He quickly helped Tina carry Robinson as Armelle helped Katrina. As they raced to the exit, they saw washed against the table the syringe and the knife. Tina pocketed the syringe while Armelle grabbed the knife. They limped together toward the door, as the vampires slowly followed the trail of blood they left behind.

33

Help People

The train was quiet.

Miles tucked himself away tightly in the corner of the booth, reflecting on the unspeakable acts he witnessed.

Armelle sat across from him, laptop on the table, scouring research sites for how to construct the UV flashlight that Sinclair had used to control the vampires.

Next to Armelle rested Katrina, and next to Miles was Robinson. Robinson and Katrina appeared to share an inversely proportional relationship, with Robinson's gradual increase in health contrasting Katrina's emotional shut-down. Neither had said anything since they had made their way onto the train.

Tina paced back and forth between the booth and the windows, searching for any trace of the vampires that chased them through the streets. They seemed to be in the clear, but she couldn't help but double back every few minutes to check. At first, she disguised these walks as gathering water for the table or using the bathroom, but after five trips to the window, she didn't attempt to cover up her anxiety. After an hour on the train, she felt comfortable enough to sit herself down in the booth. Upon doing so, she noticed that her brother seemed conscious enough to engage with.

"Robby… are you… I'm so sorry."

Even prolonged torture could not stop Robinson's contagious smile. "Sorry?" he asked with a strained voice. "Llave, you saved me!"

"But too late."

"There's no such thing," Robinson replied as he tapped his sore ribs. This drew a curious look from Miles. "I'm alive, aren't I?" This drew a curious look from Katrina.

Sensing that his sister needed time, he nursed his water and stared out his window, trying to watch Central North Carolina pass by in the dead of night. Eventually, when he felt more strength return, he turned toward Katrina and Armelle. "I didn't get a chance to introduce myself. My name is Robinson."

Katrina responded with a blank stare. Armelle fixed her gaze on his forehead and said, "I'm Armelle. Pleased to meet you."

"And what do you do, Armelle?"

Armelle relaxed with the opportunity to talk about her interest. "I run Baldwin's Books. One part college bookstore, one part rare book collection, one part cafe."

"Oh, that sounds incredible… I can't wait to check it out! I should have a bit more time to read now that my career has apparently ended, after all."

Armelle smiled at the opportunity. Tina piped in, concerned for her brother.

"What do you think you'll do now?"

Robinson looked at Tina compassionately. "Oh, you know me, Llave. I have no shortage of passions. I think I might do something different every month!" His expression turned to concern. "But the real question is, what are you going to do?"

Tina was taken aback. "What do you mean?"

"My job was a game. A fun game, but nothing more than a game. And one that I have been keenly aware was in the final phase for some time now. But your job? Your job was your everything. Has there been a time that we've talked," at this phrase, Tina dropped her gaze, which Robinson failed to notice, "when your updates weren't just your career advancement at Wakestone Trials? So what are you going to do without that?"

Tina didn't know how to respond.

Robinson answered for her. "You gotta make something! Art, inventions, stories, anything!" His excitement led to a coughing fit. Tina passed him her water, which he acknowledged with a grateful nod and a long sip. When his voice was ready, he turned to Miles, Katrina, and Armelle. "My sister is the most creative person I've ever met."

Miles realized how little he knew about this person whose life he had tied his to. But Armelle knew, and a smile spread wide across her face upon hearing such nice words about her Tina. Robinson noticed this, processed it, then matched her smile with his own.

While Robinson took this in, Miles registered the angst on Tina's face. An angst that he shared. "It's okay," he said to her. "I'm in the same boat. All I've ever known is being a priest. But I don't think I am anymore?"

Tina consoled him. "I think you are. A priest is more than a parish."

Miles wasn't convinced. But her certainty was uplifting. He thought about what else had made him feel that way, and awkwardly blurted out, "Dungeons and Dragons."

"Huh?" Tina responded.

Miles blushed. He hadn't meant to say it out loud. "Sorry. I just… I was thinking about how what we do is not who we are, and for some reason, D&D popped into my head. Dungeons and Dragons. Growing up, I would play every weekend at my cousin's house." He looked toward Tina. "I know it sounds… Well, I think you might like it. A group of friends create a story together. An adventure. Something that belongs just to that time, that place, that group. It honestly feels magical."

Tina was skeptical, but Robinson was not. "Count me in!" He pulled himself upright in the booth. "Years back there was a reliever in Charleston who was a… what was the phrase? A Dungeon Master?" He looked to Miles, who confirmed with a smile. "His passion for it was contagious, and I was so eager to play with him when we got back from our road trip. But I got moved up to Montgomery before we got a chance to do it. I need something to do, so let me learn to become a Dungeon Master. Let me put together a game for us!"

Miles, Armelle, and Tina all laughed at the thought. Mid-laugh, Tina caught sight of Katrina's eyes. As she always did, she quickly averted her gaze from those red-lined irises, but not before noticing that Katrina was assuredly not laughing. Tina realized guiltily that she hadn't thought once about Doctor Ivanov since boarding the train. She attempted to recover.

"We're only able to be here, to consider a game, because of Doctor Ivanov."

"To the doctor," Armelle replied.

"Hear, hear," Robinson said, despite not knowing her.

"She was an incredible scientist," Miles said.

"No one was better at what she did," Tina proclaimed.

Katrina scoffed. "And what was that?"

Silence.

"What exactly did she do?" she asked.

Silence.

"What a shallow grave you've dug for her. Was she only a scientist? Nothing more than her work?"

Silence.

"Well, turn it around then. What do you do?"

Tina was aggravated. "We're helping people! There is a monster out there…"

"To the monsters, we're the monsters," Katrina said, quoting a favorite book of hers.

"What does that mean?" Armelle asked.

"You say you're helping. But how? Through using people as tools? Like Maria? Like me?" Katrina waited for an answer that never came. She pushed on. "What is my last name?" Katrina asked curtly.

Tina logged her memory, thinking of the case files. She recalled her patient number, 275217, but not her last name.

"And what about Maria's daughter? What was her name?"

Tina and Miles averted eye contact. Armelle recalled the name Ivanov mistakenly called Katrina in the tank and hazarded a guess. "Anne?"

Katrina nodded sadly as she placed the colorful beads she collected at the aquarium onto the table. Tina noted Katrina's use of the past tense in her question, leaned over, and opened a new tab on Armelle's laptop. She searched for 'Anne Ivanov' and clicked on the first link, then nudged the computer back so that Armelle and Miles could see her screen. So they could read the obituary of Maria Ivanov's daughter, who died at the age of fifteen from a rare blood disorder. They noted that Ivanov was married at the time of Anne's death. Did she lose her marriage after she lost her daughter? They noted that Maria had previously worked at a powerful pharmaceutical company. Had she given up a lucrative position to devote her life to researching blood disorders? Was that what drew her to the cases at Wakestone Trials? They noted that Anne would've been about the same age as Katrina was now, had she survived. They noted just how little they had previously noted.

Tina looked deeply into Katrina's red-stained eyes. She saw the sadness. The hurt. The grieving.

Katrina stared back and replied, "If you want to help people, then help people."

34

Warrant

"Oh thank God you're all back," Doctor Contreras said as Miles, Tina, Armelle, Katrina, and Robinson entered the building in the Lemur Center where they had made their home. To their left, they could see the sun rising. To their right were three cells, one of which previously featured a lone Holy Blood Bat, but now was filled with a colony of them. The cell on the far end previously featured a lone aye-aye, but now was empty. Rufus was instead in the middle room. Katrina's room. And it was in this room that Katrina retreated before Italo had finished his sentence.

While the others looked at each other, wondering who would correct Italo, Armelle followed Katrina into her cell.

"Should we..." Robinson began as he watched Katrina and Armelle disappear behind the door.

Tina considered but then shook her head. "Armelle has this." She then turned her attention to Italo. "There's something you should know..."

Tina, Robinson, and Miles filled Italo in. On Maria's death. On Maria's life.

"I never saw her as she was," Italo said sadly. "I never tried."

"None of us did," Miles responded.

After a few moments of uncertainty, Italo said, "Well, there's something you should all know as well."

"What's that?" Tina asked.

155

Italo sighed, then looked at Tina and Miles. "There's a warrant out for two."

"For what?" they all asked.

"Kidnapping," Italo said.

"Who?"

Italo looked at Katrina's cell. They could hear her talking with Armelle. "Her."

Tina and Miles looked at each other, aware of the trap they had fallen into.

"Fine," Robinson said. "Let them come. We'll tell them what happened and get this cleaned up."

"Won't do any good," Miles stated.

Robinson stared blankly. "What are you talking about?" he asked incredulously.

"At the Blind Tiger… they were all there," Miles stated. "The Sheriff, D.A., detectives, judges… all of them. He owns them all."

"Certainly not all!" Robinson replied, his vigor returning. "They're the police. This is what they do!"

Miles looked for Armelle for an empathetic response, but she wasn't there.

"All the ones that seem to hold authority appear to be loyal to him," Tina said, before adjusting her statement. "Or at least in fear of him."

"Plus," Italo added. "There's the small matter of the Ancel Act."

"True," Tina said, then looked to her brother. "The law is…a little nebulous in terms of oversight with clinical trials."

"Nebulous?" Robinson asked. "They tortured me! They drained me! Seems pretty cut and dry to me!"

"The burden of proof for clinical trials was flipped after the pandemic a few years back," Italo pointed out.

Tina elaborated, "When the pandemic hit, some argued that we responded too slowly. Those high up in the pharmaceutical world, such as Wakestone, propositioned the government, arguing that they could have moved more swiftly without…" Tina looked for the words. "I believe it was 'the burdensome oversight of the government grinding their clinical trials to a halt, resulting in needless deaths.' Something awful like that."

"Sounds about right," Italo grumbled. "And the government eagerly relieved themselves of their responsibility. So whereas previously companies would have to provide evidence to governmental agencies that their trials were safe, now the public has to provide evidence that the trials are unsafe."

"Well," Robinson said. "I think myself and Katrina can prove that, no?"

"To whom?" Miles asked. "Everyone we would present that evidence to was in the room with Wakestone."

"So what do we do? Nothing?"

No one had an answer.

35

Bato

Armelle, who had long ago mastered the art of dodging social engagements, spotted Katrina's escape into her cell before anyone else. She quickly followed her.

"Sorry." Armelle blurted out. "And thank you."

Katrina looked up at Armelle, her expression cold and hard. Katrina stepped backward and slid herself onto the makeshift E.R. chair that had turned into her bed. Rufus, the aye-aye who had become her roommate during her recovery, hopped up next to her, paced in a circle, and curled into the nook under Katrina's arm. The only sounds that could be heard were the satisfied cooing of Rufus and the flapping of wings from the bats next door.

Eventually, Katrina responded. "For what?"

Armelle hesitantly sat on a low table alongside Katrina's bed. She rocked back and forth slightly as she searched for her words. "The… categorical imperative. By Immanuel Kant. It has a corollary of sorts." Armelle paused, then recited the line from memory. "Act in such a way that you treat humanity, whether in your own person or in the person of any other, never merely as a means to an end, but always at the same time as an end." Armelle considered how she could formulate the thoughts into clear communication. "Ivanov," she began, before restarting, "Sorry, Maria… she… well, we used her as a means to an end. I know she meant a lot to you. And she should have meant a lot to us. But she didn't. And now she's gone."

Armelle's words hung in the air, accompanied only by the rhythmic sound of Rufus contentedly tapping the bed as Katrina pet him.

"Thanks," Katrina said softly.

Armelle nodded. "And that brings me to the second part. Thank you." She tapped a tattoo on her left forearm. "For the reminder."

Katrina looked toward the word inked onto her skin. "Bato? What's that?"

"It means 'I am because we are.' Probably better known as 'ubuntu,' but we call it 'bato' in Cameroon." Armelle noticed the kindness she was giving to Rufus, a creature that Armelle had to admit she initially found somewhat disturbing, but who she now found kind of adorable. "You reminded me of this. Of how we're only as good as the impact we have on the people around us. That's what makes us human."

"But I'm not," Katrina hissed.

"Not what?"

"A human. I'm a monster."

Armelle took a moment to take this in. "Have you noticed that I'm not quite… neurotypical?"

Katrina didn't know how to respond.

Armelle continued. "Well, I personally am keenly and constantly aware of it. For as long as I can remember, I've felt… different. Othered. An outcast. As though I was dropped into this universe from a slightly different one. And each interaction just revealed that I didn't quite belong here." A flood of memories washed over Armelle. She noticed her heart rate quicken, bobbed her head from side to side, tapping her feet with each oscillation like a metronome. She caught her breath, and continued. "It took a while to realize that our humanity doesn't come from how we are like those around us, but rather how we treat those who are different." Armelle thought of how Tina made her notice what she *was*, rather than what she wasn't. "I suppose it is the bottom-up processing that comes with my autism that allows me to notice certain things that others might gloss over."

Armelle stood, and began to rock on her heels, thinking that she was out of her comfort zone. She wanted to provide the assurance that she wished she had received when she was Katrina's age. She felt like she wasn't articulating her thoughts. Her feelings. She balled her fists tightly to squeeze out the frustration, took a breath, held it, exhaled, and tried again. "Your humanity isn't based on your blood. Or your brain. Or your looks. Or your navel-gazing sense of self. It's based on your connections to others."

Armelle attempted to look into Katrina's eyes but found that Katrina's head was down, looking at Rufus.

Armelle grabbed the collar of her cardigan with each hand and pulled them against her cheeks. She felt the wool against her face, took a breath, and continued.

"I'm sorry. I don't think I'm communicating clearly. It's just that… On the train… you were the one… The one who made us look inwards and outwards. The one who made us see the humanity of others. There's no one here more human than you."

Katrina looked up. A thin smile was on her face, as was a red teardrop sliding down it. "Bato?"

"Bato," Armelle replied, before extending her arm toward the doorway. Toward the others.

Katrina looked at Armelle and held her gaze. Directly afterward, she heard what Armelle could not: Robinson asking the others what they could do. When no one answered, Katrina took a deep breath and exited her cell. Armelle and Rufus followed.

"We help people," she told the group.

36

For Anne

"Should we get started?" Italo asked the group as each entered the lobby. The previous night, when Katrina offered her support, they all agreed to wake early at 6:00 the next morning so they could get to work.

"Absolutely," Tina said as she yawned and took out her notebook.

Robinson and Armelle agreed as they prepped morning coffee and tea at the makeshift breakfast nook that Tina had constructed in the corner of the lobby.

Katrina nodded as she joined the others, followed by Rufus.

The door to the forest opened and Miles entered. "Yes, definitely," Miles said as he entered the lobby from the west, holding the doors to the woods open. "Starting with something we should have already done." He adjusted the collar on his lavender-colored button-down and then sheepishly pointed behind him. "Can we step out for a moment before the sun rises?"

The group followed him into the approximation of the Madagascar rainforest. On a platform overlooking where the Red Ruffed Lemurs had been abandoned, Miles had set up a table with candles that accompanied the diffused light from the rising sun. Centered on that table was an old stethoscope. Miles saw the curious glancing at the table and blushed. "I thought we could have a… service for Maria. I didn't have anything of hers… I didn't know what to choose." He gestured at the stethoscope. "I hope this will do," he said unconvincingly. Katrina looked down, then turned around and entered the building. Miles understood.

Too little, too late, he thought. *But still, I have to try.*

He collected himself, then said apologetically. "Maria was Eastern Orthodox, I believe. It's a different liturgy, but I found some notes. I hope I will do it justice."

Tina, Armelle, Robinson, and Contreras scooched closer to the table. Each of them had their own relationship, or lack thereof, with the idea of a higher power, but each bowed their heads reverently.

Standing behind the table, Miles glanced down at the notes he had prepared, and begun.

"Blessed is our Lord God, always; both now and ever, and to the ages of ages."

He looked up, past his friends, past the building, onto the treetops. It struck him that this canopy did not belong there. The foliage was taken directly from Madagascar, hardly native to Durham. Yet he recalled reading a sign on the property that pointed out that the vast majority of the Madagascan rainforest had been leveled. This vestige of their once thriving ecosystem did not quite belong, but it was a haven for something that once was and hopefully would be again. With this in mind, he continued reading the script recorded on the paper in front of him.

"Have mercy on us, O God, according to Your great mercy; listen, and have mercy." He caught his breath and wondered if he believed the words. He read on anyway. "Again we pray for the repose of the soul of the servant of God, Maria Ivanov, departed this life; and for the forgiveness of her, every transgression, voluntary; and involuntary. Let the Lord establish his soul where the Just repose; the mercies of God, the Kingdom of the Heavens, and the remission of his sins; let us ask of Christ our immortal King and our God. Let us pray to the Lord."

He looked up from the paper. He stretched for a feeling he once knew, but it was out of reach. "Have mercy on us, O God." He looked down at his notes, but when he tried to read the next passage, which concerned the resurrection, instead he repeated, "Have mercy on us, O God."

No words followed. Just the sound of the wind brushing by the redwoods. The distant cooing of the Sifaka. And then the opening of the door. Miles saw Katrina approach, a photo in one hand, a set of necklaces in the other. The group parted. Katrina walked up, Rufus alongside her, placed a Polaroid photo in the middle of the makeshift altar, and encircled the stethoscope around it. They all looked closer at the photo of a younger Maria carrying a young girl on her shoulders. Maria was beaming with a magnetic smile that none of them (save Katrina) had ever personally witnessed.

With the group congregated around the altar, Katrina placed the necklaces on the front of the table. Each was comprised of a Madagascan vine from the forest, and each contained a colorful bead that had been formerly a part of Maria's bracelet. Everyone took one and placed it around their necks.

Katrina looked into Miles' eyes. "Thank you. For this."

Miles looked at Katrina, down at his notes, then back at Katrina. "Would you like to say something?"

Katrina instinctively stepped back, but in doing so, a beam of the rising sun caught her in the eyes. She winced and stepped forward, shaded by her friends. She exchanged places with Miles and stood behind the table, with her hands lightly pressed against the photograph.

"She was a good person," she began. She held up a hand as if to stop an objection that she expected to be thrown her way. "I know, I know - A difficult person. But a good one." She placed her hand back down on the photo. "Anne... Her daughter... Maria talked about her. How Anne made up silly songs on the ukulele and played them for her. How Anne had her father's sense of humor. How she was a fighter, but..." She looked up, breathed in deeply, and moved on. "How when she was taken, a piece of Maria was taken too."

A thin, red tear slipped down Katrina's face.

"And how she never wanted others to feel that way. So she filled that hole in her with her studies. Not exactly healthy, I know. And she certainly knew."

"I think I..." Katrina looked up at those around her, then continued. "I think each of us has a hole that we're constantly trying to fill it with something. Just like her. Maybe some of us are healthier than she was. More whole." Katrina felt the warmth of the sun on her face before stepping over into the shade before it could irritate her. "Maybe some of us less so. I guess it's just a matter of how conscious we are of whether we're healing or hurting. Us and others. Maria... she was hurting herself. She pushed everyone close to her away. But she did so trying to heal others. So they wouldn't feel what she felt."

Katrina passed a hand over the flame of a candle. Back and forth. Then she held it there, engulfed in the fire. If it caused her pain, she didn't show it. Eventually, she pulled back her hand and continued.

"Maria was fully aware of what she was doing. She made mistakes. Lots of them. But she didn't deny them. And she didn't let them bury her in guilt. When one study failed, she simply launched a new one. Trying to fix what she broke. What was broken. In her. In...." Katrina gestured at everything around them, before extending her arms to the group, palms up. "And that's what she left us. A broken world that we can't fix. A mess of a study that we can't finish." She rubbed her hands over the hair that had unevenly been regrowing on her head. "But we can try?"

This last line was delivered with uncertainty, but when she looked at the group, they gave her the certainty she was seeking.

"We can try," they all replied.

Katrina agreed. "We have to. For..." She paused and considered, shook her head, then shared, "I'm not going to say 'for Maria' because I don't think that's what she would want from us. She wouldn't want us to do this for her. So how about this: For Anne."

"For Anne," they all said in unison.

37

A Plan

No one quite knew how to transition from mourning the dead to planning how to defeat the undead. Armelle eventually broke the silence as they aggregated awkwardly around the long table in the Nash Center lobby.

"Okay, so what next?"

Miles rubbed his neck and thought of Jonah's prayer when he was in the pitch-black belly of the beast. "Wakestone Manor," he stated, as his hand ran over the lavender bead on his necklace. "That's where they're at, right? We go there, face Wakestone, and liberate those imprisoned there."

Katrina shook her head. "Probably no one there."

"But you were there," Italo pointed out.

"Yes," Katrina confirmed. "And before that, the Tower. We outgrew each space as the trial grew. Future… patients were placed somewhere else."

Robinson paced the room, stretching his back as he considered their approach. "Any ideas where that other location would be?"

"No," Katrina said. "Sorry. When my blood was fully V, I had heightened senses, but my memory of those moments is… murky. I remember the feelings more than the facts. I remember the pain."

Tina saw the pain on her brother's face as he stopped pacing and recalled his pain. She opened up her notebook and flipped to a new page. "Everything and everyone we need is in this room. Let's take inventory, what do we have?"

Rufus hopped onto Katrina's lap while the group considered Tina's question. Katrina instinctively petted Rufus, avoiding the lump where his tracker was located. "No leads? No money?"

Robinson smiled sheepishly. "Well, I have money…" This raised their spirits slightly.

Doctor Contreras followed. "And I may have leads…" This raised their curiosity slightly.

"Tell us," Armelle said.

"Let's start with this," Contreras stated, pointing toward his laptop. He pulled up an interactive map of Durham County, with a slider at the bottom pulled all the way to the left. "It's the PIT count. Federally mandated. It's the county's dashboard of those experiencing homelessness, dated back two months." The crew gathered around the screen. It displayed the city with several triangles scattered throughout, most of which clumped around a few central locations. "This visualization is a crude census of sorts. Each triangle represents the location of someone experiencing homelessness on a given morning."

Armelle interjected. "Right. Yes. I read about this. The city sends a worker to conduct a count of parks, underpasses, and other locations, then they enter the number."

"And that accomplishes…what exactly?" Robinson asked.

Miles thought back to his ministry in D.C. "Not nearly enough. There are simply not enough beds in shelters to help each of them."

Tina frustratingly added. "No reason why there couldn't be…"

"Very true," Doctor Contreras added, bringing them back on track. "But regardless, the first step is to establish a count. It provides a baseline to gauge whether interventions are working. And look at this…" Contreras dragged the slider from April through October. The triangles remained more or less constant through the spring and summer, but as the slider passed through September and October, they practically disappeared.

"Well, that's good," Robinson said, before wondering where Italo was leading them. "Right?"

"Did we add more shelters?" Tina skeptically asked.

"I know we didn't increase our allotment of city social workers," Armelle added.

Contreras acknowledged these grimly. "No and no." He clicked on another tab. A press release. "This is what we did."

Robinson read off the title. "Revolutionary public-private partnership between Durham County and the ARC provides hope and opportunity for the city's homeless." He scratched his stubble, before adding. "Dated last week. What's the ARC?"

Miles gritted his teeth. "The Apostolic Rejuvenation Convention. They provide theological cover for monsters like Wakestone to hurt others."

"They're providing more than that," Armelle pointed out. "They're providing bodies."

"For…" Robinson reluctantly began.

Tina sighed. "Food. Blood. And possibly a next layer of vampires."

No one quite knew how to respond. One by one, each of their eyes gravitated to the cell off the lobby where the holy blood bats were housed.

Katrina broke the silence. "We need to save them."

The group all nodded politely until Armelle said what they were all thinking. "How?"

Tina added on. "We don't know where they are. And even if we did, we can't exactly traipse into a nest of vampires unprotected."

Katrina slammed her fist on the arm of her chair. "Doesn't matter. We will do it. We must."

Robinson looked at Katrina. Doing so made him recall the torture he underwent the week he was held captive, which sent a shiver down his spine. He then considered the months Katrina spent captive, and said, "We'll figure it out, Katrina. We will."

Doctor Contreras quietly cleared his throat. Everyone looked towards him. He collected his thoughts as he wiped his glasses with his pocket square, only to find that it only made them dirtier. He wished he had more of his clothes, his possessions, his space. He sighed, and continued. "I can't speak to the 'where,' but we might have some leads with 'how.'" He slid an over-stuffed notebook toward the center of the table. "Doctor Ivanov's notes. The woman was truly extraordinary. These are her reports on her work with Katrina. As Katrina began to recover, she turned her attention to a potential cure. She posited that if there is an early intervention, the V-blood might be reversible, restoring one's original blood type. Her studies were of course…" Contreras respectfully looked toward Katrina to ensure she wasn't unsettled by the conversation before continuing, "unfinished, but there's a lot to start with here." With an upturned hand, he directed their attention toward the cell next to Katrina's, where the

Holy Blood Bat was housed. "Particularly when combined with my research, as modest in comparison as it might be."

Tina suddenly remembered what she had grabbed before leaving the Aquarium. "And this!" She placed the syringe on the table next to the notes. "Sinclair was threatening to sedate Katrina with it. I'm not sure exactly what the compound is or what it does, but if it could temporarily curb the symptoms of the V-blood…"

Contreras excitedly cradled the syringe in his hands. "This could be the key that unlocks a cure!"

A spark of hope ignited in each of them. "So," Tina stated, "A group of us works on the cure."

Miles added, "While a group of us tracks down where the ARC is experimenting on the poor captive souls."

Armelle smiled. "We've got a plan."

38

Contribute

Katrina rubbed her forearm uncomfortably as she scanned the Nash Center lobby, uncertain how to help.

Miles and Armelle were sticking pins into a map of Durham hung on a corkboard, each one representing an area where a decrease in homelessness was observed. They were attempting to triangulate where those rounded up might be held. Miles contributed his knowledge of nonprofits that worked with the unhoused in the area, contacting each for information. Armelle contributed her understanding of real estate, a topic she had begun exploring when she opened her bookstore and simply continued to learn about afterward.

Katrina had nothing to contribute.

Tina and Doctor Contreras were gesturing toward a large computer screen perched atop the table at the center of the room. A cord connected the computer to a beaker which diagnosed the serum held within. Something about the microbial absorption rate. Tina contributed her understanding of scientific data analysis. Doctor Contreras contributed his understanding of biology.

Katrina had nothing to contribute.

Each of them had worked themselves to the brink of exhaustion for the sake of others, while Katrina had done nothing.

Well, not each of them. Robinson didn't seem to have much to contribute either. He was currently entertaining himself by attempting to juggle empty syringes. The uneven weight distribution made it potentially impossible, but that seemed to only motivate him more.

Katrina retreated into her cell. She plopped onto her bed, shortly followed by Rufus. She scratched gently behind his large ears. It wasn't saving the world, but he seemed to appreciate it. They both drifted to sleep with Katrina's scratches syncing up with her breaths.

She was startled out of this trance by a knock on the door. Robinson's head slipped through a cracked door.

"Grab your stuff, we've got errands," he informed her.

She sat up and quickly rolled her sleeves down, covering up the scars on her forearm. Scanning the room, she realized that other than Rufus, she didn't really have any stuff, so she wasn't certain how to respond.

"Errands?" she asked.

Robinson handed her a slip of paper that had each person's name on it alongside some items. He grimaced as he fidgeted with the yellow bead on his necklace. "They haven't stopped working for days. They're exhausted. They need something to pick them up. To take their mind off matters."

Katrina looked across the room again, this time seeing everyone in a different light. Italo was uncharacteristically disheveled, his bowtie discolored and off-center. Armelle, stuck on a problem, rocked back and forth, clicking her pen with each turn. Tina furiously scribbled in her notebook, crossing out phrases, tearing out pages. They needed… something.

Katrina nodded her consent and began to slide off the bed but paused halfway. "Wait, what time is it?"

Robinson checked his watch. "About 6:30. Why?" He suddenly realized the basis for her question and blushed. "The sun is pretty much set, but there's still some light. Is that…" he trailed off.

"It'll be fine." If her blood was still fully V, or if the sun was still fully overhead, it would have been an issue, but at this point, it would merely be a discomfort.

Robinson tossed her a hat. She looked at it strangely. "Thanks. But it won't block much."

He smiled. "We don't have warrants out for *our* arrest, but there still might be people looking for us. Pull it low." He then took out a Rays hat and placed it on his head, before smirking. "And yes, I'm well aware of the irony of my disguise."

They passed through the lobby with an unremarked-upon "Be back later" and made their way for their bikes, which they had decided were less traceable than their cars. They rode toward the closest light-rail stop. Robinson detached the crate on the back of his bike, paid for their tickets with cash, boarded the tram, and took it downtown. Once or twice, Robinson attempted to make small talk, but each time the conversation fizzled out.

The doors slid open and Robinson pointed toward a storefront. "Spud's Dry-Cleaning."

Katrina followed Robinson into the store, as he explained. "Italo is a man who takes great pride in how he presents himself. I haven't known him long, but I have noticed that his previously dapper appearance has slipped a bit. Tina thought having his shirts pressed and cleaned might be appreciated." Katrina nodded in reply.

As they approached the counter, Robinson pulled a few shirts out of the crate and placed them neatly by the register. Katrina wandered to the side of the store, with her back against the wall and placed each exit in her line of sight. A few minutes later, Robinson approached with the crate empty. Katrina stared at him blankly, not entirely certain how the process worked.

"We'll be able to pick those up tomorrow. Possibly Friday." Robinson explained to her as they exited Spud's and turned left onto Morris Street. As they did so, Wakestone Tower rose before them. Robinson froze for a moment, before continuing.

"Thank you, by the way," he said softly. "For coming with me. I, well… I just…" he trailed off.

Katrina spared him from having to finish his sentence. "Where to next?"

Robinson's smile returned to his face. "Grabbing some books!"

"From Baldwin's Books?" Katrina asked as she looked over her shoulder at the picturesque silhouette of downtown Durham set against the full moon.

"I wish. I haven't seen Armelle's shop yet. But she's got it closed down. For, ya know… Plus, it could be watched. We're going to a favorite of mine. TJ's."

Katrina thought that he lived in Tampa Bay. "You've been before?"

"Oh yeah," Robinson replied as they turned onto Warren Street. "I played minor league ball down the street," he pointed over his shoulder to the Durham Bulls Athletic Park. "I'd stop by here every home stand. Great books, of course. But I was really into movies at the time." He reflected on his use of the past tense as they were greeted by the chiming of a bell upon entering the shop. "Anyways, they had a great DVD selection. Probably not anymore…"

Katrina paused at the threshold and looked around. Shelves upon shelves of books, magazines, and board games. It was somehow both chaotic and perfectly organized.

"How about you? Have you been?" Robinson asked.

She figured she probably had a different experience in Durham than the millionaire next to her had. "We were more library people."

"Have you been to the new West-side location?" Robinson asked. Katrina shook her head. He smiled. "Oh, it's incredible. We'll have to go sometime."

Katrina smiled, despite herself. Since her mom was an only child and she didn't know anything about her dad's family, she had never had an uncle. She wondered, briefly, if this is what it felt like.

"Okay, we need a few books for Armelle." He pulled the list out of his pocket. "You find the first two, I'll find the bottom two?" Katrina nodded as she drew her hand across the red bead on her necklace.

A mischievous look spread across Robinson's face. "I'll bet you a book that I can find mine before yours?"

"Deal," Katrina stated as she darted away. She slid smoothly between customers and down aisles without them registering her. "Jemisin… Jemisin…" she said to herself as she grabbed a novel from the Science-Fiction section. She then dashed to the Non-fiction section and picked up "Walkable Cities." Armelle spotted Robinson in the poetry section grabbing a collection of Pablo Neruda's work. She held out the two books, and he grimaced theatrically.

"Already? I just found the first one! Well, a deal's a deal! Go pick out something. I'll get the last book and one other thing. Meet you at the register in ten?"

She wandered the stacks, not quite sure what she was looking for. She hadn't really read for pleasure in years. She wondered whether it was a lack of interest or a lack of time. As she was passing by a display of short stories, she overheard a customer saying "Oh I simply loved this one. Made me think of home." As they passed on, Katrina scooped up the book they were referring to. It featured a decorative candle on the cover and the title "Interpreter of Maladies." She brought it to the front counter but didn't see Robinson there.

Panic hit.

Her heart raced. With each thump, she felt as though more and more of the V blood that was hidden in her heart rushed through her veins. She frantically scanned the room, looking for vampires. But instead, she saw Robinson in the games section, lost in a bound book.

Deep breaths, she told herself as she approached.

"Oh," Robinson exclaimed as he saw her. "I'm sorry. I lost track of time." He held out two books: One with a dragon on the cover, the other with what looked to be a sorcerer. "I told Miles that I would run a game of Dungeons & Dragons, but I have no clue how to actually do so. Found some guides. Which of these missions looks better?

Katrina's breath hadn't caught back up yet, so she responded with a point. Without any thought or reason, she gestured to the dragon.

"Perfect, thanks," he responded as he brought the six books to the register. After paying with cash, he handed Katrina her book. "Let me know how that is?"

"Okay." Katrina held the book in her arms. "And thank you."

"Don't mention it," he stated as they exited the shop. Robinson placed the remaining books in the crate.

"Is Miles next?" Katrina asked.

"No, we'll have to pick up his last. Not quite sure how that one's going to work, to be honest." They turned right onto Valvano Street. "Of course, Tina didn't put anything on the list for herself, but I have an idea where we can get something for Mi Llave." He ducked his head around corners, uncertainly. "Well, if it's still there..." He spotted a brick warehouse a block away. "Katrina, look! There it is!"

Katrina smiled. "The Scrap Exchange! My mom used to take me there as a kid!" She glanced at Robinson. "Race you there?"

He laughed. "You're on!"

And they took off. Robinson started at a brisk jog, only to be passed by a shockingly fast Katrina. He laughed as he transitioned into a sprint, but even at full speed, he couldn't catch up to her. He found her waiting for him at the entrance. Panting, hands on his knees, he said through halting breath, "I know I don't have Grade-80 speed like I used to, but... how?"

Katrina scratched her forearms expecting to feel shame at what she was but was surprised to feel something else. She shrugged sheepishly as they entered. As she crossed the threshold, she was taken back in time, suddenly a child again, holding a five-dollar bill that her mom gave her. In a typical store, that wouldn't go far, but the Scrap Exchange was no typical store. It was known as a 'Creative Reuse Center,' where people could sort through donated items for creative projects.

"Ahh I wish Tina had something like this when she was younger,"

Robinson said with a smile.

This was not the image of Tina that Katrina had in her head. "Really?"

"Absolutely! Tina is wonderfully inventive. You should've seen the elaborate creations she would construct out of random Lego pieces." He paused at a bin of recycled brass brackets and picked one up. "And not just legos. To her, she could turn these into… into…" He struggled to find the end of the sentence. "Well, that's just the point! What to me is just a heap of hardware would suddenly turn into something remarkably cool. And not just cool, but practical too!" They traveled to an elaborate pyramid that someone had assembled out of old K-cups. "Like this!" He turned to Katrina. "We grew up on the Ninja Turtles. Did you watch that?"

Katrina shook her head.

"Yeah, I guess you would be a little young for that. But anyway, they had this awesome van that they traveled in. It doubled as a mobile pizza truck." Robinson caught Katrina's judgemental glance but laughed it off. "Sure, I hear it now, but it was cool! Just take my word for it! Anyway, we begged for the toy version of it, but our parents weren't exactly loaded, so they said no. Me, I shrugged it off and moved on, but about a week later, Tina showed me this wild van she created to store our Ninja Turtle figurines. Hidden underneath were mouse traps, so that when they were triggered, the van would take off! And coolest of all, she somehow set it up so that it could shoot out bottle caps painted as pizzas! It was incredible."

Katrina was surprised. "She… she's just so serious. And scientific. What happened?"

Robinson frowned as they walked through a section of the Exchange centered around woodworking. "She grew up, I guess." He picked up a jigsaw, considered it, but put it down. "Though it's not as if those skills disappeared. They just were re-routed into her scientific studies. And then into the systems she would design to track and improve other people's scientific studies. She once showed me the spreadsheet she used to chart a clinical trial on… something, I forget," Robinson winced at his inability to recall, "But it was as elaborate as her pizza truck. Just as creative. Only more…" He trailed off, unable or unwilling to classify her recent work. "But it's still there, I know it!"

As they wandered down the aisles, Katrina tried to consider what use each of the assorted items gathered in bins could be used for. But the best she could do was how to weaponize them, a thought that she found concerning. She closed her eyes, counted her breaths, and walked on, relying on her instincts to guide her. When she opened her eyes, a peculiar tool caught her attention. It had a metal base, with two sides ending in clamps. "What's this?" she asked.

Robinson's face lit up. "A lathe! Oh, that's perfect, Kat!" He picked up the machine with a grunt. "You put wood, or metal, or something between these caps, and they spin it around, like a gyro. You can then carve or shape… well, something. I'm not sure what, but I just know Tina will come up with something incredible." He looked at Katrina. "Thank you!"

She eyed it suspiciously. "I don't think that's going to fit in your bike basket, Robinson."

"We can pick it up tomorrow when we get the dry cleaning. We'll take a cab."

They took the lathe to the front desk, and Robinson talked them into holding it for him. It was the kind of request that Katrina never would've been able to make herself, but Robinson delivered it with an effortless charm that resulted in the employees responding as if he was doing them a favor.

As they exited, Katrina took a moment to bask in the moonlight. She opened her eyes and asked, "Where to next?"

"Last stop - we're headed to church." The nearly full moon illuminated the path as they walked down Mangum Street towards the tram stop, which they took eastwards towards Saint Thérèse's Church.

"And we can trust this Priest?" Katrina asked as they exited the tram.

Robinson rubbed his side uneasily. "Good question. I'm not sure. But I trust Father Miles, and he apparently trusts this new priest. So… I guess?"

Robinson wasn't able to gauge whether Katrina agreed, as she was staring off to the west. He followed her gaze and saw the silhouette of Wakestone Tower piercing the moon like a dagger. This sight froze him as well. In time, he shook his head, gave his ribs two pats, then said, "Come on, Kat. Let's head in."

Katrina took a deep breath, pulled the sleeve of her coat down over her wrists, and followed Robinson into the church.

They stepped into the church. Katrina couldn't help but notice the ornate, beautiful design integrated into every corner of the church. What she didn't see was other people. She felt a nudge from Robinson, who gestured toward the confessional where murmurs could be faintly heard. They sat in the back pew and waited for Father Michael.

Katrina waited for Robinson, who was typically quite chatty, to distract her with some inane comment or question. But he looked distant. Katrina awkwardly attempted to initiate a conversation.

"What do you think?"

"What? Huh?" He smiled apologetically. "Sorry, was in a daze. To be honest? I feel kind of weird about this errand."

"Oh, yeah, me too," Katrina replied. "But I didn't mean that. I meant about..." and she gestured at the altar, at the stained glass, at the crucifix.

Robinson exhaled. "If you asked me a year ago, I would've said absolutely, and slipped into media mode, reciting something like 'All that I've done is through the grace of God.'" He stared up at the stained glass, cocking his head to the side as he noticed that it displayed an early follower of Jesus being tortured. "But it's a bit easier to say that — to believe that — when you're making millions for entertaining millions by playing a game. But now..." he trailed off.

They sat in silence. Each looking at the series of stained glass windows depicting the stations of the cross.

Robinson eventually broke the silence. "What about you, Kat?"

"Oh I don't know," she replied deflectively, feeling herself shutting down at the thoughts popping into her head. She scratched her arm, and instinctively missed the sweet numbing feeling when the V blood would course through her veins. And what she used before that to dull her incurring thoughts. Her heart started pumping.

But then she felt the comforting presence of Robinson's hand on her shoulder.

She surprised herself when her mouth opened. "I grew up just a few blocks north from here," she shared.

"How about that!" Robinson responded reflexively, but then he noticed her downturned expression, and he pulled up a mental map of Durham. North of the church was a tough area. He grimaced empathetically.

"Yeah..." Katrina responded. "In fact, I had a good friend whose apartment was right where we're sitting now. But when they built this church, she was kicked out. Don't know where she ended up."

"I'm sorry," Robinson said.

"Every week, the rich from Southern Durham would show up in their Sunday bests, parade into this building, learn about how they should help the poor, then scramble back to their cars, trying to avoid us or the rats we shared the streets with, and retreat to their McMansions."

They sat together in shared discomfort. Robinson considered the weeks when he attended mass at this very church. Katrina considered how she hadn't actually seen any rats around the church like normal.

Katrina listened to the muted sounds coming from the confessional booth. She couldn't hear what Father Michael was saying, but her heightened sense of hearing could pick up on the empathetic tone behind the words. "So, if you asked *me* a year ago, I would've said absolutely not." She looked at the stained glass, thought of Ivan, thought of her found family. "But I suppose what I was considered religion might not have actually been religion." Her attention was drawn to a depiction of the red blood dripping down Jesus' head in one of the windows. She thought of everything that was done to her. Everything that was being done to others. Everything being done in the name of God. "I don't know if I believe, but I do know that *their* belief isn't right."

It was at this moment that the doors of the confessional opened up. An elderly woman who looked like she lived on the streets walked out. As she passed by, Robinson noticed a tear on her cheek. "Are you okay?" he asked.

The woman took a breath and wiped away the tear. Robinson and Katrina noticed that she had been clutching a worn photograph. She looked back at the booth, then at Robinson and Katrina. "Yes," she said warmly. "I think I am." And she exited the church.

A minute later, the priest left the confessional booth and caught sight of them. He smiled and approached.

Robinson instinctively liked him, though that was true of most people he met. Katrina nudged Robinson and directed his attention to behind the priest, where a brown cat with mismatching green and yellow eyes trailed behind. Robinson and Katrina collectively groaned.

The young priest heard their distress and asked, "Is everything okay?"

Katrina looked toward Robinson, who opened his mouth, but no words came out. The priest sat in the pew next to them. The cat hopped up and planted herself on his lap.

"Nice cat," Robinson said to buy time while he considered his approach.

The priest smiled. "She truly is. Her name is Naomi. And my name is Father Michael." He extended his hand. Robinson shook it, followed by Katrina.

They sat in silence, which Katrina awkwardly filled. "Does she eat a lot of rats?" She immediately regretted the question.

"What?" Father Michael asked, taken aback. He then shrugged off the randomness of the question and answered. "No, thankfully she's never brought back a rat. I'll admit, I have kind of spoiled her, and now she only eats this high-brow cat food I pick up weekly from Parker and Otis."

Robinson watched the priest scratch under the cat's chin. When Naomi decided she had enough, she bit at the priest's hand. Robinson watched as Father Michael responded with a smile, and transitioned to petting her along the spine instead.

"We're friends with Father Miles," Robinson blurted out, figuring his words couldn't be more abrupt than Katrina's.

"Is he okay? I've tried to reach him, but haven't been able to get through."

"Oh he's had some phone issues of late," Robinson replied. The phone issues being that they all had to deactivate their service for fear of Wakestone's powerful allies tracking them.

Father Michael noticed that they hadn't answered his question. "Is there anything he needs?"

Katrina waited for Robinson to ask, but Robinson looked at her sheepishly. Katrina sighed and said "Well..." as she looked at Naomi.

Father Michael followed her eyes toward the cat. He instinctively pulled the cat closer. When he did so, Naomi let out a strained meow. He relaxed his grip. Naomi repositioned herself on his lap and looked up at him. He looked across at Robinson and Katrina, hoping they might relent. They avoided his eye contact in guilt.

"It's okay," he said to them. They looked him in the eyes, but his gaze was on the cat.

"Wait here," he said to her, as he left the pew. She naturally followed him to the back room. Before the priest and the cat disappeared, Robinson made a request.

"Oh, while you're back there, let me know if you find an old leather notebook with a lavender cross embossed on the front?"

A minute or two later, Father Michael returned, with a cat traveling case in one hand and in the other an elegant communion cup that was covered with a sheet of tin foil. Naomi trailed behind him.

Father Michael placed the case on the pew next to Robinson and Katrina. "She's going to hate me for this," he said sadly. "She does not like this case."

Robinson inspected the carrier. It looked like it wasn't the fault of the case, as Father Michael seemed to have spared no expense with the model.

The young priest picked up the cat and kissed her atop her head. "You're needed more elsewhere," he said, as he placed her into the case. Doing so took some effort, as Naomi growled and hissed as he did so.

"Here," he said, handing Katrina the cup. She peeled away the tinfoil lid and saw that it was full of cat treats. "When you step outside, give her a couple of those. Not too many, they're quite rich. Each of you gives her one, and she'll forgive you."

"Thank you," they each said to the priest.

He was distracted in thought. "Oh, you'll need her food. And her bed. And her litter. She's quite particular, you know. And her..."

Robinson put his hand on Michael's shoulder. "We'll take care of her. Could we perhaps take the food now, and then come back tomorrow with a car to pick up the rest?"

"Of course," Michael replied as he left to retrieve the food. He returned momentarily and handed the bag to Robinson. "And tell Miles," he started. "Well, tell him that..." The priest grunted in frustration. He looked toward the back of the church, where he delivered his homilies each week, and said to himself. "I don't even know why I have this job. I can never find the right words." Michael shrugged, pulled an old notebook from his back pocket and handed it over. "Maybe his own words will be enough."

"Hey," Robinson said warmly as he accepted the notebook. "It looks to me like you're doing just fine."

Katrina followed up, as she looked at Naomi. "And I think Miles will get the message."

Robinson and Katrina left the church, Katrina with the carrier case, and Robinson with the giant bag of fancy cat food.

"Okay, that's all we had on the list," Robinson said. "But what about you, Kat? Is there anything else you need?"

"No Robby," Katrina replied, finally feeling like she contributed. "Let's go home."

39

The Black Hole

"Are you certain?" Miles asked as he scratched Naomi under her chin. It had been two days since Katrina and Robinson had retrieved the cat for him. She resumed her affectionate tendencies towards Miles, but was slow to warm up to the others.

"Of course not. One can never be certain," Armelle responded curtly as she rubbed her knuckles back and forth over the blue bead on her necklace. "But we are confident."

"And not the tower?" Robinson asked, looking up from his Dungeons and Dragons book, as he picked through a bowl of jelly beans, relishing being in charge of his own diet for the first time in decades.

Katrina shook her head. "Same as the Manor. In each, there was only room for a few select... vampires." She still wasn't used to that categorization, or certain whether she belonged in it. "Those spaces were set for experiments."

"And Terrance, my..." Miles searched for the word, "acquaintance in New Bern swung by the aquarium. There doesn't seem to be any sign of life there." This phrasing made everyone uncomfortable. Miles signaled his apology by raising his hands. "It seems they relocated them back west."

"Exactly," said Tina. "So we cross-referenced existing shelters with construction permits and the unhoused maps."

Miles was confused. "Why construction permits?"

Tina's face lit up. "That was Armelle's brilliant idea!" Armelle avoided the attention by marking a note down in the margins of the urban planning book she had been reading, but she did acknowledge the compliment by leaning to her side, brushing shoulders with Tina. "There hasn't been any indication of movement in the unhoused above ground, so we figured they had extended the tunnels. Of course, they're not going to broadcast where those were laid, but they do need to hire someone to do the work. Armelle was able to dig through the permitting system and map out prospective routes of the tunnels." Tina consulted her notes. "Now, each segment was tied to some dummy corporation, but we're quite *certain* we know where they're headed." She delivered this last line with a wink at Armelle.

Miles was beginning to understand. "Based on the mapping of the unhoused. Where they're congregated."

"Quite the opposite, actually," said Contreras, whose confidence had returned alongside his freshly pressed wardrobe.

Maybe he wasn't. "What do you mean?"

"Are you familiar with how astronomists identify the location of a black hole?"

Miles shook his head. "Not particularly."

Contreras reached across the table toward Robinson's jelly beans before pausing. "May I?"

"Be my guest." Robinson slid the bowl toward Italo.

Contreras promptly scattered the jelly beans across the desk.

"I mean, I was still planning on eating some of those..." Robinson said with a grin.

Contreras continued unfazed. "Black holes are, for all intents and purposes, invisible. The gamma-ray bursts they emit can be used to observe nearby galaxies, but the entity of the black hole itself is essentially undetectable." He moved some jelly beans around, clumping some together, and leaving a blank space in the center of the table. "We can, however, detect the gravitational effect they have on objects around them."

Armelle picked up his point. "Ahh, how they pull objects into their gravitational field."

Miles was getting it. "So when there's a section on the unhoused map with a dearth of homeless..."

Tina nodded. "Then somewhere there, probably underground, is where they're being held."

"And where is this location you're so confident in?" Miles asked.

"The McCaulley Shelter," Armelle stated.

Tina added in context. "It's in West Durham, on the corner of--"

"Eshcol Street and Southam Drive," Katrina said quietly.

Robinson, noticing the glances toward Katrina, spared her the inevitable follow-up question about her familiarity with the shelter. "So what's the plan then?"

Tina flipped to a page in her notebook, which featured a detailed flow chart, which branched in two atop the page. "Well, that all depends." She looked to Doctor Contreras. "How close are we to having the serum ready?"

"Theoretically close," Contreras responded, glancing over Tina's shoulder to the cell where the colony of Holy Blood Bats resided. "Based on our modeling, we believe that we have a stable dose. It was a matter of reverse-engineering the transition we can observe in Katrina's blood. The data yielded from the sample from the aquarium, and the bacterium from Bruce's saliva should theoretically be able to reverse the takeover of the V blood."

"And practically?" Armelle asked.

"We will find out tomorrow," Contreras said. "There are a few adjustments on the serum to make today, then tomorrow we'll contaminate the bats, and test out the latest batch of the serum. If that is successful, I believe we could have a stable dose that could be used on infected humans within a week. Or two." Contreras looked toward Katrina. "Would you be so kind as to donate one more vial of your blood tomorrow?"

Katrina nodded affirmatively

Tina returned to Robinson's question. "Then simply reconnaissance. Data collection. We're not ready for any interactions until the serum is ready, so we just map out the grounds, identifying points of entry, escape routes, and so on." Tina thought back in shame about the haphazard way they had previously planned. "Everything we should have done at the aquarium."

Robinson shrugged. "I appreciate you not waiting longer to perfect a plan."

Miles looked toward Robinson, Armelle, and Tina. "Okay, so we four go tomorrow."

"High noon?" Armelle suggested.

"High noon," they responded.

40

Other Katrinas

"Okay, what do you notice?" Tina asked as she looked at the McCaulley Shelter alongside Armelle, Miles, and Robinson. Armelle returned the vampire-deterring flashlight they had acquired at the aquarium into her backpack and pulled out a notebook so she could record their observations.

"It's fallen into disrepair," Miles stated. It appeared to be an old warehouse that had at one point been renovated into a shelter. Perhaps it was a tobacco warehouse that became available when the businesses left the state. But the years had not been kind to the building. The sprawling brick facade featured a multitude of windows, each one boarded up. Miles wondered whether it was this foreboding when Katrina had stayed here, presumably as a child. "This provides a bit of cover. Can't see in, can't see out."

"And that extends to the building itself," Robinson added, noticing the smattering of trees surrounding the building. "If you're a hundred yards away, you wouldn't even notice this was here." He thought about his time living in Durham. "I never even knew this place existed." As he said this, he considered Katrina's contrasting experiences in the city.

Armelle added, "There are presumably few public entry and exit points." She pointed to the barn door entrance. "Factories built in this era were infamous for funneling their workers through just one door in the front, and one in the back. Better to track their employees, though that made them a hazard if any of the dried-out tobacco leaves ignited."

Tina looked at the notes she was recording and picked up on Armelle's particular word choice. "You said *public* entry and exit points?"

Armelle gave her a wink, then bent over and dragged a finger across the sidewalk they were standing on. She lifted her finger showing the residue of the freshly paved concrete. They each visually followed the sidewalk, which led directly into the foundation of the building.

"Oh, so they're building, but underneath. They've connected this to the tunnels?" Robinson asked.

"Can never be certain," Armelle shrugged. "But I would guess so."

"Should we check the back?" Miles suggested.

A stiff mid-October breeze ran across the group as each of them waited for someone else to answer.

Tina had her necklace wrapped around her hand. She passed it over the binding of her notebook, the orange bead emitting a percussive rattle. Eventually, she responded. "I suppose."

Robinson saw the anxiety on his sister's face and tried to help by giving her some semblance of a plan that she could latch onto. "Let's use the treeline for cover. If we're a tree or two deep in the forest, we'll be able to observe the shelter while keeping us out of sight." He tagged on with uncertainty, "Not that I think there's anyone in there. It looks pretty abandoned."

As flimsy as this plan was, Tina appreciated her brother's efforts. "Good idea."

They made their own trail, zigging around the trees, keeping the building in sight, yet staying out of earshot. Armelle handed the notebook to Tina, knowing that she could more effectively map the premises. But there wasn't much to map. The shelter was essentially a giant rectangle. A row of chimneys lined the top, which would have been of use when the warehouse was running. Miles squinted and pointed to one at the far side of the building. "Is that smoke?"

Everyone paused and stared.

"Naw," Robinson said with a confidence that he didn't actually feel. "Just a low-hanging cloud."

They all moved further into the forest as they wrapped around to the back of the building, keeping a line of trees between them and the shelter at all times.

"Ow!" Miles said as he looked around at the ground. "Something bit me. Was that a snake?"

"Possibly," Armelle said. "I've seen multiple dead rats along the path. Something's eating them."

"You okay?" Tina asked.

"Yeah, I seem to be," Miles said.

They followed at a safe distance around the building. As they turned the corner, Robinson—who had the best vision out of the group—noticed that the back door was slightly ajar. No light escaped out of it, but the sound of a pained whimper did.

Armelle, who had been leading the way, froze in her tracks, uncertain how to proceed. The others each bumped into her in turn.

"What--" Robinson began to ask before his sister hastily covered his mouth. She pointed to her ear.

Each one heard the sound.

The cry for help.

"What should we do?" Miles whispered.

No one responded.

Tina cracked her knuckles and said quietly, "We need to go back. Formulate a plan. Return with Katrina. She's the strongest of us."

Each of them nodded and turned on their heels, before bumping into Robinson who was at the back of the line. "She is," he agreed while shaking his head sadly. "But she's also the one who's been hurt the most." He pointed toward the eerie noise escaping the cracked door. "In places like that."

Armelle nodded. "There are other Katrinas in there."

Miles remembered her words. "If you want to help people, help people."

Sensing that Tina was becoming overwhelmed with the decision, Armelle gently placed a hand on her shoulder. Tina nodded her appreciation and led the way towards the abandoned warehouse.

41

Interlude - Five Days Prior

"The Israelites again did what was evil in the sight of the Lord, and the Lord gave them into the hand of the Philistines sixty years," the righteous man with the long hair and the long beard said from the raised stage. "Sounds familiar?" he asked the crowd of pale figures in front of him who were boxed in by a perimeter of sunlight strategically shining through the ceiling. Their bodies twitched due to cramping, but their focus remained fixed on the man on the stage.

"So God sent a man to save them. Samson. A righteous warrior the likes of which the world has not seen." He glanced over his shoulder at the man sitting at a wooden bar, sipping from a crystal glass next to a woman with her hair in a tight bun. "Until now."

The righteous man raised his hands to the sky and his voice followed. "A man empowered by the Lord. A man who could tear a lion apart barehanded. A man who took the same vow as I myself have taken. As I beseech you to take." The man at the bar stifled a laugh while the woman next to him stifled a groan. The righteous man either did not hear or pretended not to.

"This vow strengthened him. In Ashkelon, he single-handedly vanquished thirty evil men. In Lehi, a thousand! It was the spirit of the Lord coursing through his veins that gave him this strength. And it is that same spirit of the Lord coursing through *your* veins that gives you strength. My... accomplice," the man said dismissively as he nodded to the woman to the side, "may classify it as something else.

Something that we have made." He turned his focus back toward those in front of him and warned them with a wag of his finger. "But beware! It is this prideful claiming of God's work as our own that brought about Samon's fall! Rather than following God's word, he followed his own!"

The righteous man stole a momentary glance into the eyes of the crowd in front of him, before quickly turning his back and facing the wooden cross behind him.

"I know that some of you have faltered under the weight of this cross you now bear. Being holy people in an unholy land undoubtedly presents challenges." He paused for a moment. It stretched longer than the cadence of the speech would have suggested. "But look to Samson for proof that God can still work through you. He was betrayed by the one he loved. His eyes blinded, his hair shaved, his strength sapped, his body chained. Yet he called out 'Lord God, remember me and strengthen me only this once, O God, so that with this one act of revenge I may pay back the Philistines for my two eyes!'"

His voice raised to a thunderous level. "And with that, the mighty Samson tore down the pillars on which the idolatrous temple of the Philistines rested!"

He turned back to the crowd. "Samson died so that one greater could live. Let that be a reminder to each and every one of you — the keepers of the great mystery — as you carry out God's righteous war!"

The man at the bar smiled. The woman next to him did not.

42

You Reflect Me

They peered through the opened door while they waited at the threshold. Behind them shone the light of the midday sun, but in front of them laid only darkness. The sound of screaming had faded into a low, whimpering moan.

"Wait," Miles stated to Tina as she was about to enter. He picked up a stick that had been knocked down from a nearby tree before reaching under his coat and tearing off a piece of black fabric. He wrapped the fabric around the end of the stick and then turned to Armelle. "Lighter?"

Armelle dug through her backpack and handed him an industrial-sized lighter that they had found in the Lemur Center. Miles opened up a latch on the bottom and sprinkled some of the fluid on the fabric. He closed the compartment and clicked the trigger of the lighter. The torch ignited. He stepped into the darkness. Tina, Armelle, and Robinson followed.

They huddled together and slowly walked into the shelter, following the sounds of the injured person. After a few yards, Miles stopped abruptly and tilted the torch toward the ground. They saw a pale man in tattered clothes writhing on the ground in a pool of blood. His muscles twitched, and his eyes, brown with a red halo around the irises, shifted around rapidly as if experiencing a seizure. Yet he showed no sign of consciousness.

"Never you mind him," a deep voice echoed off the walls. "He will recover. In time."

Miles frantically waved the torch around attempting to identify the direction of the voice.

"Allow me to help you," the voice responded as a plastic click was heard, followed by the grinding metal above. They looked upwards. The overlapping lumber of the ceiling suddenly parted in the middle as a section of the roof shifted out of sight, except for a few selected 2x4s in the center which were supported by metal beams. In flooded rays of sunshine forming the outline of a perfect square around the injured man on the ground, who scrambled toward the shade in the center and curled into the fetal position.

The light from the ceiling allowed them to take in their environment, which was a blend of brick and wood. The fire-red brick walls were supported throughout by wooden frames and beams. To the side of the room, perched behind an elaborately decorated wooden bar was a thin yet muscular pale man with neatly parted hair, a well-tailored black suit, and dark red eyes that featured just a hint of blue around the pupils.

"Wakestone," Tina hissed.

The man spread his arms wide. "In the flesh." He then reached toward the bar, dragging his bloody finger across the many bottles in front of him, which sang out a haunting melody as his elongated nails tapped each. His hand then wrapped itself around a bottle, which he picked up and inspected. "Care for a drink?" he asked with a smile. In response, each of them instinctively stepped into the rectangle of light. Wary of approaching the vampire at the center of it, they stopped after the threshold and glared at Jacob Wakestone.

"Just me then, I suppose," he said as he poured himself a glass. He caught their disgusted expression and grinned. "Oh, it's not what you think." He stepped closer to them and presented the bottle in the manner of a seasoned sommelier, showing them the brown liquor inside it. "50-year single-malt." His stare switched from the bottle to the vampire on the ground behind them and then onto each of them. "I find it to be an exquisite... palate cleanser between meals." He turned his back to them, paced back to the bar, and placed the bottle atop it. While he did so, Miles handed the torch to Robinson before digging his hand into his jacket, pulling out a golden cross on a chain. He ripped it off his neck and shoved it in the direction of Wakestone, who tilted his head to the side in curiosity.

"Really?" Wakestone asked bemused, suddenly back at the

perimeter of the light. "You think that stops me?" He pointed to their right, where a wooden platform raised above the rectangle of light. Behind this platform was a stylish shiplap wall that reached toward the ceiling. Centered on that wall was a crucifix that was taller than any of them.

Wakestone walked onto the platform and extended his arms wide, forming a t. "How do you think I built all of this?" He turned his back toward them and looked at the cross, before plucking it off the wall as if it was merely velcroed on. As he did so, many of the adjoining shiplap boards behind the cross scattered the ground. He stepped over them and leaned on the cross as if it were a crutch while he savored a long sip of his whiskey.

Miles let the cross fall to the ground and took the torch back, holding it tightly in two hands.

As Wakestone set the cross on the ground, a splinter cut his finger open. He stared at the blood as he took another step forward, with only the sunlight between him and them. He licked the blood off his finger and chased it with a sip of his whiskey. He extended his right hand, dragging it across the curtain of light. The blood from his skin sizzled, and smoke gently steamed off of his sharpened nails, but if it caused him any discomfort, he showed no signs of it. Armelle dug through her bag for something. Wakestone looked on in amusement. She pulled out the vampire-deterrent flashlight that they had taken from the aquarium. Recognition flashed upon Wakestone's face. He dropped the crystal glass and leaped across the perimeter of light, snatching the flashlight with his left hand before it could be ignited while his right hand slashed across her throat. All this occurred before the glass hit the concrete ground.

Everyone but Tina instinctively closed their eyes, awaiting the attack that never came. When they opened them they saw Tina cradling Armelle in her arms, whispering "Everything's going to be okay, we can fix this, everything's going to be okay..." repeatedly and they saw Wakestone somehow back across the room, leaning against the bar, pouring himself another drink.

"Oh that you will want to have checked out," he said calmly as he inspected the mix of his blood with Armelle's on his finger. He picked up the flashlight from the bartop and inspected it, before crunching it in his hand as if it was a paper cup. "You think you threaten me? Oh no. You... reflect me." He set his gaze on each of them while one by one they looked away. "I see the terror in your eyes. The awe. The...

reverence." Gratitude crossed his face. "For too long I have had to hide the best part of me, so as not to scare the sheep. But you see it. Soon I will fully reveal myself to the world and they will see me as you do. I will serve them the miracle, mystery, and authority that they crave, and they will ask for more." He closed his eyes and sipped his whiskey. "But not yet. Until that day comes, you serve a useful purpose. You remind me what is to become." He held up his index finger, still stained with Armelle's blood. "What I can do with just one finger." He placed the finger down on a button atop the bar and they heard a door open behind them. They swiveled and spotted a door opening, revealing the top of a darkened staircase. In swarmed a colony of vampires. They scrambled over each other frantically, like a pack of starving wolves chasing wounded prey.

Miles, Robinson, and Tina encircled Armelle, trying to simultaneously protect themselves inside the perimeter of light while avoiding the vampire trapped in there with them. That man began clenching and unclenching his fists. His mouth twitched.

"Ahh yes," Wakestone said across the room, looking at Miles. "Now I remember. You would make for a fine drink, wouldn't you?" He placed his glass down and stepped toward them as the vampires bordered the protective light.

Robinson jumped across the threshold and picked up the wooden cross from the pile of wood. He backhanded an approaching vampire with it, before pulling it back and swinging it toward Wakestone. The vampire effortlessly dodged the swing by leaping onto the pile of wood ten feet away. The cross had sailed by him and shattered against the bar, smashing an array of liquor bottles.

"A whiff," Wakestone taunted from where he suddenly stood across the room. "I suppose that's why you're here instead of down in Tampa?" A stream of liquor made its way across the uneven floor, making its way to the center of the room.

"Was it?" Robinson asked as he scrambled back into the protection of the light. Vampires crowded outside the box of light, waiting for Wakestone to free them with the push of a button.

"Miles?" Robinson said, looking at the torch. After a beat, Miles realized what Robinson had done, and set the torch in his hands down on the trail of liquor which had now reached them. The flames shot across the room, igniting the wooden bar.

"Tina?" Robinson said. Tina rummaged through the backpack on the ground with one arm while she supported Armelle with the other, handing the industrial lighter to her brother. Robinson wound up and flung the lighter into the flame. The reservoir of lighter fluid combusted. The fire followed the wooden beams throughout the room. One by one, each collapsed. As they did so, sections of the brick walls they were supported crumbled. Rays of light shot through the warehouse, scattering the vampires down the stairs and into the tunnel.

Robinson and Tina seized the opportunity. They propped Armelle up between them and raced toward the door. Miles shot a look back to Wakestone, horrified at the thought that he may soon be upon them. Miles looked him in the eyes and saw that Wakestone seemed to be contemplating risking a little sunlight for precisely that. Miles fell to his knees in terror, which brought a giant grin across Wakestone's face. The pale man stepped back and locked eyes on Miles, savoring the priest's fear from afar. Try as he might, Miles could not break the hold of Wakestone's red stare.

A vampire enmeshed in flames sprinted between Miles and Wakestone. As he passed by, Wakestone extended an arm and plucked the vampire up with one arm. Without breaking eye contact, Wakestone effortlessly pulled the inflamed vampire toward his mouth, drained him, and dropped the lifeless body to the ground. Miles may have been frozen there indefinitely if Robinson hadn't dragged him out of the warehouse into the light, while Tina repeated, "Everything's going to be okay, we can fix this, everything's going to be okay…"

43

Help

"Everything is going to be okay," Tina said while stroking Armelle's hand as Robinson dropped an exorbitant tip on the front seat of the taxi.

"Please…," Robinson began, but trailed off, uncertain exactly what he was requesting. The driver shrugged, took the money, and drove off as Robinson and Miles propped Armelle between their shoulders. She remained unconscious as they wove through the backroads on their way to Duke Forest.

"Here is fine," Miles said as they turned onto Erwin Road.

Armelle showed signs of life, groaning, as they pulled her out of the taxi and walked through the woods to the Nash Center.

"I can fix this," Tina assured her.

Armelle smiled weakly. "Can you?"

"We can," Tina said, looking into her bloodshot eyes. "They can," she amended as they burst through the doors into the lobby. Tina frantically looked around the lobby, and not seeing either Katrina or Italo, bellowed, "Help! Please!"

"Tina…" Armelle began.

"Yes?" Tina said as she placed her on a chair.

"I don't know what's going to happen."

Tina opened her mouth, prepared to offer a trite promise, but she recognized everything Armelle was expressing in those words. "Me either," she said softly. "I'm sorry."

Katrina and Italo sprinted into the room. "What happened?" Italo asked, while Katrina, not waiting for the answer, grabbed Armelle with one arm and raced into her former room, where the emergency equipment still resided.

"She's changing," Tina stressed. "She got his blood in her. Wakestone's. Help her. Please."

Katrina looked to Italo as she wrapped the heart-rate monitor around Armelle's arm. "Is it ready?"

"Theoretically. The first round with the bats was inconclusive, but… well — we've combined the enzymes with those in Katrina and.. Maybe?" Flustered, Italo pulled over a cart of equipment hesitantly. "But bats are bats, and it's only been a few hours and…" he rambled, before freezing. "I… I'm not certain."

A stillness hung in the air, broken by Armelle. "Can never be certain."

This shook Italo out of his daze.

"Get the vial from the bat enclosure," he said to Katrina.

"Grab me a syringe from the storage room," he said to Miles.

"Connect the laptop at my desk onto the monitor and open up the file called 'Trial_10_25,'" he said to Robinson.

"Stay with her," he said to Tina.

Without a moment's hesitation, each did as they were told.

Armelle's reached up and extended her pinky toward Tina, who wrapped her pinky around it and pulled it to her mouth, kissing Armelle's shaking hands.

"Tina, if I don't make it," she began.

"You're going to make it," Tina said.

Armelle smiled and continued. "Know that, to me, you are perfect."

Tears streamed down Tina's face. "I love you."

"I love you too."

Miles' hand was placed on Tina's shoulder. She backed away but kept her pinky interlocked with Armelle's, as Italo approached with a syringe in his hand. Robinson swapped the heart-rate monitor cord with one that traced back to the doctor's laptop.

Armelle looked toward them, said "I believe in you," and closed her eyes.

Italo slid the needle into her arm and pushed the plunger down.

The room faded to black.

44

Okay

"She's going to be okay."

45

Not Okay

"Are y'all okay?" Robinson asked, as they all silently stared at the monitor. What had previously been used to follow Armelle's vitals had been streaming the local news for the last few days. That had been about all they had done that week. Ostensibly, it was to provide rest for Armelle so she could recuperate. But her strength had returned a few days ago, and they still spent most of their time blankly staring at the screen.

The only response to Robinson's question came from the TV anchor.

"Not so long ago, Durham was a struggling city, ridden with crime, lacking investment. But now it stands tall as the medical center of the western hemisphere thanks to the generosity and ingenuity of Jacob Wakestone." The reporter gestured to a refurbished building on the banks of a river. "The beautiful building you see behind me looked quite different not so long ago when it served as a rundown apartment building. When neighbors spotted a 'new management' sign in front of it months back, they assumed little would change but the name on the door. Little did they know, that it would soon be the state-of-the-art Ethan Nock Medical Center, bringing high-paying jobs and cutting-edge research to the Triangle!"

"You got the location?" Tina asked Armelle. News had leaked out earlier in the week about the development, but they had not yet known where it was placed until this broadcast.

Robinson squinted at the screen. "That's gotta be the Eno River in the background."

Katrina nodded. "That's right. An apartment complex. Wasn't too nice." Robinson caught her rubbing her forearm in a way that he found concerning.

Armelle pulled up the Registry of Deeds on her laptop, while the anchor continued.

"Just a generation ago, Durham's population was barely 100,000, a number that has increased nearly 10-fold due to the jobs created through the city's partnership with the Wakestones."

Armelle rapidly clicked her pen with one hand as she searched on the computer with her other. "It's exchanged hands a few times over the years then and… let's see… Yep, ended up purchased by a Sedekah Organization that has no digital footprint. It's gotta be that."

"And the tunnels?" Miles asked.

"It's pretty far north," Armelle said, clicking her pen rhythmically, as she glanced at the marked-up map of Durham they had placed on the walls, covering up an infographic on the Madagascan Rainforest. "But sure, it looked like it follows the points we've logged so far. Trace that down south and it connects directly with Wakestone Tower."

The voice on the TV interjected. "Who knows just how many lives will be saved due to the generosity and genius of Jacob Wakestone."

"We shouldn't have been there," Tina said quietly.

Taking offense, Miles replied sharply, "Easy to say now."

"I said it then!" Tina responded. "We didn't have a plan. We're lucky we're all not dead."

"Or worse," Miles added.

Armelle looked down at the table, clicking the pen, which drew the ire of Katrina.

"Will you *please* stop fidgeting with that thing? Sounds like a jackhammer inside my skull."

Tina jumped to Armelle's defense. "Leave her alone. You don't think you have annoying habits?"

"I appreciate the gesture," Armelle said. "But I don't need you defending me." No one heard her.

The news anchor continued. "Truly, where would Durham be without the Wakestones?"

Italo, uncomfortable with the tension, tried to change the subject by changing the channel. But each one was covering the revolutionary research center and hospital that Wakestone Trials was opening. "Finally," he said as the television landed on a baseball game.

"Game four," Robinson said to himself. The Rays were up seven runs with just a few outs left from extending their World Series lead to three games to one. "*They* don't need me," he said.

The tension that had been building between them the past week suddenly turned to concern. They each looked at Robinson sympathetically.

"That's not true," Tina said.

For a moment, Robinson considered leaning into their misunderstanding. "Need something more than pity," he said to himself, before snapping his fingers. Rufus and Naomi, who were previously each alone in a corner of the lobby, rejoined the group. Rufus lept gracefully onto Katrina's shoulder while Naomi snuggled up against Miles' leg. "It is true." He stood up and glanced at his watch to check the date. October 26th.

"We're sorry," Miles said as he turned off the TV.

Robinson smiled. "Not only is it true, but it's also okay." He cocked his head to the side and considered it. "I mean, it's not entirely, but it will be, you know?" He considered how much planning he had left. "Tomorrow at 8:00. Meet here."

46

The Fearless

Tina, Armelle, Miles, Katrina, and Italo sat around the table in the Nash Center, awaiting Robinson. A few minutes after eight, Robinson entered the lobby carrying a dog-eared book and an overstuffed paper bag. He scanned the table, reached into the bag, and theatrically scattered four oddly-shaped dice onto the table alongside a stack of cards.

Armelle picked up a die and inspected it, noticing the sharp corners, each side with a number ranging from 1 to 20.

"Dungeons and Dragons?" Miles asked.

Robinson raised his arms wide and nodded affirmatively.

Tina smiled weakly at her brother. "I appreciate the sentiment. Really. But is this what we should be doing now? Shouldn't we be planning?"

Each considered her question. Eventually, Katrina responded. "We have no *we*." They looked at her inquisitively. "We've barely spoken to each other this week. We can't even find the spirit to fight with each other. We're each just fading away in parallel."

Silence.

"She's not wrong," Tina conceded. "But that doesn't mean we shouldn't be working on our plan."

Italo sheepishly asked, "Do we have a plan?"

"Well..." Tina began, not needing to finish the thought.

Miles massaged his neck. "It might be good for us."

Tina didn't look convinced.

"Diffuse mode," Armelle stated as she picked up one of the cards.

Tina was about to ask her to clarify when she noticed that Armelle's head was subtly bobbing from side to side as often happened when Armelle was joyfully engrossed in a task. Tina hadn't seen her like this since before the attack at the shelter. "Alright, Robby, let's do this."

"Okay!" Robinson eagerly flipped through the book, jumping from page to page, uncertain where to start. "Okay okay. So, Dungeons and Dragons. It's wonderful. Or I think it will be."

"It will be," Tina asserted.

Robinson caught his breath. "Okay. So. D&D is collaborative storytelling. I, as your Dungeon Master, am like the narrator. I'll lay out a story for you, presenting you — or I should say your characters — with options as we go. You'll make choices, and roll the dice to determine whether they're successful. The higher the roll the better." Robinson looked out at the group and saw encouragement but uncertainty. "I know. It sounds confusing. But we're going to play a simplified version. Just one set of dice and I already created your characters for you."

"How so?" Armelle asked.

"Well, there are different classes of characters. Each with their own attributes." He dealt a card to each. "For instance, Armelle: You're a wizard. Miles is a cleric. Italo a druid. Katrina a ranger. And Tina is a bard."

Tina eyed her brother suspiciously. "Which is the best?"

Miles recalled details of D&D from growing up. "It doesn't quite work that way."

Robison was heartened by Miles' contribution. "Yes! Exactly! It's not about one all-powerful character that has been leveled up to the point of becoming unstoppable, but rather a balanced team. Characters whose strengths and weaknesses complement each other." Robinson noticed that Armelle was already studying her character's attributes. "Take a minute to read your card. It gives a little profile on who you are and what you can do." Each read their card with varying levels of engagement.

"Trust me. If you embrace it, this will be great. Ready?!?"

Each of them nodded. Tina said "Yes" unconvincingly.

Robinson found a spot in his book. "Okay, you five meet in a tavern, summoned by an unknown figure in the corner." He nudged Armelle.

"Oh ummm," Armelle began shakily. "Thank you for coming. I

called you here. I'm a wizard, you see."

Robinson mimed *slow down* with his hands.

Armelle nodded apologetically. "Right. So…" she looked down at her card. "There is a great scourge upon this town! The houses have been burnt to the ground, and even before that, they were plundered for treasure! Some say there is a fearsome dragon atop the mountain to the east who is behind it."

"So," Miles said hesitantly, "Like The Hobbit?"

Robinson opened and closed his mouth a few times, not sure how to enliven the game. He looked towards Katrina pleadingly.

Katrina nodded, said quietly, "I can help." She cleared her throat, and loudly proclaimed, "I can help! I know not of what you speak, but as a Ranger, I recognize that this threat must be contained, or else the fire of this loathsome dragon named…" She looked to Armelle, who frantically read her card, and not seeing a name, panicked and shouted "Fred?"

Katrina smiled and rolled with it. "Ah yes… Fred. Across the lands, many have spoken of… Fred. Fred the Fearless."

"Ahh right," Tina added. "As a traveling bard, I have heard the songs about this Fred the Fearless."

"Can you sing one of them for us?" Italo asked.

"Sure can't!" Tina laughed. "For they are too terrible to be sung in a place such as this! What little light there is in this old tavern would be consumed by the darkness."

Getting into it, Miles added, "Yes yes… I know of what you speak. As an intermediary between this world and the next, I have felt the loss of much power and much goodness from this world."

"Precisely," Armelle said. "And that is why I called you here. For each of you have much to offer on this quest. Such as…" Armelle looked around the room.

Tina jumped in. "My lute not only entertains but creates." She glanced at her card. "The vibrations from my music can shape the world around us."

Katrina followed suit. "And though I may appear to be a rough and wearisome traveler, I am a Ranger from the North, protecting this land with my bow, sword…" As if summoned, Rufus hopped onto her lap, "And Hawk! My loyal and lethal Hawk!"

Miles snapped his finger for Naomi to join him as well. She meandered over, nuzzled her head against his hand, and plopped under his seat. "And I am a Cleric. I wield divine magic and can…" He looked at his card. "Can bring souls back from the dead. Which is nice."

Italo paced across the room and returned with a broom, which he held aloft. "I am a powerful druid! This magical staff allows me to commune with nature and command the animals!" He held his palm open to Rufus on his left, who ignored him, before swiveling over to Naomi, who responded with a disinterested hiss. "Well, not these ones, but nine times out of ten it works, I swear!"

Robinson took a beat to enjoy the moment, before throwing a curveball at them. "Just then, the door bursts open, and in storms a pair of goblins. What do you do?"

"I attack them?" Katrina suggested.

"Well, with what?" Robinson asked.

Katrina looked down at her card. "Right. Well… I have a bow. So I shoot them with arrows?"

Robinson responded, "Well, let's see. Roll the die. If the number is really high, say over a 15, it will go really well. If it's really low, it will go poorly."

"Got it," Katrina shook a die and cast it on the table. "14?"

Robinson nodded, checking his book. "A hit. One goblin is knocked back, but not defeated. The other approaches and…" he rolls a die that lands on 10, "misses with his sword, but manages to knock the bow out of your hand."

"I got your back, Kat," Miles said. "I attack with my ax." He looked toward Robinson. "Should I roll?"

"Sure," Robinson replied.

"But be careful," Tina stated. "We might need you to revive us."

Miles considered this, then rolled the dice. "Ugh, three."

Robinson chuckles. "When you heave the ax, it slips out of your hands, flies across the room, and knocks out your Druid!"

"Hey!" Italo exclaimed.

"Sorry…"

"Okay, I got this," Armelle replied while consulting her card. "One of the spells in my book is that I can direct fire, right? So I'll send the fire toward the goblins."

"Well," Robinson considered. "The town isn't currently on fire…"

"I got you," Tina added. "I play a melancholic song on my lute which sparks a flame."

Armelle's eyes light up. "And I send *that* flame at the goblins!"

Robinson scratches his chin. "You're pushing it… Both of you roll. If you each get over a 15, it'll work. If not… We'll see…"

Tina and Armelle looked at each other, linked pinkies, picked up a pair of dice, and cast them. A 17 showed up on one along with a 16 on the other."

"A direct hit!" Robinson exclaimed. "The flames engulf the goblins, who warn the adventurers with their dying breath *Fred will find you. Fred will end you.*"

"Not if we find him first!" Katrina shouted.

They played through the night, gradually being pulled further into the story as their troupe traveled the countryside, chasing down hints of Fred. In time, they came across a particularly troublesome mini-boss named Lich at the base of Fred's mountain. This monster casted projections to summon nomads to his mysterious meadow before feeding on their souls and leaving the empty husks in the mountainside. Uncertain of how to overcome him, and unwilling to gamble their quest on a lieutenant, they eventually decided to bypass him altogether and sneak up the mountain to face the dragon directly.

But Fred conquered them.

Again.

And Again.

And Again.

Each round, they attempted some new approach. Armelle's book of spells, Katrina's hawk, Italo's control of nearby predators, and Tina's songs of creation. But each time, the dice landed unfortuitously low and Robinson had to apologetically inform them that they had once again lost. After each attempt, Miles, who had been told to linger back, would revive them. Then they would proceed to to lose again.

"I don't think I have any spells left in my book!' Armelle stated.

"What if I roll a perfect 20, then can I control Fred?" Italo asked, only to receive a glare from Robinson who had already answered this question.

"Let me fight! I have my ax!" Miles pleaded, only to receive a glare from the troupe who had already answered *this* question.

"We can't defeat him," Katrina said slowly, as she itched her arm.

Tina sighed. "My character plays the sad trombone noise."

"On your lute?" Armelle asked.

"Oh yeah, I'm that good." Tina shot her brother a side-eye. "But not good enough to take down this Fred, apparently!"

Robinson scanned his book, trying to find some way he could lay a path before them that would lead to success so that they would want to play again.

Katrina considered the scene. "Well, no. Your lute isn't enough." She looked around the table. "Or your book. Your staff. Certainly not your ax, as Italo can attest." Italo mimicked rubbing a hurt shoulder. "Nor my bow. Not separately and not even together. But we don't need to." Katrina froze and stared off through the doors into the forest.

"Kat..." Miles prodded.

She responded slowly. "I know how to take down Wakestone."

"What?!?" they said in unison.

Katrina winked at Robinson. "We travel back down the mountain."

"Wait," Tina interjected. "How do we defeat Wakestone?"

"Follow me to see," Katrina shrugged.

Tina cocked her head to the side and looked at Armelle who was scanning her card for ideas. "We follow the Ranger."

"We can't beat him," Katrina said as she rubbed behind Rufus' ear. "Not directly. But maybe we don't have to. Maybe if we take down the mountain underneath him, he'll lose his power. We take down the Lich. We take down his lieutenant."

As they traveled by the mountain, Armelle piped up. "Ranger, I know you prefer the direct route, but perhaps some subterfuge would be useful here?"

"What do you suggest?" Katrina asked.

Armelle looked to Tina, who considered it for a minute, before responding. "Lich collects and corrupts souls, correct?"

"I believe so," Miles replied.

Tina nodded. "I have an idea." She proceeded to lay out her plan to the troupe, before stealing a glance at her brother to gather whether it would work. Robinson gestured at the dice and shrugged.

"We'll see what we see, I suppose," Italo stated. "I warp the thick underbrush into a cloaked tunnel around the side of the mountain."

Robinson gestured toward the dice. Italo grabbed them and rolled a 15, which drew an affirmative nod from the Dungeon Master.

"Lich stands at the edge of the tunnel, back toward you. What do you do?"

"I take out my lute and play a sorrowful song," Tina said.

"While I use my transformative spell to make that song sound to Lich like the cry of a wounded man," Armelle added.

"Creative," Robinson granted. "I'll roll for Lich and you two roll for yourselves. If your combined score is higher, he'll follow the sound. But if mine is higher..."

Tina and Armelled looked toward each other with a smile and rolled the dice. "Ugh, four and five," they said.

Robinson looked disappointed but attempted to keep a neutral expression as he rolled the dice for Lich.

"Eight!"

"Alright!" Robinson said. "He follows the sound into the nearby forest, leaving the entry to the mountain base seemingly unattended."

"I'll enter the cave with Miles," Italo said.

"Aremelle and I will follow Lich, keeping the enchantment," Tina said, before glancing at Katrina, who suddenly looked uncertain.

"I sneak up behind Lich and…" Katrina paused. "Ask him to help us defeat the Dragon."

The troupe looked at her in confusion.

"That wasn't the plan," Tina said.

"Are you sure?" Miles asked.

Katrina waived away their objections. "It will be easier to topple the mountain with him on our side."

No one contradicted her, despite not believing that was her reason, so Robinson said, "Well, roll for persuasion."

Katrina did so, then winced. "Seven."

"A miss," Robinson said sadly, before optimistically adding, "but not a critical one! Lich turns his attention to the Ranger."

Katrina looked at her item card, but Miles jumped in before she could attack. "I summon the souls he has collected."

Robinson shook his head. "You can communicate with the dead, but you can't control them. Only Lich can do that."

"We change our song then," Tina suggested.

"I pull out my bag of bones and scatter them in the meadow," Armelle said as she presumptuously rolled her die, which landed on an 18. "I meld together the souls that Miles had contacted with the melody that Tina is playing to create a projection, an illusion, of all those that Lich has devoured."

"They surround Lich," Tina said.

"Their screams bind him," Miles added.

Robinson held up his hands. "Okay, okay. For a moment, but not forever."

"A moment is all we need," Italo said. "The presence of this cave suggests the mountain is hollowed out underneath, correct? But filled with treasure?"

Robinson smiled.

"And the remains of those Lich had devoured," Katrina added.

Robinson's smile faded.

Italo looked to Katrina for confirmation, which was given with a grimace, before proceeding. "I instruct the mountain to open up at the base. On the side of the bay. This creates a chute that will drop the treasure into the ocean."

Armelle saw his plan. "And will result in the implosion of the mountain, since there will be no foundation upholding it!"

"You'll need some help," Robinson said. Before he could specify whose powers would assist Italo, the whole troupe picked up their die and cast them. 12. 17. 1. 18. In the commotion, it wasn't quite clear who rolled what.

"That will do." Robinson beamed, bypassing the fact that whoever rolled the one ought to have been gravely hurt. "The mountain bursts a seam, the treasure shoots into the ocean, scattered eventually to the corners of the globe; the mountain comes down, and the Fearless Fred comes down with it." He held his arms out. "You won!"

Armelle, Italo, and Robinson were thrilled. Miles and Tina were concerned.

"You know now what you need to do?" Katrina asked them.

Tina and Miles looked at each other, groaned, and responded, "I believe so."

47

Try

"I it is my singular honor to officially announce The Ethan Nock Medical Center!" Jacob Wakestone's words came through the television that the troupe's eyes were fixed upon, but he was speaking not from the center, but rather from one of the offices at Wakestone Tower. He was centered in a dim, diluted light that permeated the curtains covering the wall-to-wall windows. "This cutting-edge medical facility merges a hospital with a clinical trials lab, thus cutting the red tape that prevents patients from receiving the care they deserve."

"Look, on the ends," Katrina said, pointing to the television. "Our two Liches." Out of focus behind Wakestone's lectern was a long table filled with influential people inside and outside of Wakestone Trials. On one end sat Rebecca Carter, and on the other sat Saul Ferris. Each was visible when WRAL used the wide shot, which the broadcast featured alongside a long shot and the inclusion of B-roll of the new center in North Durham. A closeup of Jacob Wakestone, who was hidden behind a heavy coat of makeup and a pair of blue contacts, was never employed.

The broadcast continued, but the banal propaganda barely registered with the troupe. They were too focused on what came next.

When the report concluded, Tina and Miles squinted to inspect the faces of Rebecca and Miles as they exited out of the shot, but whatever opinions they held on what was just announced were not decipherable through the television.

Tina, who had spent the previous three days since their game of Dungeons and Dragons formulating the plan, looked to Katrina with uncertainty.

Katrina, however, was looking to the side of the Nash Center lobby where Rufus was perched in front of the door to the Holy Blood Bat's cell, captivated by the sound of their fluttering wings. "You're not doing this for them. You're doing it for all those whose lives are in their hands. They're the ones supporting Wakestone's Tower. And they're the ones who will be crushed if we take it down." She looked to Miles in case he had any doubts as well. "We have to try."

Miles held his hands up in submission. "I trust you." He looked at the clock on the wall. He had an hour until Saul's live podcast recording started.

Tina glanced at the same clock. She had half an hour to get to Alley 42. "Same." She looked up at the television to where Rebecca, Miles, and the rest of them were moments ago. "It's them I don't trust."

With that, she left the Nash Center. Armelle and Robinson followed behind her while Saul, Italo, and Katrina booted up the computer.

48

Interlude - Three Days Prior

The executive stepped back, tightened her bun, and looked at the latest arrangement for her office. Although she had been in this space for a couple of weeks, she had not been able to formulate a layout that satisfied her.

Originally, the desk was pushed against the window so she could overlook the city as she worked. But she felt uncomfortable when the window washers would appear directly in front of her on their elevated scaffold, so she scrapped that plan. Logically she knew that the coating on the window prevented them from seeing in, but that didn't make it any less awkward when each day it appeared as if they were staring at her. Judging her.

Next, she tried shifting her desk to the eastern wall, with the window to her left. Yet this left the entrance to her office behind her. She found as she worked, she was constantly looking over her shoulder to the door behind her. This too unsettled her.

But perhaps this new arrangement would work, she thought. Her desk was placed in the center of the room, insulated from those outside the door and outside the building. Distractions set aside, she tucked a stray hair back in place and sat down to work.

Methodically and efficiently, she waded through the reports of the trials being conducted, making studious notes on adjustments that she could now make with this new position. How she could use it to do good. Yet when she approached the end, she heard it again.

That muffled noise.

From the floor above. The 60th floor.

Were they screams?

She paced around the perimeter of her office three times, attempting to steady her breathing, before halting at her bag hanging in the corner. She pulled out two items: A pair of headphones and a flash drive.

Sitting back at her desk, she pulled the headphones over her ears and twisted the dial on the side to ramp up the noise cancelation. She then held the flash drive in front of her and stared at it. Taking a breath, she placed it down next to the laptop and began rummaging through files. She opened several windows, saving them neatly on her desktop into a grid. But she did not aggregate the files into one folder. She did not insert the flash drive.

She simply stared at the windows.

How long she engaged in this unproductive task, she could not say. At some point, she was shaken out of it when her eyes noticed a woman was in her office.

"I'm sorry," the executive said, as one hand removed the headphones while the other pocketed the flash drive.

"Oh not at all," the visitor said. "I need those to work as well."

The executive looked toward the visitor, then up to the ceiling, then back to the visitor. *Could she not hear it?*

The visitor continued nervously in the executive's presence. "We haven't met. Or rather, not in person. I'm the doctor from the myeloma study. I was just named the Head of Pharmaceutical Research and was dropping off paperwork. I thought I might pop in to thank you."

"To thank me?"

"Have you not read the report yet?" The doctor then hurried to add, "Completely understandable. I can't imagine how busy you must be. Congratulations on…" she gestured at the office around them.

The executive minimized the windows and pulled up her queue. The myeloma study in reference was next. She glanced at the results. A low whistle escaped her lips. "There is barely a trace of the plasmacytomas in their respiratory tracks? This is…"

The doctor finished the sentence for her. "Miraculous."

"No," the executive responded quickly.

"Sorry. Of course not." The doctor blushed. "But it is your doing. We've been trying to launch this trial for ages, and your championing of it made this happen. Just think what will happen when the Nock Center opens and we can enter the next phase!"

"Yes," the executive said distantly.

When there was no further engagement by the executive, the doctor thanked her and left the office. Immediately after, the executive pulled the headphones back on to block out the noise. She fidgeted with the flash drive, but it stayed in her pocket.

49

Alley 42

Tina sat alone in a booth in the dimly lit Alley 42, peeling the label off the bottle of Fullsteam in front of her as she alternated between looking up to the entrance and down to her phone. By the time she had removed any indication of who made the beer she was drinking, the phone lit up with a notification. She read it, slowly exhaled, then said out loud, "Robby says she's not at The Sphinx."

Armelle's voice rose from the booth behind her. "That's encouraging."

"Yes. Maybe. I don't know." Tina reached for the unopened Shiner Bock across the table, itching to peel off the label, but stopped herself. "It's been years. Why wouldn't she have changed her habits?"

Armelle popped over the top of the booth, tilted Tina's head to the side, planted a kiss on her lips, and then disappeared back to her seat.

Tina folded her hands and looked at the door. Her eyes focused on the old Lucky Strike Smokestack, once the center point of the W.T. Blackwell Factory, now a rejuvenated landmark of the upscale American Tobacco Campus.

Her attention shifted back to the foreground as Rebecca Carter opened the door. Taking advantage of the moments before she was recognized, Tina inspected Rebecca, hoping for some indication of what was to unfold, but nothing looked different. Rebecca still had the same impeccable style, perfectly placed power-bun and stoic expression. Rebecca inspected the pumpkins and candles around the bar in a way that suggested that she didn't know that the next day was Halloween. Rebecca seemed no different than when they were close. And no different from when Rebecca betrayed her.

This professional posture slipped momentarily when Rebecca spied Tina. Rebecca's eyes widened, and she froze mid-step. She glanced over her shoulder, out the door to Duke Street, but then looked back at Tina, and confidently approached.

"You shouldn't be here," Rebecca said as she slid into the booth.

"Neither should you." Tina slid the Shiner Bock across the table. "You should be at The Sphinx, celebrating your big win."

Rebecca inspected the label of the beer in front of her as if it were a short story, took a sip, then quizzically looked at the missing label on Tina's bottle.

Tina pressed on. "Or is that not how it works anymore?"

"No, it is," Rebecca admitted as she looked around at the dive bar. Tina wondered how often she came here. And if she did so with someone else, as the two of them so often did early in their careers following difficult days.

They sat across from each other, sipping their beers.

"Why are you here?" Rebecca asked.

Tina blew onto the top of the beer bottle, creating a melodious hum, as she considered what response would best suit her plan, until she remembered that Armelle was directly behind her, following each word. So she tried the truth. "For you."

Rebecca scoffed and signaled to the bartender for another round.

"And for all those you can help," Tina added. "Or hurt."

"35,000," Rebecca countered. "Do you know what that represents?"

Tina shook her head.

"That's the number of new Myeloma cases we had in the U.S. last year," Rebecca said, before shifting to her business voice. "Myeloma is--"

"I know what it is," Tina interjected. "Cancer of the plasma cells."

Rebecca smiled at Tina's familiar curtness. "And do you know how many deaths we had from it?"

Tina's eyes glanced upwards as she calculated, but Rebecca answered before Tina could guess. "Nearly 13,000. Would you like for me to describe to you what they experience?" When Tina did not respond, Rebecca continued. "Patients report that their bones feel like they're trying to break through their skin. Their appetite virtually disappears, and whatever they can stomach, they often vomit up shortly afterward. Many fail to sleep for more than an hour a night. The slightest irritation of the skin resulting in extreme blood loss." Rebecca stared at Tina. "Shall I continue?"

"No," Tina said.

"35,000 are experiencing that. And 13,000 won't survive that." Rebecca held her hands apart, mimicking a scale. "Compared to what? A few hundred in our trial that are helping us to revolutionize blood transfusions?"

The bartender dropped off their beers. Rebecca looked at Tina's Fullsteam and chuckled. "You haven't changed a bit."

Tina took a sip, then pointed at Rebecca. "And those few hundred - can you describe for me what they experience?"

Rebecca choked on her beer but then covered it up with a cough. "This has always been your problem, Tina. You become paralyzed by the pursuit of perfection." Rebecca paused at what seemed to be the sound of a growl from the booth behind Tina before continuing. "Real change comes with real costs. That's why I'm where I'm at, and you're..." she trailed off.

"Well, how about — " Tina said, preparing to trade barbs, before receiving a kick underneath her booth. She collected herself and responded. "There are costs, sure. But are you the one deciding what those are?" She looked toward Rebecca, who was reading the label of her beer attentively. "And are you the one paying for it?"

Rebecca opened her mouth a handful of times, but each time, the counter-argument she had prepared failed to materialize. Eventually, other words snuck out. "You really came here for me?"

"Yes," Tina said softly. "And those whose lives rest in your hands." Tina looked across the table but saw that her former colleague was still staring down at her beer. "Rebecca." This drew the gaze of her former friend. "We can do good."

Rebecca looked toward the ceiling and sighed, before digging into her designer bag. She placed two objects on the table: Her phone and a flash drive. She looked toward Tina coldly, with her hand hovering over the phone. "Did you know that we were given a special number to call in case one of us found any of you 'acting out of turn'?"

Tina shook her head.

"The reward," Rebecca began before her voice and eye contact faded away. "Unimaginable." After a few measures of the song playing over the jukebox passed, Rebecca regained her focus. "Everything I could ever want, I suppose. Though it comes at a cost, of course." She looked across the table at Tina. "One that I *would* pay."

Tina nodded and looked toward the flash drive. "And that?"

"I... prepared this" Rebecca's face hardened. "In case I came across you."

Tina waited for Rebecca to elaborate. When it was clear she wasn't going to, Tina pressed. "What's on it?"

Rebecca's eyes shifted off of Tina. "Everything you could ever want." With that, Rebecca grabbed the phone, placed it in her bag, swiveled, and left the bar, leaving the flash drive behind.

After a couple of songs, Armelle slid into the booth next to Tina. They both stared at the flash drive centered on the table.

"Anything could be on that," Armelle pointed out. "Once we plug it in, who knows what information it might collect." Armelle hooked her pinky around Tina's. "How do we know it's not a trap?"

"We can't be certain," Tina replied.

50

The Law

"Welcome, my Nazarites, to ARC Weekly, your destination of choice for The Word of God."

Miles tilted his head back and groaned at the ceiling. "I don't think I can do this."

The words of Saul Ferris continued to echo around the Nash Center through the speakers Italo had connected to the laptop.

"Thanks be to our Patreon supporters at the Apostle Tier, who are accessing this episode live on Sunday night. Others can join for just a small monthly tithe."

Miles turned to Italo. "You sure you're able to block the other calls?"

Italo shrugged, "It's simply a matter of flooding their systems with calls generated from random I.P. addresses. We then hang up all of those at the exact moment that you place your call, which will be placed atop the queue." He looked at Miles over the tops of his glasses, which sat upon the bridge of his nose. "You know this. You're stalling."

Miles bobbled his head to either side. "Yes. I guess. I don't think I can do this. And I don't think I want to do this."

Katrina was pacing back and forth, rubbing her arms. "I get that. I don't want to either. Did you know that as I was being drained, he just sat there, watching? Singing absurd hymns like *Washed by the Blood*?"

Miles grimaced. "I did not. So then why…"

"It's not about him," Katrina reminded him. "He's at the foot of the mountain. The mountain we're trying to topple down. How many people get crushed by that fall depends on what we do at the base."

Miles' head dropped into his hands. "The time is out of joint. O cursed spite, that ever I was born to set it right." He looked up at Katrina and Italo. "Right. Of course you're right. I know. I *know*. I just… I just… don't know if I… have what it takes."

"Exactly," Italo said as he inspected the purple bead on his necklace. "Saul's hubris is the issue; his unwavering belief. You have doubts? Good: Saul needs some of that. Maybe you can share."

Miles looked unconvinced.

"If you are willing, take this cup from me," Katrina recited.

Miles smiled. At the point she was making; how even Jesus expressed reservations; and at the fact that she was making it. She hadn't previously expressed any interest in Christianity. Where had she learned that line? Feeling fortified, he looked toward Italo for instructions, who nodded.

"We just wait for an opening." They then looked toward the laptop.

"As it says in the good book of Leviticus, oh let me find the verse…" the voice beamed out from the speakers.

"Leviticus," Miles laughed, as he skimmed through the pages of his once-forgotten leather notebook with the lavender cross on the front. "Might as well queue up the calls now."

Italo looked at him skeptically, but Miles nodded as he stopped on a page that featured the words 'The Law.' Italo began typing a few commands into a program.

"Ah yes," Saul's voice continued, "Leviticus 18: You shall not do what is done in the land of Egypt where you lived, nor are you to do what is done in the land of Canaan where I am bringing you; you shall not walk in their statutes. You are to perform My judgments and keep My statutes, to live in accord with them; I am the Lord your God…"

Italo informed the group, "Calls are in, just gotta wait for him to ask for a line."

"…And that is where we find ourselves now. The chosen few, the remnant, wandering in the desert, while heathens worship the golden gods of their own creation. Make no mistake: What once was Egypt, is now the entire world. The Lord will send the waters, but we — those who follow the Nazarite Vow — have to step into the sea!"

Katrina grumbled. Miles smiled apologetically.

Saul's diatribe continued. "Do not take my word for it, but rather look to the Word of God. In this same book, God warns the Israelites of the consequences if they lapse in their sexual relations. To be one of the chosen, you must follow these laws. Surely we see the same poisons of hedonism and sodomy running through the veins of our corrupted society today. It is up to us chosen Nazarites to extract that poison and cleanse the blood. Speaking of the chosen, Jeremy, how many Nazarites do we have following tonight?"

Another voice came over the speakers. "Over five hundred!"

Saul returned, "Then let's open up the lines!"

"Okay, Italo…"

Jeremy stuttered fearfully. "Sorry, sir. Just some issues with our system… Okay, we've got a call. Tulsa, you're on the air."

Katrina winked at Italo, acknowledging his success in masking their location. Miles cleared his throat. "Hi. Thanks for having me."

"Of course. And God thanks you for following His Word. What would you like to share with the Kingdom of Priests on the line?"

"Well," Miles began. "I wondered if we're missing the point, a little. I think a valid interpretation of Leviticus would be--"

"Ah yes," Saul cut him off. "There is that word. Interpretation. The crutch of the lame who are too blind to look God directly in the eye."

"Mixing metaphors much?" Katrina muttered.

"What's that?" Saul said, apparently having heard Katrina. The room went quiet, with only the faint cooing lemurs in the background. "And what was *that*?" Saul asked.

"Sorry, roommates," Miles quickly recovered. "Anyways, I just think that Leviticus is not a list of laws to follow, but rather--"

"Of course… you don't like the laws, so you render them incompatible with your *modern* sensibilities. Yet we see that there's nothing modern about them. The same sins that the devil paints as liberation are seen right here in the good book! You might as well be living in Canaan!"

"It's not a matter of incompatibility, but rather the underlying message of the story," Miles began, before being cut off again.

"The story! You claim that the good book is nothing more than a collection of *stories*!"

"Every book is," Miles responded. "Every life is."

"You're being obtuse, so I'll clarify," Saul stated. "I can sense your mind. You claim that the Bible is merely symbolic, to be interpreted like pagan Tarot Cards. Merely a work of fiction."

Miles looked across the table and saw the various books Robinson and Katrina had bought them the other week. "Fiction/nonfiction is a false binary. It simply wasn't how the ancient Hebrews wrote, and it's hubris to read a book that was written thousands of years ago, continents away, and expect it to be composed in a way that's personally convenient for you. And to be fair, it's even a false binary today. Every nonfiction piece has elements of fiction in it. Every fiction piece has elements of nonfiction in it. That's just how we grasp the truth; sometimes through direct observation, sometimes through analogies."

"And I suppose your distinctions of fiction and nonfiction are dogma? That your interpretations and your designations are the right ones? Now that's convenient!"

"Not at all," Miles said softly. "I suppose it's incumbent on each of us to meditate on the passages throughout our lifetime and hope that the Spirit reveals some truths to us."

Saul said snarkily, "And you feel he has done so for you?"

Miles began shakily, "I..." but then his voice petered off.

"Exactly," said Saul. "You don't know. You can't see. You blindfold yourself and then ask who turned out the light. Yet God's Word is plain to see if you would only remove the coverings of modernity! Let The Law speak to you! You who Paul warns us about! The rebellious; the ungodly and sinners; the unholy and profane; those who kill their fathers or mothers; the murderers and immoral men and homosexuals and kidnappers and liars and perjurers!" Saul's voice broke. "There is no need to seek some underlying message that more closely jives with your heathen views! You have The Law. And, if you do not respect that, then you will come to respect the Nazarites who have been chosen to enforce it."

Miles responded before he could catch himself. "'The foreigner residing among you must be treated as your native-born. Love them as yourself, for you were foreigners in Egypt.' Chapter 19, I believe. Just a few lines after your quote. Or do you skip over that rule when you're advising your xenophobic backers?"

Saul's voice could be heard in the background. "Jeremy..."

Miles felt Naomi brush up against his legs. She looked up at him with her mismatched yellow and green eyes. Miles took a breath, rubbed the back of his neck, and attempted to use grace and reason to bring Saul into the light. "Leviticus is not a list of rules that can be used to weed out the good from the bad. None of the Bible is. It's not about *you*, it's about *us*. Leviticus is a reminder of what we owe to each other, the specifics of which are constantly shifting, place-to-place, time-to-time, but the general message can be found in the very book you're quoting. When Jesus says the one rule is 'love God and love each other,' he's quoting from Leviticus. And we see there the consequences when people decide to place the *me* before the *we*. When those in positions of power, the children of Aaron, decide they'll enter into the presence of God on their own terms, for their own selfish reasons. We see how that not only hurts them but their community. Just as you are hurting others in your constant attempts to divide us." Miles looked upwards, took a breath, and continued. "But you don't have to, Saul. You have been gifted with the ability to lead others. The question is *how* you lead them. *Where* you lead them. Please don't oversimplify all this into a binary good and evil." He rubbed his temple in thought. "What is it that Octavia Butler wrote? That there isn't one magic bullet to fixing this world. There are thousands of potential answers, and you can be one of them, if you choose. So please, I beg you, choose to use your voice for good."

"Are you quite done, Father Miles?"

Miles looked toward the group. He had hoped his voice wouldn't be recognized, but he knew it was always a slim chance.

"Is it still Father? I don't recall if they defrocked you yet," Saul continued. "I graced you with your quaint little monologue so that our followers could hear the folly in your voice. So they could see how the devil obfuscates The Word of God by twisting the lines, ringing them out till they've been drained of their meaning. By your reasoning, anything can be justified. Anything can be permissible. Your subjective interpretations open up any group to defend any heinous action by saying 'That's simply how *I* read the Bible.' But we here at the ARC know that is *his* word, not ours, which will stand the test of time."

Saul paused for a moment as he shifted gears. In that space, Miles was allowed to refute this claim. To defend those who needed defending. But no words came.

Saul had no such hesitation. "Now, I think it is only right for our congregation to pray for this lost soul. Let us bow our heads--"

"Now just wait for a second," Miles pleaded, but it was no use. Saul could not hear him. The line was dead.

51

Yes and No

"So… do you think it worked then?" Robinson asked after Tina and Miles finished relaying their experiences trying to reach Rebecca and Saul respectively.

Uncertain which one of them was being addressed, they both said simultaneously, "Yes and No." Each looked to the other apologetically. Miles held out his hand, inviting Tina to elaborate first.

Tina took a sip of the green tea Armelle had brought her. She looked over her shoulder at the bat enclosure while she recollected her discussion from earlier in the night. "Rebecca could be either setting us up for a trap, or perhaps even hedging her bets by playing both sides, but I think it might be legit." She looked to Italo for confirmation.

Italo glanced over the screen of his laptop. "It seems to be. The disc is bifurcated, with one layer being a complete map of Wakestone Tower, and the other seems to be the security and access codes needed to jack into the internal communication system."

"And you're confident we're not putting ourselves at risk by using that flash drive?" Katrina asked.

Italo shrugged as he peered through the one-sided window into the cell of his bats, rubbing his thumb over the purple bead on his necklace. "I completely wiped the laptop and reformatted it through a VPN in Utah. We should be safe."

Armelle turned to Tina. "Then why do you say it didn't work?"

Tina cracked her knuckles as she collected her thoughts. "I feel better about Rebecca, but worse about myself." Tina was reluctant to elaborate until she felt Armelle's pinky loop around hers. "I know that Wakestone is hurting people. Of course, he is. But I'm just not sure that I'm going to be able to help people." She took out her notebook and inspected a page. "I've got the start of a plan. But it's..." she trailed off and closed her notebook, but then quickly pivoted to Miles before they could press her. "What about you?"

Miles scratched the stubble that had developed on his face. "Kind of the opposite, actually? I feel worse about Saul, but better about myself for having tried."

Tina considered his words and opened her notebook back to her developing plan. "Can I run this by you all?"

Everyone stopped what they were doing and turned their attention to Tina.

"Of course."

***

"What do you think?" Tina asked after they had unpacked the plan. It was still rough, but it had improved due to their input. Everyone enthusiastically assured her.

"We should probably rest," Miles suggested. "We've got a bit to do tomorrow."

Something about considering the actual tasks left each of them with a sense of unease. Robinson, despite feeling as anxious as any of them, said in an attempt to break the tension, "We certainly do - it's Halloween tomorrow! Have we even gotten any candy yet for trick-or-treaters?" His attempt to break the tension was met with polite chuckles but did little to sway the room. "Let's head to bed."

Miles stepped outside to cool off and catch his breath. Katrina followed him. Armelle and Italo remained in the lobby working at the table. Robinson headed toward his room before his sister stopped him.

"Got some time?"

"Endless," he responded.

"Follow me," she said as they exited the Nash Center. "I set up a little shop in a nearby building. I want to show you something." They walked together in silence through the replica of a Madagascan forest, guided by the cooing of the lemurs.

Robinson muttered something that Tina couldn't hear over the lemurs.

"What was that?"

A few steps later, Robinson repeated himself. "I thought I could help. But it was just a stupid game."

"You have helped," Tina assured him. "Really. I'll show you." They walked under a bridge constructed for Sifaka and entered a small building that Robinson had never noticed before.

***

Miles stepped outside, closed his eyes, and walked forward until his feet felt the transition from pavement to the dirt of the forest floor.

"Kinda nice, isn't it?" Katrina asked as she meandered next to him.

The transplanted baobab trees gently swayed in the breeze.

"Yeah, it truly is," Miles responded.

The rhythmic sound of a crowned lemur hopping from tree to tree could be heard. Off in the distance, there was the sound of a red ruffed lemur munching on fruit.

"But it's not real," Katrina said. "The trees, the lemurs, the berries: None of it belongs here."

The breeze changed direction, and blew towards Katrina and Miles, cooling off the lingering southern heat.

"True," Miles agreed. "But I suppose neither do we."

Rufus, whose energy raised as the sun set, hopped onto Katrina's shoulders. She gave him a scratch behind his long cat-like ears. "Still, it's pretty nice."

"Yeah, it truly is," Miles responded.

***

Armelle and Doctor Contreras remained in the lobby of the Nash Center. Italo tinkered on his computer, adjusting the updated antidote. Armelle was studiously annotating the map of the top floors of Wakestone Tower. A draft from the door Katrina had exited through whisked in and blew some spare papers off their desk. Italo and Armelle each hopped off their seats to retrieve them. While doing so, Armelle noticed Miles and Katrina having a deep conversation outside and saw Tina doing the same with her brother walking along the trail.

"Are we supposed to be having some heart-to-heart right now?" Armelle asked.

Italo looked at her, concerned that she had something heavy on her mind, but saw that it was purely her trying to read the room. He smiled kindly. "No, I think we're good unless there was anything you needed to say." He closed the open door to give the pair outside some privacy. A small draft still entered the room through the slot in the door originally placed for feedings.

"Not particularly," Armelle said, as she placed the papers back on the desk. The piece that happened to be on the top was her notes from their Dungeons and Dragons game. Despite her fond memories of the night, she removed the paper from the desk so it wouldn't clutter the important notes. A thought occurred to her, as she looked to the door roughly ten feet away, then back to the paper in her hands. "Think you can fly a paper airplane through that slot in the door?"

Armelle could see the Doctor running the same calculations she was. "Perhaps so…"

***

Tina held the door open and Robinson walked into the room. In the center of it was a rectangular table, with vices attached along the sides, and the lathe he had purchased for his sister perched atop it. Leaning against the walls of the room were various fragments of wood, and what looked like different prototypes of projects. Robinson beamed. "Llave! You used the lathe!"

Tina smiled. "Wait till you see this." She walked around the table and pulled out the most unique bat Robinson had ever laid eyes on. Growing up, he had played with metal bats. In the majors, he had used wooden bats. But he never had a bat that was both. He grabbed it with his right hand above the handle and appreciated the feel right away. "Ash!" he exclaimed. Had his sister known that he loved ash bats? There were very few left, due to an exotic wood-boring beetle that had depleted much of the world's supply. He had given an interview to The Tampa Bay Times years ago about his fondness for this type of wood, but he never would have imagined that Tina would have read it. Yet he knew by how she averted his eyes that she must have.

The extra weight added to the barrel pulled the end toward the ground, and Robinson noticed a small engraving of a key on the bottom of the handle.

But what really set the bat apart was the metallic elements. Spiking out from the barrel of the bat at various angles were seven metallic syringes.

"The antidote?" he asked.

Tina nodded. "We know that the injection requires a bit of pressure for it to work. Thought this might be useful."

Robinson stepped toward Tina and embraced her in the biggest hug she ever received. "Thank you," he said.

After a minute, Tina stepped away and wiped a tear from her eye. "Well, this was my way of saying thank you to you." She patted the lathe. "This was a useful reminder. It made me feel… me again."

"I know the feeling," Robinson replied as he took some practice swings, adjusting to the weight imbalance due to the syringes. "Nice to feel like I might have something to contribute."

***

Upon entering the Nash Center, Tina and Robinson had expected to find it empty with everyone attempting to sleep in their rooms. Instead, they saw Armelle, Italo, Miles, and Katrina huddled around the conference table. Tina worried that their preoccupation was keeping them from some much-needed rest until she processed Italo's curious words.

"I think we need to reconsider our draft calculation. With each degree the temperature drops, the air gets denser."

"Ahh good point," Armelle replied. "Perhaps we shift to the cardstock?"

"You're not creasing it sharp enough, give it to me," Katrina ordered, not unkindly, as Rufus sat atop her shoulder like a parrot.

"Perhaps timing accounts for part of this," Miles suggested, as he scratched Naomi behind the ears. "If we wait for the backdraft, the wind will do the work for us."

Tina and Robinson took in the scene and smiles spread across their faces. Robinson placed his bat down at the entryway and turned to his sister.

"We could stay up a little later."

52

Halloween

Knock knock knock

Each of them looked up from the Nash Center lobby where they were working on their assigned parts of Tina's plan.

"Trick or treaters?" Robinson suggested half-jokingly, half-hopingly. "I told you we should pick up some candy!"

No one responded to the knock or Robinson's jest. Tina approached the door. She cracked her knuckles as she reached for the handle. The door swung outwards to reveal Saul Ferris.

He stood on the threshold, seemingly reluctant to enter, wearing a varicolored coat that cast a ring of light around him. Tina inspected the grim expression under his long red hair, seeking some sign of remorse that would indicate that Saul had been converted to their cause. She looked back at Miles over her shoulder, who shook his head slightly, expressing his doubt. Tina returned her gaze to Saul and realized that it wasn't remorse, but rather disgust that she was seeing.

Saul scanned each of their faces slowly. The only sound that could be heard was the cooing of lemurs, which Saul registered with a smirk, before clearing his throat and exclaiming, "You shall utterly destroy all the places where the nations who you shall dispossess serve their gods."

"Ummm… who are you talking to?" Armelle asked.

"My Nazarites, of course," Saul stated as he stepped backward. With the ring of light no longer filling the doorway, a path into the building was opened up.

First, they heard the scrambling of feet on the dirt pathway leading into their home.

Then they saw the reds of the eyes of the vampires as they approached.

"Side door," Katrina ordered and each of them sprinted out the exit before the vampires could suffocate them in the crowded quarters of the Nash Center lobby. On his way out, Robinson grabbed his new bat. Upon exiting the center, they found themselves pinned between a group of vampires inside the Nash Center and a second group on the outskirts of the Duke Forest. They backed against the walls of the building as the vampires slowly encroached in their frantic, discordant manner, baring their eyeteeth as they hissed.

"Twelve," Armelle said. "Six inside, six out."

"You shall tear down their altars and smash their sacred pillars," Saul continued as he waltzed through the door, inspecting a journal that Italo had been keeping on the progress of their antidote. As he moved, the vampires hissed and tumbled away from the ring of lights projected off of his coat.

"Is that thing loaded," Tina asked her brother, looking at his bat.

Robinson looked at the empty syringes off of his bat while Italo answered for him. "No, sorry. Was testing if we could speed up the process by maturing the serum in the gut of the bats since that's where the enzymes are."

A bald, drooling vampire broke the line and sprinted toward them, his head to the side as if it had fallen off the hinge of his spine. Robinson choked up on the bat and swung with all his might, taking the creature out from the knees.

"Still works just fine," Robinson said, the last word being punctuated by a crash as the window behind them was smashed and the hands of vampires pressed them against the building.

"You shall cut down the engraved images of their gods..."

Miles screamed as he was pulled backward into the building through the broken window.

"...and obliterate their name from that place."

Robinson swung the bat powerfully but aimlessly one-handed, as a pair of vampires tore at his other arm.

"...and burn their Asherim with fire..."

The forest was illuminated as Saul ignited Italo's journal and tossed it into a pile of dry leaves. Tina's body disappeared under a pit of vampires. Armelle dove in after her, only to be tossed aside, with her shoulder popping as she hit the wall.

"There you and your households shall eat before the Lord your God..."

Italo kicked out in vain, as he was pulled into the building. A scream escaped his lips as teeth pierced his neck. Miles attempted to race to his defense, but immediately collapsed when he put weight on his ankle. As he pulled himself back up, he grabbed a shard of glass and limped toward Italo.

"...and rejoice in all your undertakings in which the Lord your God has blessed you."

Katrina plowed her way through the vampires, overpowering each one, making her way toward Saul like a running back fighting for a first down.

"To me!" Saul's voice screeched, dropping his recitation, as he saw Katrina's blood-covered body inching closer.

Eleven vampires then surrounded Katrina, with only the one feeding on Italo behind, undeterred by Miles stabbing it in the legs with his blade of glass.

Katrina swung her fists with power and precision, keeping the enemies momentarily at bay. But there were simply too many for her. Each vampire knocked aside was replaced with two more, biting and scratching and gargling. Robinson limped over as fast as he could, bat in hand.

"Help." The muffled voice of Katrina escaped from the pit. Robinson tried to do so as he swung his bat with whatever strength he had left, but it made little impact.

Content with the fall of Katrina, Saul waltzed into the lobby, just in time to see the feeding vampire toss Miles aside with a spare arm.

Saul walked around Miles, careful not to step into the pile of blood surrounding him. He looked down in pity, and said "You poor, wretched soul."

"Blessed be the poor in spirit," Miles said, uncertain if it was a statement, question, or request.

At the same time, Miles heard Katrina attempt to call for her aye-aye, only to choke on her own blood halfway through. "Ru-akh..."

Rufus, sprung from his nocturnal enclosure, lept over Miles' body like a gust of wind, and slashed across Saul's cheek with its tapping finger, before racing out the door to protect Katrina. He tore through the pile of vampires, clearing enough space for Katrina to escape.

"Go," Armelle instructed Tina, who was checking on her injured shoulder. "The bats."

Tina hesitated, but Armelle pushed her toward the building. Tina limped into the lobby, keeping her eyes on the Holy Blood Bat enclosure so that she wouldn't have to look down at Italo. In doing so, she failed to notice the vampire who, being done with Italo, pounced on Tina as she was just feet away from the door.

"No," Tina shouted, pushing the vampire away with one arm, as she reached with the other to the door. But the vampire was too strong. Dragged backward, she felt the mix of blood and drool fall from the vampire's mouth onto her face. She closed her eyes and awaited the pain.

But it never came.

The swing of her brother's bat temporarily freed her.

"Go!" Robinson strained, as he and Miles attempted to keep the vampire contained.

"Do not!" Saul shouted as he pivoted between Katrina's blows outside and Robinson's inside. But all he offered were words.

Tina grabbed the handle and pulled it down. As the enclosure door opened, a flock of bats flooded out. They instinctively flew to each of the vampires, biting whatever skin they could find, engorging themselves on the V blood they had been genetically trained to seek out. In doing so, they left behind traces of the bacteria Italo had been cultivating in the open wounds of the infected vampires.

A high-pitched screech from the attacked vampires silenced even the Red Ruffed Lemurs.

Tina, Miles, Robinson, Katrina, Armelle, and Saul looked on, wondering what the effect would be. Within a few lumbered steps, the vampires fell unconscious, one by one. All except the one who was strengthened by Italo's blood; He had managed to hit each incoming bat out of the air before being bit. Robinson approached it from one side with his bat held high. Katrina approached it from the other side with her nails extended.

Enraged, Saul screamed and charged at Katrina, who gracefully spun on contact, ripping Saul's protective coat off as she tossed him to the ground in front of his creation.

Saul's eyes grew wide as he saw the monster in front of him, and quickly dove backward landing in a damp pool nearby. His screams heightened as he looked down at his hands, now covered in blood. He did not know whose it was.

Ignoring Saul's wails, Katrina shoved the illuminated coat into the face of the vampire, who cowered backward, before being struck in the neck by the teeth of a dead bat in the hands of Tina. She twisted the jaws of the bat deep into the vampire's wounds, ensuring the bacteria would find its way into the blood. Within moments, the vampire was unconscious, lying parallel to Italo.

They each turned their eyes toward Saul, who frantically crab-walked backward until he hit the wall.

Miles led the group, hovering over Saul, who refused to make eye contact with Miles. Instead, he stared down at his own hands. Miles looked over one shoulder at the immobile body of his friend Italo. He looked over his other shoulder at the bat in Robinson's hands. Then back at Saul, considering.

Miles heard Tina's voice quietly saying, "Father..." He felt Katrina's hand rest gently on his shoulder.

"Blessed be the merciful," Miles said, uncertain whether it was a statement, question, or request.

This line finally shook Saul from his terror, as he spit out the words, "Mercy? From a collection of hedonists, sodomites, and false idols? From those that God despises?"

"You don't speak for Him," Miles shot back, before catching his breath, rubbing the back of his neck. "We offer you a choice."

A coldly mirthful laugh escaped Saul's lips. "Keep your veiled choice of death to yourself, snake!"

"No, not that," Miles said, as he looked toward his family for affirmation. He nodded at the bodies of the vampires littered across the center, silhouetted in the flames of the burning forest.

"We offer you life," Tina said.

"What you call life is only a walking death!" Saul bellowed.

Robinson chuckled. "I hope that one day you can appreciate the irony of that statement."

"Not our life, and not yours," Armelle said.

"Theirs," Katrina said, pointing to the vampires behind her without taking her eyes off of Saul, as Rufus hopped onto her shoulder protectively and glared down at Saul.

Saul did not look at the vampires, instead scanning each of the adversaries in front of him.

"Nurse them back," Tina commanded. "You have information that will help us help them."

Miles followed up, "Or flee, and drop the pretension of your

Nazarite vow." He stepped aside, clearing a path either to the vampires or to the door.

Saul's eyes were drawn to the vampire next to Italo, and for a moment, they thought he would accept their offer. But then Saul spotted the thick red blood surrounding the body. He raised a hand to the gash cutting through his beard, shook his head violently, shoved Miles needlessly, and sprinted toward the door, attempting to avoid the blood on the ground as he fled.

53

Need

Italo needed her, Tina thought as she pulled the syringe out of his vein.

In truth, Tina thought, he actually needed himself. Italo was their scientific mind. He would know what was going on with him physiologically. There was no movement. No consciousness. But there was a pulse. He wasn't dead. But what was he?

"Flashlight?" Tina asked Katrina, who retrieved one instantaneously.

"When I say so, hold his left eyelid open?" Tina asked Armelle, before registering her injured shoulder. "Sorry. Sorry."

"It's okay," Armelle responded. "Only takes one arm." She reached her right arm over Italo's impassive face while her left arm remained tucked into her midsection by a sling made from an old Duke Lemur Center shirt.

Tina nodded her thanks before turning to Katrina and her brother. "Hold him tight in case..." she trailed off, but they all knew how the sentence ended. Katrina grabbed one side while Robinson grabbed the other.

Tina cracked her knuckles once, twice, then said, "Now."

Armelle opened up Italo's eyelid while Tina directed the flashlight at it, and held it for three seconds before turning it off and saying, "Let go."

"He's going to be okay," Katrina said.

Tina shook her head. "Possibly. The pupils dilated. But that doesn't mean he'll regain consciousness."

"That's not what I meant," Katrina stated. "No red." She tapped under her own eye, and they noticed the lingering red ring around her irises.

"So he won't be like…" Tina began, before fading out.

"Like me?" Katrina asked, before pointing at the bodies behind her. "Like them?"

Tina didn't know how to respond. She would need to check back in with Katrina later to see how she was doing.

"What can we do now?" Armelle asked.

Tina wasn't certain. She looked to Katrina for the answer, only to find that she had left the lobby.

"Even if he's not…" Tina let the end of the clause linger. "He'll still need a transfusion. He lost a lot of blood. Remember what we used for Katrina?" Armelle nodded. "Let's prep that. In the meantime, be on the lookout for any signs of transition, and keep him comfortable." Armelle was slipping a pillow under his head before Tina had finished the sentence. Tina wondered what else she could do. What else Italo would need? What would Miles suggest? Prayer? She looked out the door behind her and saw Miles staring out at what remained of Duke Forest, talking with Katrina. He had gone into the forest with the extinguisher after Saul's cowardly escape, but the rain had put out the brush fire. Yet he hadn't rejoined them. Tina now saw him in physical discomfort, trying not to put weight on his sprained ankle, as he spoke with Katrina.

"I'll be back. He needs me." She jerked her head to the side. "Do the same check on each of the… well, them." Robinson and Armelle nodded and approached the vampire nearest Italo.

Tina exited the Nash Center and saddled up next to Miles and Katrina. Tina was just about to ask Miles what he needed, when Katrina bluntly asked, "Those weren't really the words in your book, were they?"

Miles stared out at the now devastated forest. Worried about Miles, Tina interjected, "You don't have to answer--"

Miles waved her off kindly. "I think I do." He then turned to Katrina and said with his hands held up apologetically, "Yes. They were. Are." The words hung in the air, merging with the smoke that remained from the fire. "Deuteronomy."

Tina didn't know what to say to soothe the pain he was in. Katrina merely stared at him. In time, Miles continued, though Tina wasn't certain whether he was talking to them or himself.

"Deuteronomy lies at the end of the Torah, and it's worth remembering, I suppose, that the word 'Torah' means instruction. Not a rule book, not a history book, but a book of instruction. Teaching. And there are different schools of thought about what exactly the instruction would be in Deuteronomy. Some say that when the Old Testament God says that He will do certain things, that this is really coded language for He will turn the people over to the consequences of their own actions."

"How so?" Katrina asked.

"Well," Miles started as he extended the arm not leaning on the branch in an arc, pointing to the devastation around him. "Look around. Saul spoke about the land being ruined, animals killed, blood being drawn, and so on." They looked at the devastated forest around them. "Did God do that? No, humans did."

Tina looked at the forest they had destroyed in front of her. Then she looked backward at the vampires — people — she had injected with an unproven serum and wondered what would become of them.

Katrina answered. "We did."

Miles looked up at the decaying vine hanging over his head. "Exactly. Humans make choices and God allows us to suffer the consequences of those choices."

As Tina searched for the words to soothe Miles, she noticed a fallen branch of a redwood tree that had fallen in the fight. She picked it up and inspected it.

Katrina pushed back. "But, if your God is real, he could've stopped it."

"Yes, I suppose He could have."

They sat in uncomfortable silence. Tina removed a whittling knife out of her back pocket and began shaving off stray twigs.

"You said there were other schools of thought?" Katrina asked.

"Yes," Miles began, "another interpretation is that these are the consequences that we as a community deserve. But Jesus, as the sacrificial lamb, took those consequences upon himself."

Tina chopped off the end of the branch about five feet down. On the other end, she sharpened it to a point.

"Right, right," Katrina stated, unconvinced. "And what is your interpretation?"

A moment passed. Then another. Tina smoothed out the sides of the branch as she waited. Eventually, Miles admitted, "I don't know. Sometimes if I squint, I can see it. Sometimes if I sit with His word, I can feel it. But then I open my eyes, look around and I see…" he trailed off as they looked at the consequences of their fight with Saul.

Miles closed his eyes and Tina wondered what was going through his head. His heart. Then Katrina placed her hands on his shoulders. Tina thought she was about to embrace him, but instead she forcefully rotated Miles so that instead of facing the devastation in the forest, he was looking into the Nash Center. She pointed inside. At his friends. His family. At Robinson, and Armelle each tending to the very people who moments before were trying to murder them. At his beloved Naomi cautiously accepting the attentive sniffs from the curious Rufus. At Italo, whose eyes slowly opened, held for a moment, then closed softly.

"Thank you," Miles said to Katrina and began to limp inside to help out. Tina stopped him by handing out the branch. Miles received it with a smile and used it as a staff to alleviate the pain of walking. "And thank you."

Tina nodded, then asked Katrina the question she had on her mind. "What do you suppose their status is?"

Katrina looked up at Tina, and studied her for a moment, before responding. "We'll have to test their blood to be sure, but I think they're reverting."

"Really?"

"Based on their pulse, respiration, and irises. Yeah. I think so. They weren't… under for as long as I was."

"Okay," Tina said. "Who's left? Who can I help?"

"Looks like they got them all." Katrina stared at Tina, then glanced through the window at Armelle, who was adjusting her sling. "Perhaps some help might be needed over there."

"Of course," Tina responded, then re-entered the Nash Center lobby. Tina patted her hand, then helped tighten the sling, not so tight to be uncomfortable, but tight enough to restrict movement. "One sec," Tina said, placing a quick kiss on Armelle's lips before heading to a closet off the east wing. A minute later she held out an aspirin and a glass of water. Armelle stared at Tina for a moment, before a sad smile spread across her face.

"Thank you," Armelle said as she swallowed the pill, then chased it with the water. Armelle then said, "How are you?"

"Good, good," Tina said, cracking her knuckles. "This pushes up the timeline, of course. We wanted another week to run a few trials on the antidote, but with our location discovered, we'll have to go. Tomorrow, I guess? I can adjust the plan. It can still work, just need to tweak a few processes, starting with…" Tina's stream of consciousness was halted by Armelle's pinky hooking around hers.

"Of course the plan can work. You created it. And you're the most creative person I have ever met." Armelle nuzzled her head on Tina's shoulder. "I've met authors. I've met woodworkers. I've met architects. Each possessing a sliver of creativity. But you, Tina, you've got each. You make art." She nodded her head toward Robinson's bat. "You make plans," she gestured at Tina's notebook, popping out from her back pocket. "You make teams," she looked around the room. But then she looked into Tina's eyes. "But all of it for others. Make some things —take some things—for yourself too. You deserve it." With her good arm, she pulled Tina's head onto her shoulder. "Or better yet, let us make some things for you."

Tina closed her eyes. "Okay. You're right. Thank you."

"What do you need?" Armelle asked.

"Just this," Tina said.

Armelle held her closer, then repeated her question. "What do you need?"

Tina closed her eyes and planted a kiss on Armelle's shoulder. She looked at her watch just as it struck midnight. "A cup of that decaffeinated green tea would be perfect." She spotted Robinson out of the corner of her eye. "And a talk with my brother."

Armelle squeezed her tight, then released. "A tea will be waiting for you in our room. Teaspoon of agave syrup, ounce of almond milk."

Tina crossed the room just as Robinson and Katrina were finishing supporting the last of the injured.

"Got a second, Robby?"

"Of course," he said jovially yet tiredly, before saying, "Good night, Kat."

"Good night," Katrina said. On her way to bed, she said "Thank you," to a confused Armelle.

"What's up?" Robinson asked as he picked up his bat and began to inject the serum into each syringe.

"There's something I need to say." Tina started to crack her knuckles, then stopped herself. "I'm sorry."

"Sorry?" Robinson looked at her. He looked around the room, at everything she had done. "For what?"

"I… I was angry. For a while. And it seeped onto you," she said, looking at the ground.

"Really?" he inquired. "I had no idea…"

"Exactly," she replied. "I bottled it up. And I wasn't really angry at you. I was angry at Mom and Dad. I tried and I tried and I tried but I was never enough for them. No matter my GPA, there was always someone with a higher one. I got into Duke? Neighbor got into Yale. I didn't do the right things, I didn't date the right… people. And then there was you. Perfect you. Effortlessly perfect you. I tried so very hard for them to love me, to the point of exhaustion. And you would just roll out of bed, do something wonderful, and they would shower you in the affection and attention that I craved."

Robinson opened his mouth to reply — to correct her — but closed it when he saw that she had more to say.

Tina continued. "I needed to tell them. But I didn't. I swallowed it down, figuring my next degree or promotion or whatever would win them over. I waited. And waited. And then one day, they were… gone. The accident. And I couldn't." The words hung in the air like a fog. It had been a decade, and they had never really discussed it. Robinson set the bat down gently and pulled himself up onto the table next to her.

Tina leaned into him. "And then *you* were gone. City to city, and I was just one of thousands trying to get your attention. So I resented you. But that wasn't fair. I'm sorry. It was always just so easy for you, and so hard for me."

Robinson gave her time before responding. "Want to know a secret?"

Tina nodded.

Robinson smiled sadly. "It wasn't easy for me. When I was in Durham I started 0 for 23. Do you remember? After the series vs Louisville, you met me at TJ's. You got me a copy of *Mother Night*. I read it on the next road trip. I couldn't tell you much about the plot (Vonnegut was a weird dude) but I vividly remember one line: 'We are who we pretend to be.' Something about that just rang true. So I pretended. And hoped that I would believe it. And hoped that I would become it." Robinson rubbed his side in recollection. "And it worked! *Sometimes*. Sometimes I would turn off my thinking and get myself into that flow state. But sometimes it didn't work. And I was alone. And anxious. And no one knew it."

Tina looked at her brother with new eyes. "I never knew."

Robinson closed one eye and looked down the barrel of the bat. "I never told you."

"Well, how are you feeling now?" Tina asked.

Robinson shuffled the bat between each hand, becoming accustomed to the weight before setting it down. "Honestly? Unspeakably scared!"

"Me too," Tina admitted, as she wrapped an arm around her brother. They stayed there for a minute or ten. "And now?"

Robinson smiled. "A little better."

54

Interlude - One Day Prior

On the morning of Halloween, the writer held the opened notebook tightly to her chest.

"It's not really good. I haven't made one of these in decades."

The second woman extended her arms and clasped the writer's hands.

"It's great."

"You don't know. You haven't read it."

As the woman pulled back her hands, she did so with the writer's paper.

"I know you." The woman looked at the writer, then down on her sonnet, with a loving, knowing smile upon her face.

Perfect, perfect, perfect, perfect, perfect…
Desperately seeking, yet what is the cost?
The more I chase, the more I neglect
The more that I seek, the more that I'm lost

I know where to go, but know not the how
Do I go from below, risk the terrain?
Or from above, but it's a long way down.

I sink or I fall, the end is the same.

My thoughts fracture and scatter with no place to land.
Maybe with force? Maybe with guile? Maybe…
The spiral is stopped with the touch of a hand.
Remember, you say, not 'me' but a 'we.'

Wherever I go, whatever I do
I'm relieved knowing I do so with you.

The woman kissed the writer on the lips, rested on her shoulder, then linked pinkies.

55

The Box

They stood in the lobby of the Nash Center, each wondering if they did so for the last time. Their respective rooms had been cleaned out, now inhabited by recovering vampires.

They each waited for someone to speak before they departed.

Katrina scanned the room and noticed the anxiety that they all were swimming in. Drowning in. "Father, you got a passage in the bank for a situation like this?"

Miles considered the question as he inspected the redwood staff that Tina had crafted for him. His eyes were drawn to the handle. Tina had carved a spiral pattern that connected the staff to the top. It brought to mind a spiraled galaxy. Or perhaps a snake. Miles traced his ring finger around the gyrating path as he recalled the Jesuitical Prayer for Guidance, which he learned in his early days at Georgetown. He adjusted his clerical collar, which he had put back on that morning, as he recalled the passage. But when he opened his mouth, other words came out. The words that Tina had written and Armelle had shared with the group afterward.

"Wherever I go, whatever I do, I'm relieved knowing I do so with you."

A calm settled upon the room. This filled Tina with pride but also self-consciousness, which she quickly covered up by shifting the attention to her brother.

"What about you, Robby? You got a pre-game pep-talk in the bank for a situation like this?"

Robinson instinctively rubbed his ribs, before pausing, smiling, and turning to his sister. "Remember what I told you last night about that hitless streak I had in Durham?"

"Sure," Tina said.

"I didn't mention how I broke it, though." He smirked to himself at the phrasing. He filled in the group on the backstory: "So there was a particularly tough stretch when I first reached AAA. Really tough. 0 for 23 tough." He held the yellow bead on his necklace between his thumb and index finger. "Felt like the ball was this big. The next time I stepped up to the plate was on a home stand. It was the bottom of the ninth, down one, two outs, man on first. I knew that if I hit a home run there, we win the game. If I get out, then we lose it. I also knew that I just couldn't do it. That season I was trying to lift my launch angle, trying to increase my barrel rate, all without elevating my K rate, and I was overly focused on the mechanics. When my brain should've been calm, it was just fixating on angles and percentages. But I stepped into the box anyway. And you know what happened?"

Italo, whose energy was starting to return, smiled. "You hit a home run, didn't you?"

"Oh God no. I flailed wildly at the first two pitches. Curve down low, four-seamer up high. Both out of the zone. My swing was an absurd uppercut, missing completely. The next pitch they tried to hand-cuff me, but the ball got away from them. Nailed me right in the ribs." Robinson patted his ribs twice. "It kind of hurt. Really hurt. Still have discoloration there. But next came Johnson, and on the first pitch, he lined a ball right by me. Past the first-baseman and past the right-fielder. Took an unexpected bounce off the wall. I swear I ran as fast as I ever had. Or at least as hard as I ever had, my ribs screaming out in pain with every step. As I approached third, I saw the coach waving me home. I sprinted toward the plate, saw the ball flying home in my peripheral vision. I dove, my ribs slamming against the ground. The pain vibrated through my whole body. But when I looked up, I saw the umpire signaling safe. We won." His hand rested on his ribs. "Two broken ribs. Not sure if it was the pitch or the dive that did it."

Armelle asked "Was your swing fixed then?" as she rotated her arm, trying to get the feeling back in her shoulder.

"No. Not for another few series. It took me a while to fine-tune my swing-path. Lots of work with the analytics department to identify the precise goal and how to measure it. Lots of work with the batting coach to figure out the right mechanics. Lots of work with the team psychologist to figure out some techniques to balance focus and calm. And then lots of work by myself in the batting cage practicing, practicing, practicing. But eventually, I got there." Robinson grimaced after an exhale, then looked at the group. "I don't know what's ahead of us. I don't know if we'll win, or if we'll lose. I expect it's going to hurt either way. But I have trust in my coach," he looked at his sister, and each of them vocalized their agreement, "and I have trust in my team," each of them again agreeing, "so let's step into the box and see what happens."

56

Stay/Go

Each of them gathered their respective items for the mission, as prescribed by Tina's plan. As Katrina wrapped herself with coverings for protection from the midday sun, she heard Italo's voice.

"I wish I could go," he said from the seat of his wheelchair.

She turned to him, then scanned the lobby. Her home. "I wish I could stay."

Italo nodded, understandingly, then looked at the others. "They need you."

"You're right." Katrina rubbed her chin with her fingers, dragging her thumb across her sharpened eye teeth. She then gestured toward the rooms behind Italo. "And they need you."

Italo looked up from his computer, where he was updating a few lines of code, and stared off at the cells. He sighed. "Good luck."

"You too."

57

Ready

They returned to the lobby as the sun was approaching its zenith.

"You ready?" Tina asked.

"Nope," said Armelle, as she rotated her sore shoulder, then placed Rebecca's flash drive in the pocket of her cardigan. She rolled up the sleeve, patted the word "Bato," then rolled it back down.

"Probably not," Robinson admitted, as he held his bat in one hand and a crowbar in the other.

"No," replied Katrina, as she placed Rufus down on the ground and picked up a pair of heavy cases.

"Same," said Miles with a slight smile, as he planted a small kiss goodbye atop Naomi's head.

"Me neither," Tina answered, as she glanced at a half-filled-out page in her notebook. She closed the book and placed it in her pocket. "Let's do this."

58

The Tower

"Here?"

The four of them circled around a sewer on a freshly paved street just north of downtown. Tina held a flat, reflective, silver stake that ended in a sharp point. Katrina, her head covered by an oversized black hood, held two large crates, each draped with a cloth (which blocked the sight, but not the noise, resulting in their unsettled taxi driver dropping them off blocks before their stop). Robinson held the bat his sister had crafted for him in one hand and a large crowbar in the other. Miles, leaning on his redwood staff, held onto one of the syringes, inspecting it before placing it in a slot Tina had sewn into his long black jacket alongside other stakes. Armelle held a map, which she studiously checked, before handing the notebook that contained it back to Tina and responding to the group.

"Correct," Armelle said while pointing behind to the North. "The Ethan Nock Medical Center." To the west: "The McCaulley Shelter." To the east: "The Manor." She then tapped her foot on the sewer cover under their feet. "The tributaries all connect here, due to the bottleneck of The Rock Quarry Park on one side and the Ellerbee Creek on the other, and then…"

No one looked behind them, but they all knew what was there.

"All roads lead to the Tower," recited Robinson, who rubbed his ribs before jamming the end of the crowbar underneath the sewer and popping it off with some effort.

Each of them hovered over the sewer, peering into the darkness below.

Armelle flashed a light downwards. If there was anyone in there, they couldn't be seen or heard.

Without a word, Katrina placed one crate on the ground, tucked the other under her arm, and climbed down the ladder out of sight. Robinson groaned, placed his bat into its holster over his shoulder, and followed her down.

"Think this will work?" Miles asked, mostly to fill the silence, as he looked downwards. His eyes settled on his lavender socks so as not to be discouraged by the darkness of the tunnel.

Armelle shrugged. "Can't be certain. But Italo seems confident. Last night the bats were drawn to the V blood. So presumably if any vampires are called, they will be stopped at this junction and not make it to the tower."

Moments later, they heard the sound of the crate being opened, then the metallic rhythm of Robinson and Katrina scurrying up the ladder.

"Did you see anything?" Tina asked, while Armelle asked, "Did you hear anything?" and Miles asked, "Did you feel anything?"

Katrina shrugged her shoulders non-committedly, as she placed the cloth cover into a trash bin and picked up the other bat cage.

"No," Robinson said without much conviction. "There was some subtle noise. I assume it was just water dropping into a puddle from last night's rain."

"I am…" Armelle started, before losing the rest of the sentence as she spotted Wakestone Tower, which broke through the Durham skyline just blocks away. Tina wondered what followed. She hooked her pinky around Armelle's, which brought a smile to Armelle's face.

Katrina looked at them, recalled Armelle's words from a few weeks prior, then finished her sentence for her. "… because we are." This got Armelle's feet moving.

Although they were slowed by Miles' limp, they reached the Tower within half an hour. They passed by the main entrance, keeping a row of shops between them, and approached it from the south. There they saw the window washers, pausing for a break as expected.

"Think she's on our side?" Robinson asked his sister.

She considered the question and recalled her drink with Rebecca at Alley 42. All their drinks there over the years. "I think she's on her own side. But that should suffice for now." Tina walked up to the group of window washers, pulled out a thick envelope, and tentatively said, "Theo?"

A man with a gray goatee and thick-rimmed glasses stepped forward. "That's me." The three behind him stared at the ground. "It's all there?" he asked.

"It is," Tina said as she attempted to steady her hand.

He took the envelope and handed it to the man to his left, who peeked inside, then nodded.

"How's this work?" Armelle asked with her eyes fixed on the wide platform connected to cables that reached the top of the 60-story building.

"You're going to the 59th?" the man asked. Upon their assurance, he continued. "Then it's easy since that's as high as it'll go. Hop on, hold on, and hit the up arrow. The cart will stop itself on 59."

"How does the 60th get cleaned?" Katrina asked.

A chill ran through the window washers. Eventually, the man in charge responded. "Only the boss goes there. Says it requires a special treatment that only he's certified to apply. Not sure how he gets there." After sharing this, the crew seemed to be ready to leave. They stepped aside, leaving the cart open.

Tina, Armelle, Katrina, and Robinson loaded onto the platform. Miles hung back momentarily to ask one last question: "Why are you doing this?"

The leader of the crew shifted the envelope from one hand to the other. "Right is right." The words settled as he looked up the side of the tower. Eventually, he continued. "Doing what we do gives us a… particular view of the world."

"What did you see?" Armelle asked.

The man with the glasses considered the question. "Well, we didn't *see* anything. Not with our product blocking the light. But it doesn't block the sound. And we heard… Well…" He trailed off, before noticing that Miles was wearing a priest's collar under his jacket. "Right is right," he repeated, before slapping the envelope against his hand. "And money is money." The crew turned and walked away.

Robinson helped Miles limp onto the platform. Tina began to ask, "Up?" Katrina had already pushed the button.

As the platform climbed floor by floor, they saw their scattered reflection staring back at them on the side of the building. Tina felt the wind on her face, heard the cranking of the elevator, smelled the steadily thinning air. Realizing that Armelle might be experiencing sensory overload, Tina gently placed a hand on her shoulder. Armelle nodded her appreciation. Tina then looked behind her and noticed Miles looking over the side. As she approached, she realized he was not looking down on the city, but rather down onto one of the syringes that was resting in his hands. She heard him recite the line "I have cause, and will, and strength, and means." She saddled up next to him and said, "Forgive me, Father. I didn't mean to bring you into this. Not like this."

Miles' eyes shifted from the stake to Tina as the platform ground to a halt, just a floor from the top. He placed the stake into his jacket alongside the others then rested his hand on her shoulder.

"Look," Miles requested. He peacefully directed her attention to the city below. The rest followed their gaze. Somewhere in the tapestry of buildings downtown laid Armelle's welcoming bookstore. The Bulls' beautiful brick ballpark just a mile southeast of the still-standing original baseball stadium. Off in the distance, their chosen home nestled in the Duke Forest. "It's an incredible city," he said.

They all agreed.

"Full of incredible people," Miles said as he looked at them.

They all agreed.

Miles straightened his collar and looked at Tina. "Thank you for bringing me into this."

Tina smiled, then turned and pushed on the window that Rebecca had indeed left unlocked. It cracked upwards at a 45-degree angle. Robinson used the crowbar to rip the window off its hinges. They each climbed into Rebecca's office.

They were alone.

It was quiet. They could hear the sounds of typing from the offices on the other side of the door. No sound could be deciphered for whatever waited for them on the floor above.

They waited there, at first to catch their breath, but afterward for other reasons. Katrina pushed them to move by saying "For Anne." They each tapped the beaded necklaces around their necks and headed to the door. On her way, Tina noticed a peeled Fullsteam label centered on Rebecca's desk.

Upon exiting the office, they drew the stares of the Wakestone Trials employees. Initially, curiosity spread on their faces, but when they saw the weapons these intruders carried that was quickly replaced with panic. Some remained frozen in their cubicles, while others ran. One of them punched a code into the control center by the exit, triggering an alarm. The lights alternated flashing white and red.

"Okay, okay," Tina assured them. "This was always part of the plan."

The troupe followed the anxious employees to the stairwell that only led down. While others were flocking to the 57th so they could take the elevator to the exit, Miles led their group through the doors to the 58th floor, where six weeks earlier he had met Saul Ferris. It looked the same. The long, wide hallway, with windowless offices lining each side, ending in the glass wall. Tina guarded the stairwell, while Armelle inspected the control panel on the wall. Robinson followed Miles down the hallway as the priest glanced at each doorway to the left, stopping at one with a scratch.

"This one," he said to Robinson, who approached it with the crowbar.

"Not yet," Katrina said, directing her ear toward the stairways. "Defensive position," she ordered.

Tina and Armelle flanked one side of the doorway, while Robinson raced to the other. Katrina placed herself directly in front of it, with Miles behind her, ready to pass out syringes as needed. Once they were set, they heard what Katrina had previously observed.

The sound of footsteps racing *up* the steps.

The stairwell door burst open. A hiss could be heard as four frenetic figures raced through, the first of which was tripped by the swing of Robinson's bat, followed by a downward hit that injected the intruder with a dose of the antidote. The second leaped over the body of its fallen comrade only to land in the waiting arms of Katrina, who threw it to the ground and drove a syringe into its neck. The next two avoided Katrina and aimed straight for Tina, tackling her to the ground. She held one by the neck, its mouth opened in a snarl with its eye teeth glistening. The other struck her in the side in an attempt to loosen her grip. The vampire in Tina's arms relinquished its attack when it felt Armelle's syringe plunged into the back of its neck. The other was knocked to the ground by the swing of Miles' cane. He kneeled over it and held a syringe up high, ready to strike it down in its chest, only to freeze, as the monster below him whimpered.

"Its eyes," Miles said, before correcting himself. "His eyes." He ripped the nametag off of the unconscious body. "Nathaniel Lewis | Senior Accountant | ARC."

Tina pulled herself up and looked at his sky-blue eyes. "Not a vampire."

Katrina shouted out from the door well. "Neither was this one," as she took their pulse.

"This one was though," Robinson said, inspecting the body at its feet.

"Here too," Armelle said, flashing a light into the pupils of the fading vampire.

Robinson looked to the stairwell, awaiting the next wave. "How do we know who's a vampire and who's staff?"

"Does it make a difference?" Miles asked.

"Somewhat," Armelle stated, as she checked the notes in her back pocket. "For dosage. One syringe will sedate a vampire, but completely knock out a human."

Robinson took the syringe that Miles handed him, replacing the one he used, before asking, "What about two syringes?"

"That will knock out a vampire," Armelle answered.

"And kill a human," Tina added, to the sounds of footsteps growing louder. Just then, a crowd of attackers exploded out of the stairwell in a hectic yet rapid manner. Armelle attempted to count as they poured in. Five. Ten. Fifteen. Maybe twenty?

Robinson swung his bat as if each was a hanging curveball. For every two hits he would whiff, and an attacker would land a blow or bite on him.

Tina, hobbled by the previous wave, did her best to hold her line but relied on the astounding athleticism of Katrina for protection. The duo held them off for a while until Katrina had to race to protect Miles, who was attempting to use his staff to immobilize the humans he identified by the lack of red in their eyes. For most, this wasn't an issue, as they seemed to be little more than fanatical staff who decided to risk their lives for Jacob Wakestone for some unfathomable reason. But when Miles tried to knock out what ended up being a vampire, he was tossed across the room and nearly impaled with his own staff, until Katrina swiped at the back of the vampire with her sharpened nails. A back-and-forth battle ensued, only to be broken up by the swing of Robinson's bat, which struck the now-fading vampire in its calf.

Meanwhile, Armelle had snuck over to the control center. She inserted Rebecca's USB drive into the port so that Italo could remotely block the main elevator before it could dock on the 57th floor. She was halfway through the task when what appeared to be a mid-level accountant restrained her, holding her arms back so that a nearby vampire could prey.

"Help!"

Katrina registered Armelle's alarm but also noted that Miles and Robinson were also now caught in a battle against human-vampire combos.

"Release them!" Tina bellowed as she raced to Armelle's aid.

Katrina looked down at the bat cage that was meant to be used on whatever awaited them on the 60th floor, then without hesitation ripped the cloth cover off and tore open the door. Twelve modified holy-blood bats flew out, and hovered in the center of the room momentarily, before sensing the V blood in the air. They dove directly at the vampires in the room, feasting on their blood, leaving the serum behind in the wounds.

Within moments, each vampire was on the ground, twitching from the transition.

All that remained were the staff, who looked at each other anxiously, wondering what was fated for them.

Robinson pointed with his bat toward the stairwell, then pulled it back, standing in his batter's stance.

"Your choice," Katrina said.

Before she could finish her ultimatum, each of them had fled down the stairs.

Tina scanned each of her friends, trying to make out their status under the pulsating red and white lights. "Are y'all okay?"

Each of them grunted their general well-being as they plodded their way to the center of the room.

"Armelle?" Tina asked, after not hearing her voice.

Armelle's head was oscillating side to side as she punched in a final command into the touchpad. "Okay, Italo should be able to patch us through." She pulled out the flash drive and turned to the group. "Miles, the secondary elevator is on the floor below. Where's the opening?"

Miles tapped on the wall of one of the offices with his staff.

Robinson leveraged the crowbar into the opening, pulled back until he heard a crack, stepped back, and kicked the door open. Behind the splintered door was an empty walkway, leading to the secret elevator. Robinson pried the elevator doors apart. They each looked into the pitch-black elevator shaft.

"The Belly of the Beast, then?" Miles asked, staring into the darkness.

Tina nodded, looking into the shaft. A foot below them was the roof of the elevator compartment, which was docked on the floor below. "Unfortunately, yes. Only Wakestone can take it to the 60th."

They each stepped into the darkness and landed atop the elevator.

"Our father..." Miles began under his breath.

Robinson held the doors open for Armelle, who plugged a final code into the command center, then raced over to join them.

"Thy kingdom come, thy will be done..."

Robinson let go of the elevator doors, which screeched shut, leaving them without any light.

"..Our daily bread..."

The elevator shook below their feet and began to rise. Each of them clutched one another.

"...Forgive those who trespass against us..."

"It won't go all the way to the top, right?" Tina asked with uncertainty, as the roof of the elevator shaft inched closer and closer, threatening to crush them. She reached her pinky towards Armelle, knowing she would struggle with the sensory deprivation.

"It shouldn't..." Armelle stated as she reached her pinky towards Tina, knowing that she would struggle with the unknown. Their hands met in the middle.

By the time Miles reached "...deliver us from evil" the elevator halted. Robinson reached forward and felt the seams of the elevator door in front of him.

"Step into the box," he said to himself as he shoved the crowbar in the crack and pulled to the side. As he wrenched them apart, a beam of light temporarily blinded them. As their eyes adjusted, they saw sitting behind a large mahogany desk, the blood-red eyes of Jacob Wakestone staring at them.

59

We

"Welcome," the syrupy words poured out of Wakestone's mouth as he rose from the rich mahogany desk. The room comprised most of the 60th floor, and featured a marble kitchenette to one side and a living quarters on the other. Tucked in each corner were four rooms, harboring God knows what. Armelle noted the internal security cameras on each wall, as Italo had predicted. Underneath one of those cameras stood Saul Ferris, but without his long red hair and beard, which had recently been shaved. He instinctively raised a hand to the scar across his cheek that Rufus had given him. Rebecca was nowhere to be seen.

Wakestone tapped on the screen of a tablet with his elongated nails, before handing it to Saul. "What you did below was... impressive. Truth be told, I was rather hoping that you would make it here. I longed to see you again. I longed to... be *seen* again." He raised himself from the desk. Miles looked at those around him as they stepped out of the elevator shaft. They no longer had the Holy Blood Bats, as Tina had planned. Robinson had his syringe-embedded bat. Tina had her reflective stake. Armelle had her flash drive. And Miles his staff and seven remaining glass syringes. He prayed that was enough. That he was enough.

Miles looked at Saul, and stated softly "One cannot serve two masters." Saul's eyes were cast downwards. Miles then looked at Wakestone, whose eyes were now nearly entirely red. Miles couldn't hold Wakestone's piercing gaze and instead looked out the windows to the city behind him. "It's not too late."

A guttural laugh escaped from Wakestone's lips. "You're saying this to me? Just how do you think this ends?"

Miles responded as he traced his thumb around the spiral atop his cane. "Not well for you, regardless. But it doesn't need to be that way. For one reason or another, you have found yourself in a position of great power. Economic, political, scientific power. You have used that to persecute the very people you should be helping. You've been blinded by your own glory, but please, I beg you, for all of our sakes, open your eyes. It's not too late. It's never too late."

"You are correct." Wakestone stepped the desk, leaving Saul behind, and methodically walked toward them. "It is not too late. In fact, it is only the beginning."

Robinson and Tina stepped in front of the hobbled Miles, while Armelle stepped behind. Tina grabbed the reflective stake from her back pocket and shoved it upwards, the flat side facing Wakestone.

"How… quaint." In a flash, he gripped Tina's wrist and pulled the stake toward him. He tilted his head, taking in his reflection. A piece of dried blood lingered on the corner of his lip from a recent feeding. He wiped it away, keeping his eyes on the mirror. "You thought I wouldn't see myself?" He glanced over the edge of the blade and locked eyes with Miles. "From you, I expected such small-minded superstition." Then he looked at Tina, then in an instant his hand was atop hers. He clenched it tight, shattering the bones in her thumb, before pulling back with the blade. He turned his back on the group, unconcerned, and kept his gaze on his reflection while addressing Tina, who hunched over, holding her broken hand. "You have a keen scientific mind. Why do you fall in with such a pathetic lot?"

Wakestone dropped the blade as he crossed the room and paused in front of the window. With its freshly coated exterior, a thin image of himself was reflected back. He stared through that onto the city below him. "Oh, I most certainly see me. Everytime I look down on this city, I see *me*. After all, what was this city before me? A cesspool of poverty, crime, and chaos. I single-handedly raised it from the ashes." He pointed down at some far-away buildings. "That block there? All mine. The libraries? Mine. The infrastructure? Mine. Not to mention the previously ineffective cops and courts. I *brought* order."

"We never asked you to," Katrina spit out.

Wakestone paced the perimeter of the room tapping at the glass saying "mine, mine, mine," as he spotted his possessions. He returned to behind his desk and placed a hand on Saul's shoulder, which dipped under the weight. "When your people were in the wilderness, they pleaded for God to send them back to Egypt." He looked back at the rest of them with a thin smile. "But a steadfast God knows what his people need."

"You don't speak for them," Tina said as she massaged the hand that Wakestone had struck, trying to get the muscles to function.

"No, I suppose not," Wakestone admitted. "But in time, with their blood coursing through my veins, they will speak for me. They will act for me. My people, patrolling and protecting my city. They crave authority. Miracle. Mystery. I will gift them this trinity and they will beg for more." Wakestone reflected for a moment. "And I will think for them, as is needed. I think therefore I am. So all of them, all of this, is me."

"That's not true," Miles said, as he stepped to the side with his cane in an attempt to shield the distant Armelle from view. "That can't be true. There's more of us."

Wakestone shook his head. "The masses aside, there is more of *me* than there is of you."

Tina stepped forward, her injured hand tucked to her side. "That's kind of the problem, isn't it? You operate in this zero-sum manner. In order for you to become more, others must become less. But us? We realize that we only become more through others."

Katrina picked up where Tina left off. "I am because we are."

"And our *we* is bigger," Robinson said, unable to withhold a smirk at his juvenile joke.

"You are nothing," Wakestone shot back, venom slipping into his silvery voice. "You have been a distraction. A momentary inconvenience as I assemble the assets from the shadows while the... character of Jacob Wakestone is in the light. But with the Nock Medical Center, the true me can now step forward, as I will soon have a limitless supply of staff. Of prey. Of power."

"But the law..." Katrina began, before being cut off by Wakestone.

"Whose law?" Miles locked eyes with Saul, who closed them slowly.

Wakestone continued. "Haven't you noticed? Every step along this path has been paved by the law." He pointed aggressively at the city behind him. "The law is by the people and for the people. The people are mine. So the law is mine. And I will mold it, bend it, break it if I must, to bring everlasting life."

"Whose?" Miles asked again.

"All those who accept the life-altering medicine that I alone can give them." He looked back upon the city. "In time, all of them. They will all be mine. This will all be me." He spun on his heels and walked toward them. As he did so, he caught his face on the mirrored blade that laid on the floor. "And you thought I wouldn't see my reflection."

"No," Tina admitted. "I thought you would be distracted by your reflection."

Wakestone looked confused, then turned toward Miles. "Oh, you thought that my image would make me change my path? That you would convert me? All you did is remind me of my power."

"It's never too late," Miles shrugged. "But no, to be honest, I did not hold much hope that we could convert you. Perhaps, however, we were able to convert them," Miles pointed to the ground beneath them.

"We got it?" Tina asked Armelle, who was at the control panel by the entrance. Armelle nodded. Tina then pointed at the cameras around the room. "Streamed for everyone in the building."

Armelle rejoined the group. "And Italo relayed that stream over the Wakestone Trials' video platform for the whole world to see who you truly are."

Miles turned toward Saul intending to convince him that this would not reflect well on the ARC. Saul's face turned pale. His legs became weak. His knees trembled. Then he slinked away, hoping to minimize the inevitable backlash on his precious Nazarites.

Tina peered into the security camera and tsked. "Can't imagine that's going to help attract pharmaceuticals…"

Rage spread upon Wakestone's face as he saw staff flood out the exits 60 floors below. "You fools! Do you realize what you have done?" He pointed to the window. "You have doomed them all! Think! Each death that would have been preventable with my medicine… is on you. Their blood is on your hands." He then pivoted and pointed at each of them. "But most of all, you have doomed… yourselves." He slowly walked forward, each word punctuated with a step. "You have cost me dearly. It is true." Tina, Armelle, Miles, Katrina, and Robinson bunched up, each holding their respective weapons closely. Wakestone paused, mere steps away. The setting sun placed a dim, diffused light filtered by the windows around Wakestone. He held his arms outwards, closed his eyes, and collected himself. "But… I suppose… you have also liberated me. The world sees me for the God I am? That is… glorious. I must admit, I grew impatient waiting for this moment.

You have my gratitude for bringing it to fruition. They now see me for what I am? So be it." He dragged his thumb across the nails on each hand while staring directly in one of the cameras. "Prior to… this moment, if I wanted to see my reflection, I only had you. I suppose this now renders each of you… expendable." He slowly scanned their faces, deciding where to begin. He paused at Miles and licked his lips. "You have O- blood, I have been informed. Perhaps my next… acolyte would be better suited if they had some extra… incentive to fall in line."

Robinson stepped into the light. He tightened his grip around his bat. "No."

"Ah yes, Robinson Sanders." Wakestone glared at him. "I do recall your career. I am an investor in the Bulls, after all. I will grant you this: You always did know when to swing, and when it was more… prudent not to." A thin, knowing smile appeared. "Always had quite the eye."

Wakestone fixed his red irises on Robinson, daring him to act. Robinson's wrists shifted ever-so-slightly backward, bracing in preparation for a swing to Wakestone's skull.

The instant Robinson's bat tilted forward, Wakestone's hand sprung forward like a snake, snapped at Robinson's face, and pulled back.

"And now it is mine," Wakestone cackled.

Robinson dropped to the floor, face in his hands. Their attention shifted back to Wakestone, who was inspecting an object in the palm of his hand. Robinson's eye. Wakestone squeezed his fist tightly. Aqueous humor oozed out, dripping onto the floor. He opened his fist and beckoned them to engage.

Katrina leaped forward and landed a blow to Wakestone's side, which he rolled with, turning backward from his hips, bracing himself on the desk behind him. As Katrina reached forward with her syringe, Wakestone recoiled, wrenching the mahogany desk off the ground with one arm and flung it at Katrina. The desk and Katrina were launched clear across the room.

As Tina and Armelle grabbed extra syringes from Miles, Robinson scrambled to his feet, swinging the bat wildly as blood poured from his eye socket. Wakestone reached forward, dexterously grabbing the bat with his two hands in between the exposed syringes. He pulled the weapon toward him, while he kicked out, sending Robinson back alongside Katrina.

Tina and Armelle raced towards Wakestone. Miles set down his staff, grabbed a syringe from his pocket, and limped after them. Tina and Armelle flanked Wakestone, but before they could impale him, he snapped Robinson's bat over his knee, rotated his wrists, and drove the shattered ends into each of them. Their bodies hit the floor, complemented by the sound of broken glass.

"You reflect me," Wakestone said grimly, looking down at them, before smiling at the approaching Miles. "You believe you have the power to stop me?"

Miles limped forward and attempted to respond, but only a strained noise escaped his lips, one cut off when Wakestone gripped him around the neck. Miles was raised off the ground, his legs fruitlessly dangling. Wakestone reached with his other arm and ripped Miles' collar off to expose his throat. Miles stared directly into Jacob's blood-red eyes. Wakestone pulled Miles into him over the screams of all in the room.

His teeth dug deep into Miles' neck.

Blood flowed into Wakestone's mouth.

Wakestone let go. Miles' body landed with a thud and did not move.

The satiated smile on the vampire's face slowly faded as Wakestone looked curiously at the three empty syringes trailing behind Miles.

60

Interlude - One Minute Prior

The priest tried to help. But he couldn't.

Tina.

Armelle.

Robinson.

Katrina.

All down. All defeated.

He laid his staff down.

Closed his eyes.

Breathed in.

Tapped the lavender bead on his necklace.

Breathed out.

He saw Italo, beaming as the old man adjusted his newly gifted bowtie.

And Robinson, blissfully scheming as he laid out traps in Dungeons and Dragons that he desperately wanted them to overcome.

Then he slid one of the syringes into his neck, pushed in the plunger, and took a step forward. The sounds of glass was heard as the syringe fell to the floor.

He saw Tina, in her workshop, making tools and toys for all of them.

And Armelle, by her side, sharing her multitudes of passions with the person who mattered most to her.

Then he slid a second syringe into his neck and took another step forward. The syringe fell to the floor.

He saw Katrina on the train, teaching him what loving others means.

And Naomi, purring rhythmically on his lap, teaching him what accepting love means.

Then he slid a third syringe into his neck and stumbled another step forward. The syringe fell to the floor.

The light in the room slowly faded as he attempted to answer Wakestone's inane question.

Darkness surrounded him as he was raised up.

A flicker of light remained as he fell to the floor.

61

Feel It

The two men lay on the floor, dying.

Wakestone withered in pain as the serum he had drank from Miles' neck spread through his blood. He cursed them all. But no one heard. No one was there.

Tina, Armelle, Robinson, and Katrina encircled Miles, their voices swirling together. Their faces fading out.

"Are you okay?"

"Can you hear me?"

"Please speak to me!"

Miles scanned their faces. A thin smile spread across his face. His last words fought their way to his lips, but no sound was heard. Reading his lips, Tina thought he said, "I can see it. I can feel it."

61

Epilogue - One Year Later

"Forgive me, Father..." Tina said breathlessly as she raced into Saint Thérèse's, patting out the wrinkles in the black dress she had recently designed.

"There is nothing to forgive," Father Michael said, as he sat in a pew with Naomi on his lap. "The service hasn't started yet. We were just catching up."

Tina took in the crowd. It was larger than she expected. Big enough for Tina to prioritize a task.

"One minute, Father. Thank you again for hosting."

Tina found Armelle in a corner, pretending to be reading a book that was written in Latin. Tina apologetically wrapped her pinky around Armelle's. Something about the feeling of Armelle's silver engagement ring comforted the pain that had remained in her hand, despite multiple surgeries. "I'm sorry, I'm sorry, I know I was supposed to get here first. I lost track of time finalizing the new window display for the memoirs that arrived today." Armelle didn't lie and say that it hadn't bothered her but knew that crafting took Tina considerably longer due to her nearly useless right thumb. Armelle demonstrated her understanding and forgiveness with a kiss.

"What did I miss?" Tina asked, as she placed a hand on the back of Armelle's wool cardigan.

Armelle scanned the room, considering the correct order for recounting. Knowing that Tina wouldn't be able to focus on the positives until her anxiety was addressed, she began with Rebecca, who appeared impeccably professional as always, addressing a group of visitors. "She's in recruiting mode for Anne's Trials."

Tina nodded and looked for Italo. A step ahead, Armelle pointed to the man leaning on a four-point cane. "Two feet to the left. Setting up the ofrenda with pictures of Miles and Maria for tonight, but also eavesdropping on Rebecca's pitch."

"I still don't know if she can be trusted."

Armelle shrugged. "They've been co-partners for months. Obviously, the established CROs scooped up most of Wakestone's larger clients, but they've done admirable work identifying community-focused trials. And they've made quite a bit of progress building on Maria's blood transfusion studies." She rocked her head side-to-side. "He trusts her. And I trust him. So I trust her."

Tina pulled Armelle close. "And I trust you, so I suppose I trust her too?" She laid her head on Armelle's shoulder. From this new angle, she spotted her brother, sporting his stylish eye patch with his admirable blend of self-confidence and self-deprecation.

"He's already raised over two thousand for The McCaulley Shelter," Armelle pointed out. Tina smiled as she spotted an unlikely pair alongside her brother. Two of the many people were supported by the organization that Robinson and Katrina started. Two of the many people that had attempted to kill Tina a year ago.

Robinson graciously accepted a check from a prominent community member and handed it behind him to Katrina with a grateful smile. Katrina looked at the check, and placed it in an envelope, before pulling out a notebook and recording the total on a marked page. Tina thought she saw a sparkle in her eyes, which had settled into a cosmic swirl of pink and hazel. Katrina ran her hand through her thick, curly hair, allowed herself a second of self-satisfaction and retreated to a backroom in the church.

"Rufus?" Tina asked.

Armelle nodded. "Yep, he's waiting for her there. As is a text Father Michael recommended for her next op-ed."

Tina nodded. "How is it coming?"

Armelle stated matter-of-factly. "Great, of course. Unassailable logic." Armelle bumped her shoulder against Tina's. "Could probably use a little bit of your creative touch to spice it up before sending it to the News & Observer though, if you wouldn't mind."

"Of course," Tina immediately responded.

"I suspect we'll see another five percent drop in the ARC Weekly's listenership rates after this one. She's made quite the dent."

Tina smiled, as her eyes scanned the rest of the room. Some of the faces she recognized. Dean, the troubled man on the train, alongside Terrance, the social worker who helped him. Maria's Teaching Assistant from Duke. Lindsey, the intern from Wakestone Trials. Theo, the window washer with the thick-rimmed glasses. But many faces she did not recognize, and she wondered if Miles or Maria would have. People who benefited, either directly or downstream, from their words. From their actions.

She closed her eyes and nuzzled her head deeply into the nook of Armelle's neck. She remembered them. It helped. It hurt.

Father Michael interrupted this recollection with a clear of his throat as he began his service, with Naomi weaving a figure eight between his legs as he did so.

"We are gathered here together…"

MEET THE AUTHOR

Spencer is an educator in North Carolina whose students pressured him to finally start his debut novel, *The Staff and the Stake*, in retaliation for him assigning them countless creative writing prompts. As an autistic author, he strives to create stories that celebrate diversity, acceptance, and grace.

For more, check out his website at
www.spencermakesstuff.com